Silence of My Love

Kay D. Rizzo

Pacific Press® Publishing Association
Nampa, Idaho
Oshawa, Ontario, Canada
www.pacificpress.com

ISBN 978-0-8163-2993-9

9 780816 329939

Cover design by Gerald Monks

Originally published in 1993.

The author assumes full responsibility for the accuracy of all facts and quotations as cited in this book.

Heritage Project
This book is part of the Pacific Press® Heritage Project, a plan to re-publish classic books from our historical archives and to make valuable books available once more. The content of this book is presented as it was originally published and should be read with its original publication date in mind.

You can obtain additional copies of this book by calling toll-free 1-800-765-6955 or by visiting www.adventistbookcenter.com. You can purchase this as an e-book by visiting www.adventist-ebooks.com.

ISBN: 978-0-8163-2993-9   0-8163-2993-1

Table of Contents

Chapter 1

Alone on the Prairie

Black as a thunderhead, the Union Pacific roared behind McCall's Feed and Hardware, devouring the steel ribbons with a savage hunger and leaving behind a trail of soot across the sky. Each morning at nine o'clock, the eastbound train steamed into Hays and picked up the mail and passengers heading for Kansas City, Chicago, and all points in between. And each afternoon at four, the westbound express train rumbled into town, slowed enough to toss three mailbags from the mail car, then continued its journey toward Denver.

During my first few days in Hays, I walked to the railway station each morning to mail a letter: the first to Pa, the next to my sister Hattie, then to Joe in California, and to my mother. I couldn't have managed the seventy-five cents postage if James McCall hadn't called me into Aunt Beatrice's study our first morning in Hays.

He sat in front of a large roll-top desk, papers and ledgers spread out before him. When I entered the room, he stood and handed me a large brown envelope.

"Miss Spencer, I hope this will reimburse you for your services thus far. Also, you will find the ticket to San Francisco, as you requested."

"There was no hurry, Mr. McCall. I agreed to stay for a few weeks, and I will." I blushed and glanced down at the envelope in my hand. "By the way, have you heard from Mary's sister?"

He shook his head. "Not a word."

"Well, thank you very much for the money. I need to mail a letter home as well as pick up a few personal items in town." I was stalling. Mr. McCall had no interest in my shopping list. "Uh, I am sorry if I offended you yesterday."

He lifted his hand and waved off my apology. "No, I thought about what you said. And now that Mary has told me your story, I realize you were wise to ask for your ticket before

4

we left town. In your position, I'd do the same." It was the first time I'd seen his expression soften.

"Thank you."

He paced to the window and back. "I know you are eager to continue your journey to California. For that reason, I think we need to be specific about the length of your employment. Would you be willing to stay until the second week of September?" I couldn't help but smile. I'd seen the same pleading look many times on the face of his son. "That's about six weeks from now. You'd reach San Francisco long before the first snow."

"That sounds reasonable, I suppose."

"By the way, my aunt insisted that I wire your parents of your whereabouts yesterday before we left the station. So you might want to check whether you have a reply waiting."

"Oh, thank you, Mr. McCall. That was so thoughtful."

In the distance a train whistle sounded. My employer smiled and cocked his head in the direction of the incoming train. "It's the eastbound express. If you plan to mail that letter today."

"Oh! Yes. Excuse me. The letter's in my room."

The man smiled again. "You'd better hurry. I'd have Sam take you to the station, but I think you have a better chance of catching today's train if you cut across the cornfield behind the store."

"Thank you. Oh, thank you, Mr. McCall."

"James, call me James. Now go!" I dashed down the hallway to my room, grabbed the letter, and bounded down the stairs and out the back door.

"Through the cornfield," I mumbled as I plunged into the broad-leaf jungle.

Flip, flap, flop. I beat the dark green leaves back with my hands as I ran and reached the edge of the field before I heard the train whistle again.

As I darted past the startled travelers standing on the station platform, I realized I'd forgotten my sunbonnet. My free hand flew to my head, unsettling the hairpin that had been holding my hair in the wad at the back of my neck.

Oh, no. The hair tumbled down about my shoulders and to my waist in wild disarray. I considered stopping long enough to rescue the hairpin and my dignity until I heard the hiss of steam and the screech of metal on metal beside me. Without a glance over my shoulder, I burst up to the ticket window and thrust Pa's letter into the startled agent's hands.

"You made it just in time, little lady. That will be seventy-five cents." The white-haired ticket agent with the mustache and goatee chuckled as he slammed the stamp onto the ink pad, then onto my envelope. He turned to a blond-haired boy, about my age, who was sorting mail. "Here, Willy, give this to the postmaster."

The agent turned back toward me. "Is there anything else?"

"Um, yes." I leaned on the windowsill and tried to see past him into the tiny mail room. "Would you see if there is a telegram for Miss Chloe Spencer?"

"Miss Chloe Spencer. Hmm." His helper returned, dragging a heavy mailbag. "Willy," the ticket agent chuckled and turned to the red-faced boy. "Did you hear that? Her name is Miss Chloe Spencer."

The boy's face reddened more, causing the agent to chortle, "No, ma'am. No messages of any kind for a Miss Chloe Spencer. Sorry."

Mumbling a thank-you, I turned and strode across the boardwalk. At the end of the building, I slipped around the corner and wove my hair into a long braid down the middle of my back. At least it will be out of my face!

Then I turned to watch the mail boy heave the heavy mailbags onto the train. A pang of emptiness jabbed at my insides when the giant locomotive chugged east toward Pennsylvania and home. One glance at the remaining coins in the envelope, and my list of wants dwindled in importance. I could make do with the clothing I had, but I couldn't survive without news from home. No answer yet? What is going on?

Why hasn't either Ma or Pa replied to my telegram ? Something must be terribly wrong!

My imagination went wild as I trudged back toward the hardware store. Accident? Illness? Death? What terrible tragedy had occurred at home to prevent them from contacting me? The more I thought about it, the more worried I grew.

James and Sam left that morning for the ranch and didn't return until the weekend. Aunt Bea went back to running the hardware store, leaving me to care for Jamie and Mary during the day. Mary spent her days in bed, mourning the loss of Agatha. I watched over her with growing fear. While I tried to tell myself that she was improving each day, her cough worsened. She spent more and more time curled up with her pasty white face toward the wall. When I coaxed Mary to come down to meals for Jamie's sake, she buried her face in a pillow. When I suggested I read to her from her Bible as we'd done on the train, she snapped at me.

"Take that book from my sight. It's lies, all lies. If God cared for me, He wouldn't have taken my baby from me."

"Mary, you know better than that."

She glared at me through puffy, red eyes. "No, I don't know better than that. I want you to take that Bible from this very room. In fact, if you want it, it's yours to keep."

For a moment I was afraid to speak. I took a deep breath. "Mary, I'll tell you what. I'll keep the Bible in my room until you want it back, all right?"

Her eyes narrowed. She ground her teeth in fury. "That day will never come! Never! Any God who could steal my baby from me is no God of mine."

Tears sprang into my eyes as I remembered the gentle young woman I'd met less than two weeks earlier. What could I say? I remembered the conversations I'd had with my father about death. I'd asked some of the same questions and hadn't received answers. So how could I answer her? I shook my head and left the room.

Mary rejected every attempt I made to encourage her or help her help herself. Once after one of her particularly bitter outbursts, I threatened to pack up my things and leave. She only snarled, "Do what you have to do."

I wanted to scream at her and shake her. "What about Jamie? Don't you care about Jamie?" But even Jamie couldn't break through to the woman submerged beneath the pain. Whenever I brought him to her, Mary held him for a few minutes, weeping and fussing over him, then handed him back and asked to be left alone.

After such a visit, I would have to coax the little boy back into a playing mood.

Since Mary refused my help, Jamie occupied most of my time. We fashioned blocks out of wood scraps from Aunt Bea's store. We built forts out of shipping crates. We played with Muffin, Aunt Bea's yellow-and-white cat. Walter, the clerk in Aunt Bea's store, helped us hang a swing from the eaves of the barn behind the hardware store. Even when the child hit his thumb with a hammer, he didn't utter a cry. Jamie enjoyed our daily walks to the station to check the mail. He helped me carry Aunt Bea's mail back to the hardware store, all without a sound.

During the night, I thought about Jamie's stubborn silence. Perhaps Mrs. DeMarko was wrong. Perhaps he has a physical problem instead of an emotional one.

On my first weekend in Hays, Aunt Bea asked me if I'd be interested in touring the fort. James had ridden into town to see Mary, so he could watch over his wife and son. Aunt Bea said it would be good for Jamie to be alone with his mother and father for an afternoon.

Walter hitched up what Aunt Bea called her Sunday-go-to-meeting surrey to her team of matching grays. We climbed into the surrey, Aunt Bea in the driver's seat, and circled the south edge of town.

"There've been squatters on the land since the War Department abandoned the fort in 1889. There's talk of granting it to the state of Kansas to be used as a normal school to train teachers. Representative Curtis is lobbying in Washington right now.

"When the fort was founded in 1865, they called it Fort Fletcher. The following year the post was moved to its present location and renamed Fort Hays, in honor of Major General Isaac G. Hays, who was killed in the Battle of the Wilderness."

She pointed west of the fort. "See the White Caps." I strained but could see only grass-covered rolling hills. I admitted that to me, one rolling hill looked much like the next.

"They were called that back in the days when the buffalo roamed the area. The massive herds would climb the hills in the heat of the day to escape the pesky flies. In the process they'd eat the hillsides bare."

"Have you ever seen a buffalo herd?" I'd seen sketches of the shaggy, massive creatures.

"Oh, yes, when my husband and I first arrived, there were still many around. Up ahead you can see what's left of the fort that was once considered the healthiest military post in the United States."

The fierce white July sun trapped the cluster of buildings in a stagnant immobility. I'd expected to see spiked poles and guard towers, a sentry at each corner. Instead, I saw children scampering about in front of long wooden barracks. Lines of clothes waved in the breeze. The squatter families eyed us suspiciously as we passed.

"See that squared-off building on your right? That's the old stone blockhouse. If the plans for the school go through, that will be the dormitory."

Aunt Bea pointed at another building. "That white clapboard building over there was the commandant's home. Just imagine, this was one of the main forts the U.S. government set up to fight the Plains Indians." She chuckled as she noticed my startled look. "When the soldiers weren't fighting Indians, they were chasing roving bands of renegades from the Civil War or bandits bent on destroying the railroad, or the local beauties.

"General Custer's Seventh Cavalry spent time here in '68. Back then, Hays was a wild and dangerous place to live - saloon brawls, gunfights in the streets, fancy ladies from New Orleans …"

I let my imagination fill in the sights erased by time. I could see wooden buildings lining three sides of a large parade ground. At the far end of the field, a United States flag hung limp in the dusty heat. Five partially dressed soldiers in scraggly beards and dusty boots sat playing cards in the shade of an unmarked building. Another man, dressed like a cowboy, slept hunched over, his hat shading his face. Over by the hospital an Indian, in buckskin breeches and a beaded buckskin shirt, lounged in the shade of a buckboard. I snapped my mind back to the present. No teams stood hitched along the wooden sidewalk in front of the weathered buildings.

By the wistful smile on Aunt Bea's face, I knew she'd done the same. "Chester loved the vibrancy of the West. The day our train pulled into Hays, there was a shooting right in front of the sheriff's office. We heard a pistol shot." Aunt Bea chuckled to herself. "A woman dressed in a low-necked, short-skirted dress ran screaming out of Dalton's Saloon and Gambling House. A man chased after her, firing his pistol at her feet. She disappeared into the general store, and the man returned to the bar."

Shocked, I gasped, "What did you do? Why was he shooting at her?"

Aunt Bea grinned. "Chester and I stood there, our mouths agape. A railroad man leaning against a water trough explained it was just a drunk cowboy having a little fun."

"Fun? Shooting at people is fun?"

"Honey, things are different here than back East. Why, just a few years ago, four gunmen robbed the bank, killed the teller, and made off with the railroad's money. In Kansas, even today, strong feelings exist against the railroad."

I still marveled at the change in Aunt Bea's attitude toward me since we had arrived in Hays. She'd been so hostile when I first met her in Kansas City. Now, less than a week later, she was positively effusive. But I didn't mind. Her tales of Fort Hays and life on the prairie fascinated me. When we returned to her home, she gave me a stack of books to read on the cattle towns of Kansas.

At the supper table that night, James announced that we would be leaving the next morning for the ranch. "Mary's eager to get settled," he explained.

I agreed with him. Mary needed something to occupy her mind. At times I wondered if she would recover faster if Jamie was completely in her care. I'd seen my mother mourn the loss of one of her babies, but she hadn't languished in bed. Aunt Bea insisted Mary needed more time to get her strength back. Her protests went unheeded.

For my sake, it was agreed we would leave for the ranch immediately after the morning mail train. Aunt Bea suggested I take the stack of books with me to enjoy. "I never have time to read them anyway. When you get those read, come back and get some more. We have a library in town now, you know."

I thanked her. Later, I carefully packed each of the leather-bound volumes in a wooden crate. While Sam loaded our luggage onto the farm wagon, I helped Mary and Jamie dress. James walked to the station to pick up the day's mail. By now, the entire family knew I hadn't heard from my parents. They were almost as anxious as I.

Aunt Bea and I were helping Mary down the stairs as James McCall bounded into the store.

"Miss Chloe, do I have a surprise for you! Two letters and a big brown envelope! Is this a beautiful day, I ask you?" He handed me the mail and scooped a surprised Jamie up into his arms. "We're going home, son. We're finally going home!"

He danced in circles with his son. "I can hardly wait to show you the swing Sam and I hung in the front yard. And, Mary, the rosebushes I planted for you last spring are thriving. I bet we get roses before the frost."

I shuffled through the stack of mail: a fat letter from Hattie; a skinny one from Joe; and the brown envelope - though there was no return address, I would have known that sweeping scrawl anywhere - Pa. I sighed with relief. Everything was all right, after all.

I decided to wait until we reached the ranch before reading my letters. Even though I was eager to read my family's words of love, I preferred to do so in private, for I feared I might cry.

The farm wagon bulged with trunks, food stuff, and gardening tools. After Mary had mentioned that she might like to try her hand at an herb garden, James purchased almost a dozen gardening tools from his aunt.

I climbed into the carriage behind Mary. James set Jamie in the front next to the driver. Aunt Bea placed her hand on my forearm. Tears glistened in her eyes. "Take care of my precious ones, won't you, Chloe?"

Before I could reply, James bounded into the driver's seat. "Now, Aunt Bea, your crusty image is slipping. Where is that pioneer grit you always talk about? You wouldn't want Miss Chloe thinking you've gone soft in your old age."

The woman chuckled and pounded her nephew on the leg. "Soft? I can still outrun you any day of the week. Go on, get along out of here."

James clicked his tongue and flicked the reins. We were underway. Sam, driving the farm wagon, followed far enough behind to avoid eating our dust. As we crested the first rise, I glanced back and waved at Aunt Bea's lone figure, standing in front of the hardware store.

The road dipped beyond the first rise, and the settlement of Hays could no longer be seen. I glanced at Mary, her form rigid against the seat, her eyes closed. I watched Jamie gawk first at one side of the carriage, then past his father to the other. I felt the child's excitement as the carriage rolled over the rutted roadway. I wondered how Mary could be so disinterested in the land that had become her home.

Only the clopping of hooves, the creaking of wheels, and an occasional small animal or bird sound broke the prairie silence. The corn gave way to fields of grain, then to sparse scrub brush. An occasional clump of cottonwood trees marked the spot where a homestead once stood. Broken wheels and couplings, tin cans, medicine bottles, and rusting kitchen utensils littered the sites that bore a dismaying testimony of defeat in the western migration.

As we passed a dilapidated farmhouse rising crookedly from the tall grass, James pointed and shouted above the rumble of the wheels. "The Godfrey place - gave up and moved back to Maryland ten years back."

The two-story house, naked of paint, with its gaping, paneless windows and sagging porch, had clearly been built with an eye for the future - ample room for a good-sized family. A screen door swayed on one hinge. An abandoned wooden rocker leaned, slats up, against the side of the porch. I wondered what dreams had died there.

We'd ridden less than a mile farther when the carriage shuddered and skidded to one side. James slowed to a stop. Sam pulled alongside in the farm wagon and called, "Right back wheel loose."

James eased the team over to the side of the road and climbed down. Sam joined him. Standing in the carriage, I looked out over the tall prairie grass toward the northern horizon. "Look, Jamie," I pointed to my right. "There's a real sod house. Can you see it? I wonder if it's abandoned."

"Yes, it is." I jumped at the sound of Sam's voice behind me.

"I'd love to see it up close."

Sam grinned and nodded toward the carriage. "We've gotta repack the wheel. It will take us a spell."

"Really?" My eyes lighted up. "Do you think we'd have time?"

"Ask the mister." Sam nodded toward James, who was digging under a tarp in the back of the farm wagon. I glanced over at Mary's inert form, then hopped down from the carriage.

"Jamie, you sit tight while I talk with your daddy." I walked back to the wagon. "Mr. McCall? Would you mind if I took Jamie over to see the abandoned soddy while the wheel is being repaired?"

He lifted his head from under the tarp, looked in the direction of the homestead, then back at me. "Sure, but watch for snakes."

I cringed. Snakes? Honest-to-goodness snakes? Next to my aversion to mice, snakes ranked a high second. I remembered the spotted adders and the green garden snakes in Ma's kitchen garden. I'd wanted to kill them with my hoe, but Ma wouldn't let me. She said they were God's creatures and had as much right to live as we.

I battled my fear and won. I couldn't miss seeing an honest-to-goodness sod house. Hurrying back to the wagon, I placed Jamie's wide-brim felt hat on his head and lifted him from the carriage. "Let's go on an adventure. Maybe we'll find a treasure or an Indian arrowhead on the way." I paused and looked at the silent woman in the carriage.

"Mary, would you like to come too?" She didn't stir.

Thinking once more of the snakes, I grabbed a hoe from the wagon. I figured if I saw the snake first, the creature wouldn't stand a chance - Ma or no Ma. The sun beat down on my head and shoulders. I pulled on the bonnet resting on my back; it would supply me with a little shade. We located a narrow path leading to the sod house. "Now, stay on the path and watch for treasures as you walk."

Single file, Jamie followed me along the overgrown cow path. Once out of earshot of the carriage, I started singing, thinking my voice might scare any creatures that might be lurking nearby. "Oh, my darlin'; oh, my darlin'."

I swung my arms and twirled about in a circle. Catching my jubilant spirit, Jamie's face glowed. He skipped and fluttered his arms about in perfect rhythm to my song. Hm, I thought, there's nothing wrong with his hearing, is there? Maybe his taste in music, but not his hearing.

Nearer the soddy, the grass grew sparsely. An assortment of tools and utensils lay rusting in the Kansas elements. Using the hoe, I pawed through one of the larger mounds of rubble, unearthing only more rubble. Jamie spied a glint of metal in the center of the pile. He picked up the shiny object and handed it to me.

"It's a button, Jamie, a button off a military uniform. See the star in the center. And," I rubbed the button against my skirt to remove the caked-on mud, "look, here's a T, an E, X, A, S. It's off a Confederate soldier's uniform! You should keep this - it might be worth something someday." I turned it over and read the words, Wildt and Sons, Richmond. "That's the company that made the button - Wildt and Sons."

I returned the button to Jamie. The boy ran his grimy fingers over the raised brass star, then grinned up at me and stuffed the button into his pants pocket. We walked over to the soddy and peeked in the opening where a door had been. Sunlight streaked through the partially caved-in, pole-and-dirt roof. At the sound of our approaching footsteps, insects scuttled for cover.

A cookstove, cot, table, and a chair with a broken leg were festooned with cobwebs. An empty whiskey bottle lay atop a pile of old blankets. With the hoe, I poked at the blankets and gasped as a colony of mice scrambled behind the cookstove. I shrieked, picked up my skirts, and ran from the house. A few seconds later I gathered my courage about me and I peeked back inside to find Jamie covering his mouth with his hands to hide his laughter. His eyes danced with merriment over my discomfort.

"You think that's funny, do you? Well, I don't!" I sashayed about in mock irritation. Suddenly I stopped and slowly turned back toward the little boy. Had I imagined the little squeal when he tried not to let me see his laughter? I took his hand and led him out into the sunlight. Step number one, little friend. Step number one. And if you can take one step, sooner or later, you will take another.

We skipped back along the path to the wagon. As Jamie reached the side of the road, his hat flew off in the breeze. Jamie and I chased it down the roadway, past Sam and James as they reloaded the repair equipment. "Catch it," I shouted. "Catch the hat."

Each time I got within range, a capricious breeze sent it sailing twenty to thirty feet down the road. The men recognized my dilemma and gave chase. With my side aching from running and laughing, I had to stop to catch my breath.

Sam dashed by me. "I'll get it," he shouted. Confident he'd saved the hat and the day, he reached for the hat, only to have the breeze catch it once more and send it sailing farther down the road.

"Don't worry, I can get it." James sprinted past, laughing at Sam as he ran. Thirty feet down the road, the same thing happened to him. Two more attempts to catch his son's felt hat failed. On the third, James tackled the hat, belly first. Slowly he got to his feet and waved the flattened object in the air.

By the time I reached Sam, tears of laughter ran down his black, weather-beaten face. My sides hurt from laughing so hard that I doubled over beside him. We waited for James and walked back together, laughing and talking at once about our strange adventure.

I couldn't read the expression on Jamie's face when James returned the boy's hat. "I rescued it, son." James punched the center of the hat, then popped it back onto the child's head. "A little worse for the wear, but a hat nonetheless."

We climbed aboard the vehicles and resumed our journey. I babbled to Mary about the chase, the soddy, and the button Jamie found. She turned her face toward the canvas, disinterested. Exasperated, I turned my attention to the passing countryside. It's as if she's willing herself to die - after being so eager to reach Kansas. I don't understand her.

We arrived in a broad valley filled with thick green grass and an array of wildflowers. Their colors of red and yellow, violet and white rippled in the wind like the waves of an ocean. Off to the right, a white two-story house with red shutters proudly oversaw a white picket fence surrounding an expansive green lawn. Dangling from the limb of a massive cottonwood was a wooden swing.

I patted Mary's arm. "Look, your new home. Isn't it beautiful?"

She glanced at the structure for a moment, then closed her eyes. "It's not my home. It will never be my home. My home is in Boston, next to my precious Agatha."

"Oh, Mary, don't say that. Your husband will be so disappointed."

Jamie hopped down as soon as the carriage had completely stopped and ran straight to the swing. Because his legs were too short for him to climb onto the seat, he pushed the wooden seat back and forth.

James leapt out of the driver's seat and hurried to his wife's side. His eyes glistened with excitement. "Do you like it, Mary? Do you like it?"

Mary smiled weakly and held out her hand. Instead of taking her hand, the eager young husband swept her into his arms and ran up the front steps onto the porch. Sam bounded ahead to open the front door.

I took my time climbing down from the carriage - James and Mary needed a few minutes alone in their new home. Picking up my pack of mail, I strolled up the brick sidewalk to the porch steps. I sat on the steps and watched a goldfinch land on the fence. Another bird, this one less colorful, joined the first. Looking around at the beauty of the McCall land, I wondered if Mary realized how lucky she really was. She wasn't moving into a one-room, dirt-floor soddy like so many of the frontier women had. James couldn't have given her a more desirable home.

After what I hoped was a respectable time, I called Jamie to come and see the house. Immediately the little boy abandoned the swing and came running toward me. His face glowing with happiness, he threw himself into my arms.

"This is your new home, Jamie. Do you like it?"

He started to speak, then caught himself. I took his hand and led him inside to the cool, dark entryway. A colorful Oriental carpet interrupted the deep tones of the highly polished oak floor. A tall mahogany coat-and-hat rack with a built-in mirror stood on the left of the doorway. On the right was a carved mahogany table. The mahogany-railed staircase led up to the second floor. Straight ahead, the first floor hallway disappeared into the shadows. Sliding doors opened on both sides of the entry.

Curious, I laid my mail on the table and peeked into the room on the right. "O-o-oh, Jamie. What a beautiful parlor. Look, an organ. See? My mama has a similar one back in Pennsylvania."

Beyond the parlor was the library lined with shelves and shelves of books. Jamie watched as I twirled in the center of the room. I whispered to the child, "If I lived here, this would be my favorite hideout."

I took his hand and led him back through the parlor and across the hallway to the formal dining room. I couldn't believe my eyes. I'd never imagined such luxury existed on the Kansas prairie. I ran my hand over the edge of the glossy mahogany table.

"Imported from England." Startled, I whirled about to face the smiling James. "It's beautiful, Mr. McCall. Mary must have loved it."

His face clouded. "I really don't know. She glanced inside the room once, then asked me to take her upstairs to her room. Her room, not ours." The muscles in the man's jaw flexed as he held his emotions in tow.

"She's just tired. Later, after she rests a bit ..." My voice trailed off. "But tell me, how did you get these beautiful pieces of furniture here from England?"

James strolled behind the table to the marble fireplace. "I didn't. My father bought the house already furnished."

I stared incredulously. "Everything was here, just as I see it?"

He leaned against the mantel. "That's right. A number of years ago, this ranch was part of the dream of Sir George Grant, a wealthy London silk merchant. The Englishman purchased fifty thousand acres of land from the Union Pacific Railroad and sold parcels of land to his neighbors back in the old country. This was one of the parcels." James ran his hands over the pink veined marble. "Throughout the seventies and eighties, more than two hundred Englishmen, as well as groups from a number of other European countries, immigrated to this area of Kansas and transplanted a bit of old Europe to the prairie, right down to top hats and morning coats."

I looked around the room, appreciating the intricately embroidered wall hangings and framed oil paintings.

"Dreams are funny things, aren't they? Never turn out like we imagine." I wondered if he was referring to Grant's dream or his own.

"Imported from Brittany." James waved his hand toward the massive crystal chandelier hanging over the center of the table. "Regardless of their wealth and the splendor of Europe they imported from the old country, the prairie beat them. In the first three years, the town was demolished by a prairie fire, the crops destroyed by a plague of locusts, and disease wiped out their herds of sheep. And their prized racehorses became easy targets for horse thieves."

He walked over to one of the long, narrow windows. "Austrian lace and beige brocade from the Orient ..." His hand drifted across the satiny fabric. "The climate, the unskilled labor, the disease and disaster proved to be formidable enemies and, one by one, the Englishmen abandoned their dreams and returned to England."

"How sad. Such a beautiful house." I admired the fine bone china behind the leaded-glass doors in the breakfront. "How did you learn about this place?"

"From my Aunt Bea. My brother Ian and I yearned to move west. My father, a Boston financier, purchased this estate. At the same time, he acquired three gold-mining sites from a bankrupt company in Colorado. Ian chose the gold; I chose the ranch. Everything was pretty much as you see it when we arrived."

"Incredible." Catching my reflection in the massive gilt-framed leaded mirror over the fireplace, I cringed. I looked like a wild-haired street waif lost in a museum.

He slid the door open between the dining room and the kitchen. "Come on out here. The kitchen is the original section of the house." I followed him through the swinging door into the large open kitchen. Bright copper pots hung overhead. Red gingham curtains framed the long, narrow windows. A wooden rocker sat on each side of the fireplace hearth, a red-and-yellow braided rug between them.

"This was once a cabin for the first settlers on this land. See the whitewash?" He brushed his hand against the rough textured walls.

"What a bright and cheery kitchen. Mary is going to love this place."

James smiled, but the sadness in his eyes told me he had doubts. "Come on, son." He lifted Jamie into his arms. "I want to show you the bath closet. It even has a built-in heater to warm the water in the holding tank."

The large bath closet, as James called it, included a giant copper tub with brass feet shaped like bird claws. On the other side of the room was a porcelain sink and matching indoor toilet. "There's another bath closet upstairs."

The tub itself slanted downward toward a small hole that could be blocked during one's bath by a rubber stopper . I couldn't believe it. Mary would never have to draw water for baths or carry the used water out of the house and dump it. It was all done for her. And no outhouse to clean! I hated cleaning the outhouse.

"It's beautiful, just beautiful."

James grinned at my enthusiasm. "The former owners spared no expense, I assure you. Jamie, let's go find your room. Sam has probably already taken your luggage upstairs, Miss Chloe."

I reclaimed my mail and carried it up the stairs. James showed me the six bedrooms on the second floor, as well as the bath closet. "Why don't you go read your letters and rest up? Jamie needs to help me check on the horses in the corral, right, son?"

Jamie nodded and grinned. I returned to the room that for the next six weeks would be home and closed the door. I barely noticed the yellow-and-cornflower-blue appointments of the room. Finally, I could read the letters from my loved ones. Eagerly, I tore open the brown envelope first, the one with my father's familiar handwriting scrawled across the front.

Chapter 2

Wounds to Heal

A small envelope fell to the floor at my feet. Eagerly, I bent down and picked it up. It was the same envelope I'd mailed from Hays. Scrawled across the front were the words Rejected! Return to sender! I turned it over and looked at the seal. It had never been broken. By the weight of the envelope, I knew the twenty-dollar gold piece was still inside.

I sank on the bed, not wanting to believe. My father had refused to read my letter, let alone forgive me. The writing blurred before my eyes. The hundred-pound bundle of guilt I'd shed the day I mailed the gold piece to him dropped onto my shoulders once again. I peered inside the brown envelope, hoping to find a message - any message. Even anger would be preferable to silence. Nothing.

Stunned, I tore Hattie's letter open and scanned the opening lines.

Dearest Chloe,

I am writing this letter in defiance of Pa's order. No, I'm not going behind his back. He acted shocked that I would tell him to his face that he was wrong. You are my sister. I'll never let anyone take you from me. If the boys hadn't picked up the mail at the post office the day your letter arrived, I doubt Pa would have given it to me or mentioned one had come. It's pretty quiet around here. No one is allowed to speak of you. Ma cries a lot. And I miss you terribly. Wash days aren't the same anymore - ha, ha.

You were right about Emmett. Last week, he beat his son Charlie senseless. Jack Bennett, their next-door neighbor, said Emmett almost killed the boy. Sheriff Daniels threw Emmett into jail until he cooled down. Rumor has it Charlie ran away and joined the army. So, see, you didn't need to run away after all.

Little Franklin is growing like a weed …

I skimmed the rest of the letter, picking out the highlights. Then I read it again slowly to savor every tidbit of news.

I reached for Joe's letter from California. Instead, my eyes rested on my father's bold handwriting scratched across the large brown envelope. My eyes filled with tears, and I choked back the massive lump of loneliness forming in the base of my throat. Pa, I'm sorry, I'm sorry.

I knew my father. For generations, the Spencer clan had prided themselves on their code of honor. My father's rejection of my repentance was evidence of that code. By running away, I had brought shame on the family name. There would be no forgiveness. In his mind, I was dead.

He used to joke about it. "God may forgive ya, but don't expect a Spencer to." I recalled the story he had told about his great-grandfather and his great-great-uncle immigrating to the United States more than a hundred years before. Soon after they arrived, the two brothers argued over the borderline between their properties. Neither had any other family in the New World, yet they broke off all contact. And to this day, the two branches of the Spencer family stubbornly maintained that schism.

I collapsed face down onto the blue-and-yellow patchwork quilt covering the bed and crushed a fluffy white pillow to my face. After saturating one side of the pillow with my tears, I turned it over and did the same to the other side.

I jumped at the sudden knock on the door. It was James. "Miss Chloe, are you all right? Is everything all right?"

I sniffed back my tears and ran to the door. "Yes, I-I-I'm fine."

"Can I do anything to help?"

"No, no. Thank you anyway." I covered my mouth with my hand.

James paused. "Mrs. Paget and Mrs. Simons, our nearest neighbors, just arrived at the kitchen door with a hot meal. Do you feel well enough to come downstairs for supper?"

"Give me a few minutes to freshen up."

"All right. Jamie is outside playing with the Paget twins. And Mary, well, Mary refuses to come down."

"I'll be right down, Mr. McCall." I hurried over to the oak washstand and looked at my blotched face in the mirror. I splashed water on my face, then patted it dry. You can do this, Chloe. You can do this.

Then I searched the valise for my hairbrush. I couldn't go down to meet the neighbors with my hair awry. By the time I brushed the tangles out of my hair and rebraided it, I felt in control again.

I straightened the quilt on the bed and stacked my mail on the small writing desk beside it. A tingle of guilt prickled at my neck when I realized I'd not yet read Joe's letter. I'll read Joe's letter after supper.

On my way past Mary's room, I paused to look in on her. She appeared to be asleep. I took a deep breath at the top of the stairs, then descended with all the grace I could muster. In the kitchen, James sat on a stool by the hallway door while two women as different as midnight and noon bustled about the room. When James saw me, he leaped to my side.

"Miss Chloe, I'd like you to meet two of our neighbors. This here's Mrs. Zerelda Paget. You met her at Aunt Bea's place the day you arrived."

Zerelda grabbed my hand and pumped it. "Chloe, the name's Zerelda. Landsakes, Jim, when did you start calling me Mrs. Paget?"

A bit abashed, James stepped back and let Zerelda take over. "And this here's Amy, Amy Simons. Amy, have you ever seen such a mite of a gal in your life? It wouldn't take much of a breeze to pick her up and carry her to the Missouri border!" The two women laughed at my expense.

Mrs. Amy Simons, a short, amply rounded woman with a bright, cheery face, greeted me shyly. "Call me Amy. Jim tells us you are a midwife. We could really use one around here."

"Yeah," interrupted Zerelda, giving a hearty chuckle. "Come spring, and babies appear around these parts as sure as newborn lambs."

Amy laughed nervously. "Zerelda! How you go on, and in front of Jim!"

Zerelda removed a hot baking dish from the oven. "Jim don't mind, do ya, Jim? It's mighty good to see a new female in these parts, especially one of good character and breeding. The boys are goin' to be hangin' around your ranch, Jim, once they take a gander at her."

I blushed. I heard James chuckle. Glad he's having fun at my expense.

Amy counted out a stack of plates and set them on the round oak table in the center of the kitchen. "Where are you from, Miss Spencer?"

"A little town in Pennsylvania."

Zerelda placed the hot casserole on the table. "Chloe, now don't take offense, but you're far too pretty to be a midwife. Some say I was pretty when I was young - I'm twenty-four, in case you wanted to know. The West has a way of aging folks."

She returned to the oven. I tried not to stare. Zerelda Paget wasn't much older than Hattie and Myrtle, my oldest sisters. The lines on her face and the wisps of gray in her dull brown hair aged her by ten years.

After taking a hot tin of muffins from the oven, Zerelda shook them into a gingham-lined basket. "Well, everything's hot and ready to eat. We'll be headin' home as soon as I round up the kids."

"Aren't you two staying to eat with us?" I asked.

Zerelda laughed. "Oh, no, we've got to get home. The men will be coming in from chores as hungry as bears." She shook her finger in James's face. "As soon as that little wife of yours is up to it, you let us know. We want to welcome her into the community properly. Come on, Amy, your chariot is waiting."

After the two women tied their bonnets, Zerelda rested her hand on my shoulder. "Chloe, why don't you drop by tomorrow around four in the afternoon for tea. Bring Jamie along. Amy will be there too, won't you, Amy?"

The second woman blinked. "Well, I guess I will." I turned toward my employer. "If it's all right with Mr. McCall …"

Zerelda snorted. "Mr. McCall? Of course it's all right with Jim. You'll make sure she gets there, won't you, Jim?"

He nodded and opened the kitchen door for the women. I stood watching as James escorted the women to a farm wagon. The wagon wheels had already started turning when the two boys ran toward the wagon and leaped on the back. James waited until the wagon turned onto the main road. Then, taking Jamie's hand, he climbed the back steps and entered the kitchen.

Awkwardly, the three of us gathered around the table, and James asked the blessing over the food. Without Mary present, conversation was strained.

Shyly I asked, "Doesn't Sam eat with us?"

"Usually." James nodded between bites of fried chicken. "But tonight he and the boys decided to heat up a can of beans in the bunkhouse. I think they wanted to avoid running into the county's two biggest matchmakers."

I laughed. "Jamie, did you show your father the button you found?"

The little boy's eyes lighted up as he dug deep in his pocket and took out the shiny brass button. He handed it to his father. James studied the button carefully, nodding his approval.

"Looks like a Civil War relic. Some Texas cavalryman wore it, perhaps. It will be worth something someday." James handed the button back to his son. "Better put it in a safe place, son."

The child beamed with happiness at earning his father's approval. He stuffed it into his pocket and tackled his muffin. When our hunger took over, the conversation lagged.

James leaned back in his chair and rubbed his stomach. "My, those were good victuals. Don't you agree, son?"

Jamie looked up from his plate and grinned.

Excusing myself, I cleared the table, then filled a kettle with water. "Would you like me to take a tray of food up to Mary? She needs to eat something."

James shook his head. "She said she didn't want anything. She's been coughing a lot since we got here. I guess the road dust got to her."

Without thinking, I planted my hand firmly on my hips and said with the authority of a drill sergeant, "She needs to eat something, Mr. McCall."

"I know that! Don't you think I know that?" Irritation knitted his brow. "And, please! Stop calling me Mr. McCall. That's my father's name, not mine."

Startled by his vehemence, I took a linen napkin and dabbed at the gravy on Jamie's face. "Oh, I'm sorry, er, James. Would you mind if I fixed Mary a pot of tea and a slice of bread with jam?"

James arose to his feet and pushed in his chair. "Do what you like. Maybe you'll have better luck than I."

He turned and strode from the room, letting the screen door slam shut. I glanced over at Jamie's chair, but it was empty. Hopeless, the situation is hopeless!

Bertha's advice about breaking problems down to size came to mind, so I decided, as far as Mary was concerned, anything was better than nothing. The worst thing she could do was scream and kick me out of her room. Left to my own devices, I did a cursory check of the kitchen cupboards and the pantry. I took a canister of mint tea and a loaf of freshly made bread from the shelf. One step at a time.

Step one, I washed the supper dishes. By the time the second kettle of water came to a boil, I was ready to lead the attack against my finicky patient. Searching through the dining-room buffet and breakfront, I found a silver tray, along with a tea set of white English bone china.

In one of the drawers in the bullet, I searched through a stack of fancy work and c hose a round crocheted doily While the mint tea leaves steeped in the teapot, I ran outside and picked a handful of daisies and arranged them m a vase I d found in the breakfront.

After slicing off a healthy slab of Zerelda's homemade wheat bread. I spread it with a thick layer of blackberry jam, cut the bread in quarters, and arranged it on a dessert plate. A slight adjustment of the tallest daisy, and the tray was perfect I walked up the stairs to Mary's room, stopping oft" in my room long enough to stuff her Bible under my arm.

I took a deep breath, then pushed open her bedroom door. "Hi. there. I bet you're as ravenous as a church mouse by now, so I fixed you a little something. You have great neighbors." I placed the tray on a round table next to a large Queen Anne chair by the window. I laid the Bible beside it.

The window was shrouded with both a shade and heavy brocade draperies. I didn't wait for her response. Tying the draperies back, I raised the shade and threw open the window.

"It is such a glorious evening. I think evening is my favorite time of day. How about you? Just look at the streaks of sunlight bathing the world in gold."

I heard a discontented murmur coming from under the bedcovers. I looked at the multicolored down-filled quilt and wondered how she could breathe on such a warm day. "Oh, look, Mary, Jamie has managed to climb into the swing all by himself." I giggled aloud at the boy's attempts to pump the swing into action. "Ya gotta see this."

Mary broke into a wrenching cough. I rushed to her side and handed her one of the linen hankies stacked on the bedside table She struggled to catch her breath.

Helping her sit up, I massaged her back as she wheezed in pain. When her coughing subsided, I handed her a tumbler of water. "This should help."

The dark rings around her eyes and the hollows in her cheeks stabbed at my heart. I remembered a proverb my father often quoted about "a merry heart doing good like a medicine." The disease eating at her lungs had also consumed her spirit.

I shook off the moment of despair and resumed my stream of cheerful chatter. Before she could protest, I threw back her bedcovers and swung her feet over the side of the bed. "Let me help you over to the chair. It will be easier drinking the mint tea there. And wait until you taste Amy Simon's blackberry jam."

My exuberance must have overwhelmed Mary, for she didn't protest as I led her to the chair. As she sat down, I grabbed a knitted afghan and placed it securely over her lap. "Would you just look at those daisies! They're all over your backyard. Lots of brown-eyed susans too!"

"I-I-I don't feel much like eating." Mary lifted a limp hand. "I'm not up to this."

"Isn't this house incredible?" I ignored her whining and poured the steaming mint tea into the teacup. "Some woman poured a lot of tender, loving care into every room. My mother once said, 'A house doesn't become a home for a woman until it speaks of her unique tender, loving care.'"

I hoped the momentum of my enthusiasm would break down her resistance. If she would only eat a few bites of bread and drink a few sips of tea. I skipped over to the bed and straightened the sheets. "O-o-h, would you look at the detailed embroidery on these sheets and pillowcases. Some bride spent many hours stitching this cutwork."

I stole a glance toward Mary and smiled. One of the bread squares was missing from the plate. I saw her lick a spot of jam from her fingers, then take a sip of the tea. "Zerelda or Amy must have aired this room before you arrived. Either that, or James is a much better housekeeper than I would have imagined. Everything is spotless."

Mary sucked in a noisy breath. "And baby Agatha will never get to enjoy - " A coughing fit swallowed up her tear-filled words.

I grabbed one of the clean hankies and ran to her side. I wanted to remind her about the little boy on the swing outside the window. I wanted to say, "Jamie is here, needing you right now."

When the attack subsided, she blew her nose on the cloth and threw herself into my arms. "Oh, Chloe, please don't give up on me. No matter what I do or say, don't give up on me."

"Don't worry, Mary. I'm here for you as long as you need me." As I uttered the words, my California dream slipped tantalizingly beyond my fingertips. We clung to one another a few seconds longer, each gaining strength from the contact.

We both heard the sound of footsteps on the stairs. Releasing her, I held her at arm's length. "However, there is one thing I'm going to ask of you in return. You've got to try to regain your strength - not for me, but for your son and your husband. Will you promise to at least try to cooperate?"

She nodded and wiped the tears from her eyes.

"Ahem, I, uh, just wanted to see if you are needing anything, Mary." We turned at the sound of James's voice. "I brought Jamie in for the night. He's getting ready to take a tub bath. Can you imagine, he's actually looking forward to it?"

After one look at the giant tub, I could understand why. I, too, could hardly wait to submerge myself to the neck in warm, sudsy water. I stood up and straightened my skirt. "I'd better go help him."

"I already started heating the water," James informed me. "When you ladies have time, I'll teach you how to do it."

I picked up the Bible and tucked it under my arm, then lifted the serving tray to return to the kitchen. "How about teaching me as soon as Jamie finishes his bath?"

James smiled. "All right, I'll be downstairs in the library. In the meantime, you tend to Jamie, and I'll return that tray to the kitchen." He took the tray from my hands and turned to Mary. "Honey, it's so good to see you up and around on your own."

A wan smiled crossed Mary's face. I slipped out of Mary's room, dropped off the Bible in my room, and hurried to Jamie. The water had cooled before I could coax him from the tub and into his nightclothes. After our usual good-night prayer, I tucked him into bed and kissed him on the forehead. "If you need me, Jamie, come to my room and get me."

Then it was my turn. James taught me how to operate the water heater. I waited impatiently for the water to get hot again. Finally, I released the water into the copper tub.

As I eased into the oversized tub, I couldn't believe my good fortune. I luxuriated in the tub until the water became tepid, then dried off and hurried to my room. I still had one more letter to read - Joe's. It proved to be no surprise. I skimmed it quickly. He scolded me for detouring to Kansas and insisted I join him in San Francisco immediately. He told me that Pa had written a long letter berating my behavior. By the time I finished the letter, I felt I'd been battered by a Holstein bull. Only the postscript brought a smile to my face. "Cy sends his regards. He says he looks forward to seeing you soon."

I put Joe's letter in the desk and picked up my father's. Removing the coin from the tattered envelope, I placed it in the desk drawer. On top of it, I placed the railway ticket to California and the money James had paid me. Mary's Bible sat unopened on top of the desk.

Running my fingers across the leather binding on the Bible, I stared into the gathering shadows of the room. An overwhelming sadness welled up inside of me. Feeling far older than my years, I sank into a chair.

Is it possible for a human heart to actually break from grief? I didn't used to think so. Now I'm not so sure. What have I done to my life? How many more stupid mistakes can I make? Will Pa ever forgive …

It seemed natural to open Mary's Bible to the Psalms. I needed comfort. I needed assurance. While I was searching for the twenty-third chapter, my eyes paused at Psalm 27:10. I read the words aloud. "When my father and my mother forsake me, then the Lord will take me up."

I stared at the words until they blurred before my eyes. Do You mean what You say, Lord? Even when my parents forsake me because of my sins, You can forgive me?

If I was expecting a verbal answer, I was disappointed. For none came. I read through the rest of the chapter, then read verse 14 a second time. "Wait on the Lord: be of good courage, and he shall strengthen thine heart: wait, I say, on the Lord."

I closed the Bible and watched the sun disappear beyond the western horizon. Darkness shrouded the valley. The only man-made light I could see came from a window in the bunkhouse. Soon stars appeared in the night sky. The evening breeze ruffled the curtains. I stepped away from the window, ready to sleep.

I climbed into the featherbed and closed my eyes. The words from verse 14 circled in my brain. Wait. Wait on the Lord. Be of good courage. He shall strengthen thine heart. Wait. Wait. Wait…

I awakened to a meadowlark singing outside my bedroom window. Go away. No one should be that cheery at such an early hour!

I snuggled deeper under the sheet and wrapped a pillow around my ears. But it was no use. Like it or not, I was awake. I dragged myself out of bed and slammed the window shut. The bird flew away.

Since the stay at Aunt Bea's, my wardrobe had increased beyond anything I'd ever had before. Aunt Bea had made it her business to replenish my wardrobe. She delighted in dragging me to the dressmaker for fittings on several new dresses. And when we left, she insisted I use her Saratoga trunk to transport my new wardrobe to the ranch.

I opened the trunk and took out the dresses of calico and gingham. While the dresses Mary had given me were lovely for travel, they wouldn't stand up under day-to-day chores.

I chose to wear the blue calico. Then I placed the rest of the dresses on hangers in the dark mahogany wardrobe in the corner behind the door. I arranged the smaller items in the dresser drawers, then pushed the empty trunk to the corner by the window. After arranging my hair, I hurried downstairs to start breakfast. Sam was already at the stove flipping pancakes. His eyes twinkled as he read the consternation in my face. "How many can ya eat, missy?"

Before I could reply, James, who was transferring fresh milk from a large milk can into a pitcher, laughed. "Find a place to sit, Miss Chloe. Miss Chloe, meet the boys. This here's Jake and Darcy and Shorty and Bo." I blushed as the men leapt to their feet and fumbled with their table napkins. "Boys, this is my son's nanny, Miss Chloe Spencer. Miss Chloe, we took a vote and decided to let you sleep in your first morning here."

"Uh, well, I don't know what to say."

Shorty, a grizzly bear of a man, chuckled, "Say you'll do the dishes afterward."

"Yeah," interrupted Darcy, a short, wiry man with wavy brown hair and a twirled mustache, "especially since it's Shorty's turn."

Shorty laughed along with the other men.

James filled my tumbler with milk. "I hope you realize we're all joshing you. You aren't expected to play chief cook and cleanup girl around here. Jamie and Mary are your responsibility - nothing more." He eyed each of his men to be certain they understood the arrangements as well.

"I wouldn't mind taking my turn. That's if you gentlemen think you can stand my honey-buttermilk biscuits."

Sam set a platter of pancakes in front of me and patted his stomach. "M-m-m, wanna start tomorrow morning? Nothin' against Darcy's grits, of course."

Darcy arched his eyebrow. "You aren't complaining, are you?"

Sam retorted, "Me? I'd be the last to fuss."

James laughed and thumped Sam on the shoulder. "Especially since we have a rule around here. 'He who complains about the food prepares breakfast for the next week.'"

Between mouthfuls, I nodded my approval. "Sounds like a reasonable rule to me." I noticed the men watched me as I ate, hints of grins tugging at the corners of their mouths. Bewildered, I thought it was because they weren't used to having a woman at the table. But when I took my first sip of the milk, I knew better.

"EEuuoo!" I choked and sputtered. Only my mother's strict code of etiquette forced the foul-tasting liquid down my throat. "What is wrong with that milk?" I blurted.

Everyone laughed. Sam chortled the loudest. "Not a thing. It's goat's milk from Jake's herd out behind the barn. Makes great cheese too."

Bo, a boy around my brother Joe's age, glanced across the table at me and blushed. "Don't worry. You'll get used to the taste."

"Well, it will take some getting used to." To myself, I added, Maybe in a million years!

A pleasant glint of amusement twinkled in James's eyes as he took his place at the head of the table. The conversation switched to the day's chores.

Sam announced, "The wheat in the south forty looks prime for harvest, boss. I ain't never seen such plump and heavy heads."

James spooned honey onto his stack of pancakes. "We'd better get it in before a freak rainstorm hits."

Jake interrupted. "What about the fence that needs repairing down by the creek? If Paget's cattle come visitin', there won't be no wheat crop either."

"Jake, you and Bo mend the fence. The rest of us will start harvesting the wheat crop. I'll be down in an hour or so to help you, Sam."

Once the assignments were made, the men excused themselves, carried their dishes to the sink, and rinsed them under the pump. After drying their hands, Jake, Darcy, Bo, and Sam grabbed their hats from the hooks behind the back door and left. Shorty filled the teakettle and put it on the stove.

"Don't worry about the dishes, Shorty," I said. "I got to sleep in this morning, so I should do the cleanup. Besides, what better way is there to learn where everything belongs, right?"

Shorty's bearded face broke into a grin. "Thank you, Miss Chloe. You don't know how much I hate doing dishes. By the way, Sam made extra batter for the boy's and Mrs. McCall's breakfast." He twisted his hat nervously in his hands. "You're one good sport, Miss Chloe, do you know that? Taking the teasing and all."

Laughing, I told him I was used to a whole lot worse. "I have big brothers, you know. And little ones too. I'm not sure which was worse."

He grabbed his hat and left. When we were alone, James asked me to sit down. "I think we need to outline what is and what is not expected of you around here."

"Mr. McCall, er, I mean, James, I grew up on a farm. I am used to hard work." I folded my hands on the table in front of me. "While I would never neglect either Mary or Jamie, I do need tasks to keep me busy."

"I really don't want you to ..." His dark eyebrows knitted together. "I've been paying Zerelda to come in three days a week to clean the house and do the laundry. She bakes up a storm when she's here."

By the stubborn look on his face, I knew it was time to negotiate. To tell the truth, I wasn't too crazy about doing the laundry anyway. But there were other tasks I would enjoy. "At least let me do the day-to-day cleaning. Dusting, sweeping, general tidying."

James mulled my words.

"And what about meals? I should do my share."

His frown softened. "At breakfast maybe. The boys take care of their own noon meal and eat their night meal in the bunkhouse."

"What about you? You need to eat."

"My lunches are pretty much the same as the boys, usually leftover biscuits and beef jerky. For supper, I eat whatever I can piece together, or on the days Zerelda has been here, I eat the food she's prepared for me." His resolve was wavering.

"Obviously Mary and Jamie will need a more balanced diet than that. Since they are under my charge, I will want them to eat properly. It certainly won't be any trouble to fix a little extra for you, at least at suppertime - and at lunch, when you are here."

The lure of hot meals overpowered his stubbornness. "But I don't want you overdoing it - for Mary's sake and for Jamie's."

I laughed aloud. "I won't overdo. Just ask my ma. Overdoing is not one of my talents. And, James, please understand. I am here because this is where I belong right now. Thank you for caring."

He smiled and rose from the table. "Guess I'd better check on Mary before I leave."

I hopped up from the table. "How about taking a tray of food up to her? Here, let me make a couple pancakes and a pot of tea while you go outside and pick a handful of brown-eyed susans for the vase."

I'd griddled the pancakes and topped them with butter when he returned with a handful of flowers. I arranged the flowers in the vase and stood back to admire our handiwork.

"Looks good, huh?"

He grinned at me. "Sure does." He picked up the tray and started from the room.

"Send Jamie down for breakfast, if he's awake."

"Right."

Chapter 3

Just Plain Polk

I twirled in front of the hall mirror one last time to be certain the green lawn dress fit the occasion. I'd never before attended an afternoon tea. My overworked mother never took time out from her busy day to sip tea and nibble cookies with the ladies of the community. "Too English," she would say, "for an Irish lass."

Mary's reaction had been the opposite. Her eyes sparkled as she recalled afternoon teas and luncheons she'd enjoyed while growing up in Boston.

"It was at an afternoon tea of the Beacon Hill Literary Guild when James proposed to me, you know. I slipped away from his mother's parlor and met him at the gazebo next to the pond." Her eyes glistened with happiness as she told about their rendezvous. "He was about to kiss me when Drucilla, my sister, called to us from the house."

About of coughing ended her storytelling. The attack left her weak and limp. I helped her back into bed, refilled her crystal tumbler with fresh water, and hurried down the stairs. In front of the hall mirror, I adjusted the bodice, tipped my head to one side, and coyly touched the sides of my face with my gloved hand. I felt like a little girl playing dress up.

Instead of preparing for Zerelda Paget's afternoon tea, I imagined myself back in Shinglehouse attending a tea at the Chamberlain estate. I fluttered my lashes at the mirror and crooned, "Good afternoon, Mrs. Chamberlain. Isn't it a lovely day?"

I glanced behind me at Jamie and saw him cover his mouth to hide his grin. "Pretty silly, huh?" I picked up the matching hat and pinned it atop my head. "Are you ready to go? My, what a handsome escort you make. Is the buggy waiting?"

He nodded and took my hand. Sam stood waiting for us beside the one-horse buggy. The foreman helped us into the

37

carriage. "Now you're sure you won't need help handling Effy?" He patted the brown-and-white horse on the head, then handed me the reins. "She's a good horse, but ya gotta show her who's boss right off."

I thanked Sam for hitching Effy to the runabout and assured him I was comfortable driving horses. I glared at the beast, clicked my tongue, and flicked the reins. Instead of going straight down the roadway, Effy chose to turn back toward the barn.

"Oh, no, you don't, little lady. We're going to the Paget place, like it or not." I pulled firmly on the reins and cracked the whip over the horse's head. One crack was all it took to convince Effy that I meant business. She turned and trotted down the road with the grace of a thoroughbred. Relieved, I whispered a quick prayer of thanksgiving.

When I arrived at the Pagets, I discovered Zerelda had invited a number of the neighbors. She had already regaled them with the story of Mary's premature delivery, greatly exaggerating my skills as a midwife.

"You just forget about all this California stuff," Mrs. Weatherby exclaimed. "We'll help you find yourself a good man, and you can settle down right here in Kansas where you're needed."

At first it seemed strange to be accepted by the women as an adult. Back home, I felt trapped in a never-never land between childhood and womanhood. Sometime during the last month, I'd passed over the line. If I'd had any doubts earlier, they were erased when the tales began, the childbirth tales, stories that would convince a single woman like me never to have children. And for some reason, the Kansas women's stories were worse than most.

Mrs. Meta Archer, the forty-seven-year-old mother of seven, closed her eyes and shuddered. "I remember in seventy-two, the year we arrived from Arkansas, Jesse Tipton, barely eighteen she was and the mother of twins, went into labor for her next child when a blizzard hit. The storm stranded her husband in a line shack, leaving poor Jesse to deliver her own child."

"The early days on the frontier weren't very kind to women," Minna Kline, Zerelda's closest neighbor, said as she passed a tray of oatmeal cookies around the circle. "Remember Prudence Warren? Poor Prudence! Her husband had to make a trip to Abilene in November, leaving her alone in a one-room soddy with three little ones and expecting a fourth. While he was gone, she miscarried. By the time he returned, Prudence had gone plumb loco."

I stared unbelieving at my hostess. "That's terrible. The poor woman. Did she recover?"

Minna shook her head. "Her husband sold out and took her back East to an asylum."

Mrs. Archer nodded sadly. "I can think of a large number of people, both men and women, who have been destroyed by the frontier. Isolation, grasshoppers, prairie fires, bandits, Indian uprisings, border raids by rebel renegades - a harsh heritage, to be sure."

I looked at the middle-aged woman who'd traveled to Kansas in a covered wagon as a bride. "Then why do people stay?"

A soft smile spread across the older woman's face. "It's home. It grows on you."

"That's right," Amy Simons interjected. "I took a trip East a few years back to see my parents in Delaware. I could hardly wait to get back to the big skies and the golden fields of western Kansas. I felt crowded by the cities and the large number of people."

"You wait, Miss Chloe," Mrs. Archer predicted, "if you stay in these parts long enough, you'll understand. Kansas is Kansas - big, broad, and brassy, but definitely Kansas. Not another place like it on earth."

I smiled to myself and thought, From what I've seen, you can have the prairie. I'll take civilization on either coast, thank you. Aloud I said, "I hope Mary McCall learns to like it here.

That's what's important. Me, I'll be gone in a few weeks, to California, then on to China."

"China?" Zerelda asked the question I read on each of the other women's faces. "Why China?"

I told them about my dream to go as a missionary to the women of the Orient. Suddenly I felt foolish, like a child again, defending my errant behavior to an angry mother. Mrs. Archer huffed indignantly. "Missionary to China? Well, if you ask me, there's enough to be done right here."

Zerelda calmed the older woman. "Who can know what the good Lord has in mind for Chloe? As long as she's willing to do whatever He asks and go wherever He leads, she'll be fine."

Suddenly the back door slammed, and seven children bounded into the parlor, with Jamie and Amy's five-year-old, Shane, trailing behind.

Amy's older daughter Ginny announced that Wayne Archer was trying to dunk Mrs. Lucy Gates' daughter Melinda in the duck pond. The women scurried from the room. Zerelda and I stayed behind.

"Zerelda, do you really believe that? Do you honestly think God cares whether you live in Kansas or Georgia."

She looked at me, surprised. "Oh, yes. I've never doubted it. My daddy used to say - he's a preacher, you know - 'God has a special plan for you, if you're patient enough to let Him show you what it is.' "

"This is going to sound a little strange, but what do you think about death?"

"Death? I beg your pardon?" She blinked in surprise. "I don't like it."

I laughed. "No, I don't mean that. I mean, what happens? Does the Bible say?"

We heard the sound of voices and knew that the other women were returning. "Mary's terribly confused since she lost the baby. And I don't know how to help her. Would you help me find some answers?"

"Sure, I'd love to. How about after I finish cleaning on Monday?"

I took her hand in mine. "Any time."

Amy burst into the room. "Meta left her purse by the chair. She's rounding up her brood and heading home."

Picking up on the cue, I gathered the teacups onto the tray. "I need to be going too. Let me help you with these dishes first."

"Oh, no, I can manage everything just fine." Zerelda threw her arm around my shoulders and escorted me toward the front door. "I hope you had a pleasant afternoon getting acquainted with everyone."

I assured her I had and thanked her for inviting me to her home. I added, "I know Mary will fit in beautifully with you ladies. She's a very special person; you're going to love her."

We joined the women, children, horses, and buggies in the roadway beside the house. After all the appropriate farewells, Jamie and I climbed onto the buggy and started Effy in the direction of home.

That evening as I shared the experience with Mary, I thought of how good it would feel to belong again. All afternoon, I'd forced myself to remember that everything in Kansas was temporary. Would I find such friendliness and neighborliness in California?

As the days passed, I developed a routine at the McCall home. After breakfast each morning, I did dishes, dusting, and general tidying. Later, I would play with Jamie, often on the front lawn. I put on my brother's trousers in order to teach the little boy how to do somersaults and cartwheels. Sometimes we would lie on our backs and stare up at the clouds. But Jamie's favorite activity was the swing. Yet, nothing I did convinced him to speak.

The closest he came to making a sound was the day he and I packed a picnic lunch and headed toward the creek across the road from the house. I had awakened long before dawn, my body layered in sweat, my bedding in tangles. And no matter how I tried, I couldn't fall back to sleep. I puttered about the house all morning, doing only what absolutely needed to be done.

As the August sun climbed overhead, so did the temperature. An oppressive humidity replaced the prairie's usual dry heat. I decided a dip in the stream would make it easier for the little boy to rest during his afternoon nap.

I set the basket under a clump of cottonwood trees and spread the blanket out on the grassy bank. Jamie plunked himself down on the blanket and extended his feet toward me. I removed his boots and stockings, then his outer clothing.

After I slipped out of my shoes - I hadn't bothered to wear any hose or petticoats underneath my skirts - I lifted my skirts to my knees and stepped into the stream. The cool water swirled gently about my calves. I fastened the hem of my dress into my sash and beckoned for Jamie to follow. Instead of cautiously stepping into the water, the child leapt into my arms.

"Hey, cowboy," I squealed. The impact of his tiny body caught me off balance. I struggled to maintain my footing, but my feet slipped on the mud in the bottom of the stream. I shrieked as we hit the water. While my face didn't go under, the back of my head did. The weight of my waterlogged hair loosened the hairpins, and my braid tumbled down my back.

"You scamp, you!" Laughing, I splashed water at the delighted little boy. Jamie gave a tiny squeal and splashed back. Startled, I paused momentarily, then scrambled toward the shore so he wouldn't see my surprise. He followed. I lifted him in my arms and clambered out onto the bank. "Oh, that felt good, didn't it?"

Jamie wriggled free and rushed for the picnic basket. While he munched on an oatmeal cookie, I sat on the blanket and wrung out my braid. As always, I chatted throughout the meal, ignoring his silence. He took another dunking in the stream and then, at my insistence, lay down with his head in my lap while I read to him from a storybook I'd found in the library. Within minutes he was asleep.

He slept with his head in my lap until I remembered it was Monday. Zerelda would be done with the cleaning soon. If we were going to study the Bible together, I would have to head back to the house.

Reluctantly, I let Jamie sleep on the blanket while I packed the picnic basket. Then I slipped the basket handles over one arm and scooped up the little boy with my other and trudged back to the house. I placed the sleeping child on his bed and hurried into Mary's room. Mary greeted me with a wan smile.

"If you're not up to this today," Zerelda began, "we can wait until later." When I'd told Mary about Zerelda's offer to study God's Word with us, she'd readily agreed. Zerelda and I pulled up two chairs beside Mary's bed and sat down.

Mary handed Zerelda a list of questions she'd compiled. Zerelda read them silently. When she finished the list, she took a deep breath. "Understand, I don't have all the answers just because my father is a preacher. And not everyone agrees with my beliefs. I can only give you texts that satisfy me."

"Anything you can tell us will be helpful," Mary told her. "My parents read the Bible and went to church every Sunday. But you know kids; we didn't listen to the grown-ups. I just remember a lot of shouting about fire and brimstone." The ailing woman shuddered. "I guess I want to know if it hurts to be dead."

Zerelda glanced over at me. "And you, Chloe, what do you think happens when one dies?"

I shrugged. "I guess I believe you go to heaven and float on a cloud or something."

Zerelda shuffled through the pages of her Bible as she spoke. "Well, let's see what the Bible says. Chloe, why don't you find the texts for Mary?" She turned a few more pages. "Find Ecclesiastes nine. Ecclesiastes is a short ways after Psalms - Psalms, Proverbs, Song of Solomon, Ecclesiastes." She looked over my shoulder. "Yes, that's right. Would you like to read it, Chloe? Verses five and six."

I skimmed down to the fifth verse. "For the living know that they shall die: but the dead know not anything, neither have they any more a reward; for the memory of them is forgotten. Also their love, and their hatred, and their envy, is now perished; neither have they any more a portion for ever in any thing that is done under the sun."

"Oh, that's terrible!" Mary gasped. "Does that mean my baby Agatha is gone forever from me? I barely got to hold her in my arms."

Zerelda shook her head and turned toward the back of her Bible. "I don't think so. I think to get a clearer picture of death you also need to read First Thessalonians four. Here it is - First Thessalonians four: thirteen to eighteen. 'But I would not have you to be ignorant, brethren, concerning them which are asleep, that ye sorrow not, even as others which have no hope. For if we believe that Jesus died and rose again, even so them also which sleep in Jesus' - did you get that? - 'sleep in Jesus will God bring with him.'"

I brightened. "Oh, then little Agatha is in heaven with Jesus, like I said."

"If one stops reading here, that would be the conclusion. But listen to verses sixteen and seventeen, and then tell me what you think. 'For the Lord himself shall descend from heaven with a shout, with the voice of the archangel, and with the trump of God: and the dead in Christ shall rise first - "

I knitted my brow in confusion. "Rise from where? If the dead are already with God in heaven, where do they arise from? I'm confused."

Zerelda smiled. "Let's go on to verses seventeen and eighteen; then I'll see if I can answer your questions. 'Then we which are alive and remain shall be caught up together with them in the clouds, to meet the Lord in the air: and so shall we ever be with the Lord. Wherefore comfort one another with these words.'"

I listened to the words she read and remembered bits of sermons I'd heard at the graveside funerals I'd attended. "Isn't there someplace in the Bible that says, 'From dust thou are; to dust thou shalt return'?"

Zerelda nodded. "Yes, many places. Psalm twenty-two: fifteen talks about being 'brought… into the dust of death' and Job thirty-four: fifteen says man shall turn to dust again."

Mary had been silent for some time. Suddenly she did the unexpected - she giggled. We looked at her in surprise.

She bit her lip, trying to swallow a sheepish grin. "Just remembered something my mother would say if my sister and I hadn't cleaned our rooms thoroughly, especially under the beds. In complete seriousness, Mama would lift the edge of the bed's dust ruffle and ask, 'Who died?' " Mary thought for a moment. "I never did understand what she meant by that, until now."

We laughed. Zerelda closed her Bible and suggested we pray together. During her prayer, my mind tossed the words of the texts about with others I'd picked up here and there. I was still confused. When she said "Amen," Mary thanked her.

"Zerelda, if death is a sleep, as these texts indicate, then what does Psalm twenty-three mean: to 'walk through the valley of the shadow of death'? Is that the time just before you die or something?"

"That's a pretty deep question. It will take some time to answer it adequately. What if I give you a list of texts to read on your own, and we can talk about them together next week?"

Mary sent me to the mahogany secretary by the window for paper, pen, and inkwell. I watched Zerelda skillfully flip through the pages of the Bible. I was impressed. She seemed to know right where to turn. I wished I could do that. My Bible study seemed to be so hit and miss. From the bed, Mary raised one hand. "Chloe, don't you read ahead of me. I want answers too."

I laughed and assured her we'd read the references together. Mary's bout of coughing ended our afternoon visit. When the attack subsided, she wheezed, "Do you realize that was the first time I coughed all afternoon? Isn't that amazing?"

One morning, I awoke before dawn. I'd never been so uncomfortably hot in my life. Thinking it might be cooler out on the front porch, I dressed and tiptoed outside to the porch. A warm breeze caressed my face and ruffled the hair cascading freely down my shoulders and back. I sat down on the porch steps. Pulling my knees up to my chin, I watched the fingers of sunlight skitter across the prairie. Overnight temperatures had dropped less than five degrees; it would be another sizzling-hot day.

Silhouettes of the barn and bunkhouse loomed stark against the glowing new morning. Silently, I watched Sam and the other ranch hands trek toward the house for breakfast. I thought of mornings I'd sneaked out of my parents' home in Pennsylvania in order to watch the sunrise. The six weeks since I left Pennsylvania seemed like a lifetime ago. Hmm, six weeks - that would be about right, I thought. Six weeks?

I counted the days on my fingers. Stunned, I counted them again. Leaping to my feet, I bounded into the house and rushed into the library, still engulfed in morning shadows. There on the corner by the crystal kerosene lamp, I spied a calendar. A third count proved I'd counted correctly the first time. Today is my seventeenth birthday! I don't believe it.

I sank into the leather desk chair. Imagine forgetting one's own birthday! I remembered my sixteenth birthday: Ma's luscious huckleberry cobbler, the diary Hattie gave me, the younger kids' cards, and Pa's gift - a copy of a book by Mark Twain I'd seen advertised in the Buffalo newspaper. My homesickness returned. The only contact I'd had with those I loved back home was through Hattie, faithful Hattie.

I'd tried again to return Pa's twenty-dollar gold piece inside a letter I wrote to Hattie, but when she answered, I knew by the weight of the envelope that I hadn't succeeded. Footsteps on the staircase reminded me that I still was less than presentable for the breakfast table. I waited until Jamie and his father disappeared into the kitchen before dashing upstairs to brush and rebraid my hair. When I took my place at the breakfast table, Sam asked me if anything was wrong. "You look exhausted, like you've been crying."

I rubbed my eyes and yawned. "I am tired. Doesn't this Kansas heat ever let up?"

Bo, the youngest of the ranch hands, joked, "Come October, you'll wish you'd put up a few jars of this heat along with Amy's blackberry jam."

"Right now, I can't imagine ever wishing for such a thing!" I sniffed.

Later, after sending Jamie out to play in the front yard, I gave the house a quick touch-up and hurried into the library to write a letter home. I took out a sheet of paper and began to write.

August 12, 1898

Dearest Hattie,

I received your letter last week and, what with helping Zerelda can fruit for winter and keeping Jamie out of trouble, I am just getting around to answering it....

I told her about Zerelda's visits, about how Mary's spirits seemed to improve afterward. I told her about the violent attacks that racked Mary's body with pain and left her exhausted.

I wish Pa were here to give Mary a few doses of his cough elixir. While Mr. McCall and I don't discuss Mary's weakened condition, we both know the truth. Maybe that's why I'm still in Kansas instead of on my way to San Francisco. Oh, yes, I started my own herbal pharmacy in the pantry. Jamie helps me collect the herbs and string them up to dry.

After finishing the letter, I placed it on the hall table for James to take into town. I glanced out the front screen door at Jamie stalking a squirrel. He looked my way and put his fingers to his lips to shush me. I waved and walked to the kitchen. Tying an apron around my waist, I took the flour bin down from the shelf. I used to laugh at my mother when she said that baking bread was the best cure she knew for depression. Now I understood - I could hardly wait to knead a batch of bread dough.

I was up to my elbows in flour when James strode into the kitchen, his face looking strained.

"Good," he said, sitting on the chair across the table from me. "When I saw Jamie outside, I knew I'd find you alone. Last night, Mary and I talked late into the night."

I continued to knead the dough.

"Mary wants to go back East to a lung specialist in Boston. Both of us realize that she'll never make it through a harsh winter here. This is her only chance." He drew circles with one finger in the dusting of flour on the table.

I paused. "I think that's an excellent idea. When will you leave?"

"As soon as possible."

"Good."

"Our problem is Jamie. With Mary in her condition, I could never handle him too. It's taken weeks for him to allow me to hold him." He sighed and frowned.

I continued kneading the dough.

"Chloe, what I'm going to ask is unreasonable, but for Mary's sake, I've got to. We considered asking you to accompany us East, but Jamie is already confused. Would you be willing to stay with Jamie until we return? You could move into Aunt Bea's place so you wouldn't be alone out here at the ranchhouse."

I inhaled sharply. "Stay here? I thought Mary's sister was coming to help."

"She is. She'll return with us. We shouldn't be gone for more than a month." He stared down at the table.

The truth was, I knew James was right. Like it or not, the little boy depended on me. During the past few weeks, I'd seen so many hopeful changes. "In for a penny; in for a pound. All right, I'll agree, but only if we can stay on the ranch. He's happier here."

James hesitated. "I don't know, a sixteen-year-old girl and a five-year-old staying alone?"

"Don't Sam and the other hands count? And besides, I'm no longer sixteen, I'll have you know. I recently had a birthday." I placed my hands on my hips and grinned a self-satisfied grin. "I understand that Mary was seventeen when you married her, was she not?"

The grim lines about his mouth told me I'd won my point.

Chapter 4

And the Rain Must Fall

Dark, ponderous clouds welled up in the western sky as the eastbound Union Pacific chugged into the Hays railway station. Already, flashes of lightning played hide-and-seek with the clouds and the prairie. Sam eyed the pending storm, then looked at James. We all knew Sam should be back at the ranch helping the men gather in the last of the hay crop instead of standing on the railway platform, waiting for Mary and James to board the train for Chicago.

For no apparent reason, Cy's jovial, slightly cynical face flashed before my eyes. I struggled to recapture the sights and sounds of the delightful day we'd shared in the Windy City. So much had changed since then. In many ways, that adventure in Chicago was my last day as a kid.

Allowing myself the luxury of one deep sigh, I then stuffed the memories away for a sunnier day. I glanced over my shoulder at Mary sitting on the bench beside the station house. We'd said our goodbyes at home, praying the words Pa had prayed when Riley left for the army. "May the Lord watch between me and thee while we are absent one from another." Lately, tears came whenever I thought of my father.

Jamie sat on Mary's lap. She held his face in her hands and whispered in his ear. I wondered how he would do once he realized his parents were gone. With a stiff breeze whipping my skirts about my ankles, I hugged myself and strolled to the end of the platform, where I could better view the drama of the impending storm. I'd never seen a lightning storm on the prairie. Long-time residents warned me of the potential for violence and disaster these summer storms contained. As Zerelda put it, "They don't call 'em storm cellars for nothing."

"Miss Chloe?" I hadn't heard James approach. I turned slowly to face him. He held Jamie in his arms. Mary was nowhere in sight.

50

"We're ready to leave. Mary's already on board. She didn't want to say goodbye again. She knew she'd cry."

I nodded. With his free hand James reached into his jacket pocket and withdrew an envelope. "The ticket agent asked me to give this to you. It came in on yesterday's train."

I glanced at the envelope, then slipped it into my skirt pocket. "Thank you. It's from my brother."

He smiled and turned his attention to Jamie. "Be a good boy for Miss Chloe until Mama and Daddy return, you promise?"

The little boy nodded, then stretched out his arms toward me. Reluctantly, James handed me his son. "I still don't like leaving you at the house alone. Aunt Bea isn't too happy about the arrangement either. She's helping Mary get settled in the sleeping car."

Again I nodded.

"Oh, yes, I left an envelope of cash in the right-hand drawer of my desk to use however you wish. Now remember, anything you need, Sam will take care of for you. And what he can't do, Aunt Bea will." James's grim expression softened into a teasing grin at the mention of his forceful and determined relative. "I don't know how Mary and I can ever repay you for all you're doing for us."

I shook my head. "I'm only doing what any caring person would do. Besides, Mary's like a sister to me. And then, of course, there's Jamie ..."

"Yes, Jamie ..." His voice caught. The silence between us spoke of the fears we couldn't discuss. At that moment we both saw time stretching ahead as an untrustworthy companion.

"You remembered the basket of food, didn't you?" I asked. "I baked some sweet rolls this morning, Mary's favorite."

James nodded, smiling. "Aunt Bea carried it on board." Tenderly, he brushed a stray curl from his son's face. "I hope we're doing the right thing, not taking him with us. If only Mary were feeling..." The noise of the steam engine swallowed up the rest of his words.

I shrugged and avoided his gaze. Over James's shoulder, I could see the conductor conferring with the station master. I knew it wouldn't be long before the train pulled out of the station.

When the conductor cried, "All aboard," Aunt Bea emerged from the sleeper car and stepped down onto the platform. Spotting me, she strode in our direction. Before she reached us, James kissed his son on the cheek and climbed on board.

The bell sounded, and the train's hissing grew insistent. Slowly the monster of the prairies chugged forward, gathering speed with each turn of the massive iron wheels.

An overwhelming sadness settled on my shoulders like a lead weight. What have I done? What have I agreed to? Have I let my heart get ahead of my head again like Pa always says I do? Oh, Pa, if only you were here, if only you'd forgive me, if only I hadn't…

For a moment I imagined Pa standing beside me, whispering in my ear. "Once you make a decision, accept the consequences and move on, Chloe Mae. Vain regrets guarantee self-fulfilling defeat."

Without warning, Jamie squirmed from my arms and ran after the disappearing train. "Jamie, come back," I shouted, chasing after the child. Aunt Bea instantly joined chase.

Jamie had almost reached the end of the wooden platform when Sam darted out from the shadows and lifted the little boy into his arms. "Hey, where do you think you're goin'?" Jamie silently pummeled the man's chest with his angry fists. "It's all right, little man. It's all right." The rangy cowboy held him close.

Relieved, I hurried over to Sam and reached out for Jamie, but the wiry black man shook his head and mouthed the word "Wait." I glanced at Aunt Bea. She lifted one eyebrow disapprovingly. However, during the previous weeks, I'd come to respect the strong, gentle man. Soon, Jamie's tantrum subsided, and a shower of silent tears dampened Sam's chambray shirt. The man whispered soothing words until the sobbing child heaved a ragged sigh and wilted in the foreman's strong arms.

Sam cast a wink at me and strode toward the waiting carriage. Aunt Bea tried once more to convince me that Jamie and I should move into town with her until her nephew and niece returned. I attempted once again to explain my reasons for staying at the ranch. "Jamie has never been happier than he is at the ranch; his life has been in a turmoil ever since he left Boston, two months ago. James and Mary agree he will accept their absence quicker if he's at a place he's come to love."

"Well," the agitated woman huffed, "I never believed one should kowtow to a child's whims."

I rested my hand on her arm. "Aunt Bea, you are such a special lady to care so much. I promise if it gets to be too much for me or for Jamie, I'll have Sam bring us to your home immediately."

She stopped walking and studied my face for a few seconds. Convinced I wouldn't budge, she shrugged her shoulders in defeat. "For such a young lass, you can be stubborn."

I giggled and squeezed her arm. "I guess we're two of a kind, huh?"

"Hmmph!" A twinkle in her eye and a hint of a grin told me I'd struck pay dirt. I climbed into the back seat of the surrey, and Sam handed Jamie up to me. "Thank you again for all you've done, Aunt Bea. Can we give you a lift home?"

She shook her head. "My carriage is waiting on the other side of the depot. Young lady, I expect to hold you to your promise! Samuel, you take care of these two children, ya hear?"

"Yes, ma'am." Sam tipped his hat and climbed into the driver's seat. The horses responded instantly to the flick of his wrist, and the carriage wheels rolled forward. I blew a kiss at Aunt Bea and settled myself for the long ride home. Jamie snuggled under the protection of my arm. As we passed Aunt Bea's hardware store, he curled up on the seat, with his head on my lap, and instantly fell asleep.

With my hands steadying Jamie, I leaned my head against the carriage's leather-upholstered seat and closed my eyes. The gentle rocking of the carriage lulled me into a stupor. My mind retraced the events of the morning. That's when I remembered the letter in my pocket. Trying not to waken the sleeping boy, I reached into my pocket and withdrew the envelope.

I tore open the seal and took out the sheet of expensive linen note paper.

San Francisco, California August 1, 1899

Dear Chloe Mae:

I was very happy to hear from you once more, though I found the news of your decision to stay with the McCalls for a while gloomy indeed. Kansas is such a raw, forbidding country, too dangerous even for you and your adventurous spirit, which is why I see no use trying to dissuade you....

Hattie told me about Pa and the gold piece. I am so sorry. Give him time; he'll soften. You were always his favorite, so you can understand his pain at what he considers your betrayal of the family. She also told me about the cad, Emmett. Guess you were right about him anyway. Cy sends greetings. He said to tell you that the family sent his brother Phillip to New Orleans to study banking from the inside....

Grudgingly, Joe wished me good luck, then added,

Try to make it over the Rockies and the Sierra Nevada before winter storms close the passes. Except for the parties Cy drags me to, I love California. He has leased a house on Nob Hill. It makes his parents' home in Shinglehouse look positively shabby! Ha, ha. Looking forward to seeing you soon.

Your brother, Joe

In the Kansas heat, snow was the farthest thing from my mind. One glance at the billowing clouds told me I should be more concerned about a summer thunderstorm. Sam must have spotted the advancing cloud bank at the same time, for with a shout and a snap of the whip above the horses' heads, the carriage lurched forward.

"Hang on to the boy, Miss Chloe. We're in for a rough ride." The carriage tore down the rough county road, shaking, rolling, bouncing over every rut and pothole.

Jamie awakened, wide-eyed and terrified. "It's all right, Jamie," I comforted. "We're just racing a storm home. Hang on to me."

The wind whipped my bonnet from my head. Only the ties under my chin prevented it from flying out of the carriage. Over his shoulder, Sam shouted out a string of commands. "Lower the canvas flaps on each side of the carriage. There's a blanket stored under the front seat."

I leaned forward and acknowledged his instructions. "Doesn't look good, does it?"

"The horses know. I can't hold them back; they're running flat out."

I drew Jamie closer. My heart seemed to beat to the rhythm of the pounding hooves. "Is it dangerous?"

He shrugged and wrestled with the reins.

"We've got to get home." Anxiety caused my voice to come out higher and louder than usual. I breathed deeply several times to fight back the panic growing inside me. I hated lightning storms.

A flash of lightning announced the first water droplets. Before I'd finished lowering the second canvas flap, the heavens opened up into what my father called a "gully washer."

I turned and looked through the small window behind my head in time to see a long finger of a cloud separate itself from an upper cloud and begin to rotate.

With each rotation, the cloud enlarged as its spinning funnel skimmed the earth like a top.

"Sam, is that a tornado funnel?" He glanced quickly over his shoulder.

"Yep!" The snap of Sam's whip sent the frightened horses plunging ahead. "Hold on," he shouted. The carriage careened off the main roadway. Purposely, I slid to the floor of the carriage with Jamie clinging to my neck. The tall prairie grasses whipped the sides of the carriage as we sped by. I peered out the side of the carriage and realized Sam was taking us to the abandoned soddy. While the crumbling structure didn't inspire my confidence for safety, it was better than being hurled through the air in the carriage.

Sam brought the wagon to a halt on the eastern side of the shack and leapt from the driver's seat. I watched in horror as he unhitched the horses to set them free. With no time to shout orders, he lifted Jamie from my arms, clamped his viselike hand on my wrist, and dragged me toward the sod house. Instead of ducking inside the roofless structure, he darted past to a crumbling storm cellar.

He shoved Jamie into my arms and attempted to lift the heavy door. For some reason, it had been nailed fast. While he pawed through the rubble for something he could use to break the door, I watched the advancing funnel. It moved steadily forward in a graceful, swaying motion, rising and falling like a kite.

A sudden crash returned my attention to the problem at hand, the storm cellar. Wood splintered in every direction as Sam stood astride the opening, crashing a rusty plowshare against the rotting door. With one motion, he tossed the plowshare over his shoulder and hauled open what was left of the wooden door. Seizing my hand, he dragged me into the damp, spider-infested cavern and lowered the door over us.

The timbers overhead groaned with the pressure of the wind. As a little girl I always imagined our storm cellar had a secret trapdoor that led to the other side of the earth or to hell - I wasn't sure which. My teeth chattered uncontrollably from fear. Jamie buried his face in my shoulder and clung to my neck with incredible strength for a five-year-old. I shrank back against the wall and felt something cool and slimy on my back. Moss covered the earthen sides of the cellar. The broken door did little to protect us from the torrential rains. I pulled the soggy blanket around our shoulders and closed my eyes, reminding myself that, for the moment, we were safe.

The tornado roared like a Union Pacific on a mail run. Then it hit. Wood screeched as it was ripped apart over our heads. Then the bed of an abandoned farm wagon fell over the opening, casting us into darkness.

Sam chuckled. "Praise God. At least we won't get wet."

Drenched, frightened, and cold, I groaned. The last thing I wanted was humor. "Sam, doesn't anything ever get you down?"

Though his face wasn't visible in the darkness, I could imagine his broad, easy smile. "Child, if I'm alive and in one piece, I have all the reason I need to praise my Creator."

"I don't understand." My voice broke off in tears.

An arm of iron encircled my shoulder. "Miss Chloe, a little tornado is nothing compared to the violence I've seen." Then without warning he started singing. "Nobody knows the troubles I've seen ..."

His heavy bass voice echoed off the cellar walls and for a while drowned out the storm overhead. "... nobody knows but Jesus." When he stopped singing, an eerie silence settled over us.

Self-conscious, I pulled away from his protective arm. "The storm must be gone. We can get out of here."

I moved toward the stairs, but he grabbed my arm. "Wait, not yet. I think we're trapped in the eye of the funnel right now."

As quickly as the silence fell, it dissolved into a furious maelstrom. Discouraged, I dropped to the floor and leaned back against the grimy wall. Sam offered to hold Jamie, but the child refused to let go of my neck.

"So all your kin is back in Pennsylvania?"

Appreciating his attempt to get our minds off the present danger, I told him about my family and how I came to be in Kansas. When I finished, I asked him about his family.

"Oh, can't say as I know. I left Georgia and headed West after the war." He paused and took a deep breath. "My father died at Antietam, and my ma, well, she and my two-year-old sister died in a house fire set by local ruffians. They barred the door so she couldn't escape."

I waited until I realized no more information was forthcoming. "How did you get away?"

"The mob dragged me from the house and hogtied me. They intended to string me up in a tree in front of our house, but the flames attracted the townspeople."

"Why? Why would anyone do such a thing? You must hate them."

A silence fell between us. Finally he spoke. "No, I won't stoop to their level by hating too. After the war the South was a frightening, lawless place to live. Remember, Miss Chloe, fear and hate always go together."

"But you're always so happy. I'd be miserable if I were you."

A deep resounding "Aw," filled the cellar. "The way I look at it, I have two choices: I can spend the rest of my life eaten up with anger, or I can let my hate go and give thanks for having been given a second chance at living." What a remarkable man.

"That's enough reminiscing for today. Let's get ourselves out of here." Sam struggled to his feet and strained to lift the plank over our heads. By the sound of his groaning, I knew he was having little success.

I disentangled Jamie's fingers from my neck and set the child on the moist dirt, then rose to my feet. "Here, let me help."

"You help?" Sam snorted. "How much help can a slip of a gal like you give?"

I turned toward the stairs and felt my way up two steps. "You might be surprised. When I say, 'push,' push!"

Once certain of my footing, I pressed my back against the wooden plank. "Now push."

I squealed as the first shaft of daylight spilled into the cellar.

"Move over a tad." Sam pushed me to one side. "You might be a scrawny little thing, but you've got brains. If we combine your brains and my muscles, maybe, just maybe we'll get out of here. On the count of three. One, two, three."

The door inched upward. With one powerful thrust, Sam lifted the wagon bed and slid it to one side. Jamie followed me as I scrambled out of the storm cellar and started to where we'd left the carriage. The shiny black vehicle lay like a heap of bones beside the soddy.

Sam ran his hand along the carriage's luggage boot. Tears surfaced in the foreman's eyes. "I sure did like driving that carriage. After I get you two safely home, I'll come back and see what I can salvage."

I inched closer to where he stood. "You did the right thing. We're alive, remember?" I reminded.

He shrugged, then whistled for the horses. It took a second whistle for the matching set of roans to come galloping across the flattened prairie grass. Sam examined both horses carefully. While one had been cut near her right eye by flying debris, the other escaped the tornado unscathed.

Running his hands over the injured horse's muzzle, he glanced over his shoulder at me. "Ever ride bareback?"

I sized up the animal before answering. "Once, uh, not very successfully, however."

"Well, Nellie's as gentle as they come. I'll put Jamie on Nestor with me. Here, step into my hand, and I'll give you a hoist up." He knelt beside the horse and cupped his hands.

"I'd really rather walk."

Sam took off his hat and ran his fingers through his damp hair. "Miss Chloe, I'm tired. I'm hungry. And that good humor you commented on earlier is in great danger of slipping, so get on up there!"

Instantly I obeyed, straddling the mare, long skirt and all, while trying to maintain my dignity and my modesty.

"Here, hold on to the reins." He handed me the reins, then lifted a wide-eyed Jamie onto the back of the other horse and leapt on, Indian style, behind him. Sam glanced over his shoulder and grinned. "Come on, let's ride."

Clinging to the mane with one hand and to the reins with the other, I followed Sam's horse to the main road. We rode side by side along the wagon road, with the foreman setting an easy pace. While I never completely relaxed, I did make it back to the house without mishap. When we rode onto the ranch, the ranch hands rushed to meet us. Jake lifted Jamie down while Bo helped me down.

"Boss," Jake thumped Sam on the back, "sure is good to see ya. I hate to tell you this, but we lost at least a third of the hay crop in the south forty. We had to hole out in a gully, horses and all, until it passed over."

Sam turned the horses over to Darcy. "Any injuries?"

"Nope, to neither man nor beast." Jake's bush of a mustache stretched to accommodate his grin.

Feeling as irritable and uncomfortable as a wet cat, I hurried toward the house. "Give Jamie and me an hour for hot baths, and supper will be ready. I have a pot of chili that just needs to be heated."

Sam caught up with me. "Now, Miss Chloe, Mr. McCall left firm instructions that you were not to wait on us while he was gone."

I glared at him and kept on walking. "Mr. Sam, I am cold, tired, filthy, and hungry. And this good nature you see is threatening to explode into a screaming tantrum, so don't mess with me. You get your boots in here in one hour, you got that?"

The ranch hands froze. No one used that tone with Sam. Sam drew back in surprise, then bristled. I felt my chin quiver in my effort to contain my laughter. Suddenly he winked and broke into loud guffaws. "Yes, ma'am, in one hour. I'll be there, boots and all."

I strode through the front door, letting the screen door bang behind me. I rushed Jamie through his bath, then let the tub refill while I dressed the little boy and told him to play in the parlor with a set of blocks his father had bought for him in Kansas City.

Grabbing a change of clothing, I hurried into the bath closet and slipped out of my clothing. I held my dress up to the window to assess the damage. Streaks of brown and green covered the back of the dress. Similar smudges decorated the front. I dropped it into a pile and climbed into the copper tub. A hot bath had never felt so good. After sudsing the dirt and grit off my skin and giving my hair a thorough cleansing, I sank deep into the tub and filled my lungs with the hot steam coming off the water.

I could have stayed submerged much longer except for the sound of four pair of boots stomping about the kitchen. I reluctantly pulled the tub stopper, dried myself off, and pulled on clean clothing. Wrapping a towel about my hair, I ran downstairs to the kitchen.

I stopped at the door and stared. Bo was setting the table while Jake stood by the baking shelf, whipping up a batch of corn bread. Jamie sat on a tall stool, watching the action.

"I'm sorry. I guess I got carried away in the bath."

Sam stuffed a log in the stove and grinned. "Just take your time, Miss Chloe. Everything's under control here."

"Just give me a few minutes to brush out my hair." Upstairs in my room, I yanked the brush through my wet tangles. Knowing it would never dry if I braided it, I pulled it back and fastened the front portion back and let the rest hang down to my waist. I eyed the sad results in the mirror. Can't be helped.

I charged back down the stairs and into the kitchen. When all eyes turned to watch my unladylike entry, I felt conspicuous as I joined the men at the table. When we finished eating, Sam called me aside. "Miss Chloe, I appreciate the meal tonight, but James left strict orders. He doesn't want the men hanging around the house. We'll continue our breakfast schedule as usual, but suppers are out."

I started to protest, but Sam silenced me instantly. "No arguing, Miss Chloe. Young Bo already thinks he's in love with you. Now, I'm here whenever you need me, but the boss's orders must be obeyed."

I reluctantly agreed. I cleaned the chili off Jamie's face and hands, then led him out to the front porch. Since the grass was still wet from the storm, I suggested he run up to his room for his box of metal soldiers and play fort.

It was strange indeed for me to sit on the porch steps while the men finished the supper cleanup as agreed. The picture of my father and my brothers helping Ma and Hattie either prepare a meal or clean up made me chuckle. Pa had definite ideas about women's responsibilities. It wasn't all bad, though - he never made Hattie or me muck out the cattle stalls.

Jamie spread out his set of hand-painted tin soldiers on the porch floor. With the sun still high in the sky, I decided to answer my brother's letter. Retrieving a large book, a pen, a bottle of ink, and some paper from James's desk in the library, I settled myself on the top porch step and scribbled the date and salutation on the paper.

But after thinking about the events of the past few days, I decided to wait to write until I heard from James. After all, I reasoned, what can I tell him at this point except that I've postponed the rest of my journey a while longer? He won't understand.

I studied the little boy left in my charge. No, Joe will not understand.

Chapter 5

A Little Faith

Jamie washed down his pancakes with a second glass of milk.

"Slow down, honey," I warned. "The goats will still be there ten minutes from now."

The little boy nodded and lifted his glass toward Jake.

"Want more, son?" Jake laughed and poured him another glass. "How about you, Miss Chloe?"

I grimaced and swallowed the last of the goat's milk in my glass. "I will never get used to this stuff." I shook my head vigorously to erase the memory of the gamey-tasting liquid.

Jake laughed again. "Maybe you should come along and meet your benefactors, Faith, Hope, and Charity."

"That's all right. Spare me the pleasure."

"What?" Shorty snickered. "You've been here for more than a month, and you haven't met Satan yet?"

I gulped. "Satan?"

"Satan's my billy goat," Jake explained.

Sam warned, "The name says it all."

"He's not that bad," Jake shot back.

Darcy's eyes twinkled, his Arkansas drawl thicker than usual. "Yeah, as long as he's on one side of the fence and you're on the other."

"A silly little billy goat! Ya just gotta let 'em know who's boss," Jake scoffed. "Seriously, Miss Chloe, you are welcome to come along and meet the 'family.' "

I pushed my chair back. "If you gentlemen will excuse me, I will start the breakfast cleanup, since it is my turn to do so. And, Jake, thank you for the invitation, but - "

I felt a tug on my hand and looked down into Jamie's pleading brown eyes. "I guess the dishes can wait a few minutes while I meet the 'family.' "

Jamie's face lighted up. He slid from his chair and ran to the screen door. Jake carried his dishes to the sink, then extended his arm toward me. "Are you ready for the royal introduction, Miss Chloe?"

Untying my apron, I slipped it over my head. With a proper curtsy, I took his arm. "It would be a pleasure, sir.

As we stepped out onto the back steps, I caught Sam's frown.

"We'll be loading hay in the north field near Simons' place," Sam called. "We want to unload the first wagon before noon."

"Yes, sir. I'll be right along." Jake grinned, picked up a bowl of breakfast scraps, then led me down the back steps. Jamie bounded ahead toward the bunkhouse. By the time Jake and I reached his side, Jamie had climbed three rails high on the fence.

In the pen behind the bunkhouse, Faith, a gray doe; Hope, a gray-and-white spotted doe; and Charity, a pure white doe, waited by the fence for their morning fare. Satan, a solid black buck with yellow slits for eyes, peered from behind a lean-to shack at the far end of the pen.

When Jake opened the gate, Jamie climbed down from the fence and ran to Jake's side. I frowned as Jake led Jamie into the pen. "Will Jamie be safe in there?"

The man nodded and emptied the scraps of food into the trough. "As long as I'm here to control Satan, he'll be fine. The does are as gentle as lambs. James uses them to keep the grass around the house trimmed." I cast a wary glance at Satan still lingering in the shadows of the building.

"You can come too," Jake suggested. "Old Satan's not as bad as the boys make him sound. Like most animals, he just has to know who's boss."

I waved off the invitation and leaned over the fence. "Thanks anyway. I have a perfect view right here."

Hope came running when Jake called to her. Cautiously, Jamie extended his hand and patted the animal's head. When the spotted doe turned her head and licked the boy's face,

Jamie gasped in surprise. Jake strolled over to the fence where I stood. "See, they're gentle creatures; they love children."

I laughed. "Kids, you mean."

Jake groaned.

When the other two does saw the attention Hope was getting, they bounded over to Jamie and nuzzled him from every side, causing the little boy to stagger to maintain his footing.

"Talk about butting in!" I giggled.

Jake cast me an exasperated look. "I've heard them all, Miss Chloe. You can't possibly out-pun Sam."

I grinned and arched an eyebrow. "Now, Jake, stop goading me."

The cowboy opened his mouth to speak, then stopped and looked at me curiously. "Did you hear what I heard?"

I nodded and glanced over Jake's shoulder at the little boy and the three playful goats. "Jamie giggled, didn't he?"

Jake didn't have time to answer, for suddenly, out of the corner of my eye, I saw an ebony blur dart past. "Jake! Watch out, Jamie!"

Jake whirled about as Satan charged at Jamie, sending the little boy sprawling face down on the grass. The animal backed up, then pawed the ground, preparing for his next attack. Jake quickly stepped between Jamie and the bullying billy goat. "Satan, Veto! Veto!"

The goat lifted his head, then shook it in disgust. "I mean it, Satan. Veto!"

The animal snorted, then strutted back to the lean-to. In one motion, Jake scooped Jamie into his arms and handed him over the fence into mine.

"Veto?" I asked as I dusted off Jamie's overalls. "Veto? I understand how he got his name, but veto?"

Jake laughed. "Yeah, I bought old Satan from a Missouri State congressman. The congressman trained him to be a guard goat, so to speak. I got butted a few times before I could remember the command to make him stop."

"I've got to tell Pa about this. He will …" I paused, remembering the miles and barriers between us, then continued. "My father loves politics. He'd get a laugh over a butting goat that only a veto can stop. Well, Jamie boy, you and I had better be getting back to the house and let Jake join the rest of the men in the fields."

"Jamie," Jake called, "any time you want to come and play with the goats, let me know. I'll be glad to bring you, but never, ever, ever come down by yourself, all right?" The child slipped his hand into mine and nodded solemnly.

As we walked up to the house, Aunt Bea's carriage whipped around the corner and up the driveway. We paused by the gate and waited until she halted the team. "A telegram for you, Chloe. It's from Boston."

Before I could help her from the carriage, Aunt Bea jumped to the ground. The back of her skirt caught on the brake handle. Disgusted, she lifted it free, then handed me the telegram. I tore the envelope open while she tied the horses. This was the first message we'd received since Mary and James had left more than a week before.

"Arrived in Boston, stop. Mary hospitalized at Boston General, stop. Her condition - stabilized, stop. Kiss Jamie and Aunt Bea for us, stop. James McCall." I stared at the yellow sheet of paper for a few seconds.

"Well, that really tells us a lot!" Aunt Bea frowned.

I showed Jamie the telegram. "See, honey, this is from your daddy. Your mommy's in the hospital, where the doctors can make her feel better." I searched his steady gaze, trying to discover whether he understood. All I found was that strange, dark emptiness I'd seen on the train after his baby sister had died. I planted a tender kiss on each of Jamie's cheeks. "One is from your daddy, and this one is from your mommy."

Folding the telegram, I slipped it into my pocket and suggested Jamie go play in the front yard. A smile reappeared on his face, and he nodded and skipped away. Aunt Bea and I entered the house.

"It's so good to see you." I gave the woman a hug. "You didn't have to come all the way out here to deliver the telegram. One of your clerks at the store could have done it for you."

"I wanted to see for myself that you and Jamie are faring well. And from what I see, you are. I hate being wrong, you know." She chuckled. "That doesn't change anything, though. I still wish you would reconsider. Your room is ready any time."

I laughed at her honesty. "I know. And I will keep my word if it gets too difficult. Jamie's well-being is more important than my pride."

She squeezed my hand, then walked back onto the porch. "I think we both feel that way." We paused to watch Jamie swinging in the yard. "And you were right, I've never seen the boy so happy. He seems to be settling in nicely!'

"Would you like to sit on the porch for a few minutes? I sit out here often, to relax and keep an eye on Jamie at the same time."

"I can't stay long. I left Walter in charge of the store. And you know Walter."

"Even for a glass of fresh apple cider?" I coaxed.

She paused and eyed me carefully. "I don't want to be a bother."

"Aunt Bea, since breakfast, Jamie and I have been in the company of goats. The hired men are out in the fields. As you can see, Jamie is occupied. Believe me, I would gladly welcome your company."

"Well, I'm not sure if preferring my company over that of goats is much of a compliment, but I'll take it as such anyway. And, yes, that cider sounds delicious."

"Wonderful. You just make yourself comfortable. I'll be right back with the juice." I hurried into the house and filled three glasses, then took them out onto the porch.

I told her about Jamie and his surprising squeal that morning and the earlier one at the stream. "I wish I knew what to do next."

She pursed her lips in thought. "I've never been a mother, but I think I'd ask him questions he had to answer."

"I've been trying that. Sometimes it frustrates him, though."

"Maybe one of these days, he'll get frustrated enough to speak."

We talked about the books Aunt Bea had loaned me.

Her insights and humor surprised me. "In the carriage, I have four new books for you to read. I also brought a stack of newspapers you might find interesting. I know it's difficult to keep informed out here so far from town."

I reached over and patted her hand. "You are so good to me, Aunt Bea."

"I'm going to miss you when you leave for California." Tears filled her eyes. "Oh, I almost forgot. Remember that missionary preacher you told me about? Elder Van Dorn? He will be speaking in Hays next Saturday. He and his wife have completed their speaking tour and are on their way back to China."

"What?" I squealed. Tingles of excitement raced up and down my spine. "Really? How did you find that out?"

She shrugged, assuming an air of disinterest. "There are posters all over town. You would have seen them, too, if you'd ever come to visit."

"You can expect us this weekend!" I assured her.

"I thought so," she teased. "Tell Sam I have his room ready too. But now, I really must get back to the store. I've enjoyed this morning so much, Chloe."

"Me too. Thank you for bringing the telegram and for staying awhile."

I caught the twinkle in her eye as she turned to go. "Of course, we could do this every evening if you moved back into town. I know, I know ..."

"You never give up, do you?"

The older woman chuckled. "Frontier women never say die."

I called Jamie over to kiss his aunt goodbye. We stood beside the driveway, waving until her carriage disappeared over the rise. Jamie and I ate lunch together; then while he napped, I gathered up the books Aunt Bea had left and took them to my room. While I knew a sink full of dirty dishes awaited me, I couldn't wait to begin reading.

At the sound of the hay wagon rumbling up the road, I realized the afternoon was gone. Hurrying down to Jamie's room, I found him quietly playing soldiers on his bedroom floor. He looked up from his toys and smiled.

"Ready to eat a little supper?" I asked. He nodded, scooped up his toys, and carefully placed each one on a shelf in his bookcase.

By the time we reached the kitchen, Jake had already delivered the evening's supply of goat's milk for Jamie and me. I poured a glass for each of us. I admit it's good for me, but I don't have to like the stuff!

After we ate, I took Jamie for a walk to the rise. Together we sat under a spreading elm and watched the cloud shapes change. I saw Sam later that evening and told him about Aunt Bea's visit and her invitation. "Sounds fine, Miss Chloe. The team and I will be ready to travel right after breakfast."

When Zerelda arrived at the house the next morning, she was bubbling with excitement. "Imagine, real live missionaries from China are coming to Hays! And what are the chances they'd be the same ones you met in Pennsylvania at the beginning of summer?"

"Pretty good, I'd say, since the railroad has been their main means of transportation around the country." I tried to sound reasonable. I glanced across the room to where Jamie and Zerelda's sons, Billy and Benny, sat eating jam sandwiches. "I remember them saying that they landed in San Francisco and headed east. When they stopped in Shinglehouse, they were on their way to New York City."

Suddenly in the middle of measuring out the flour for the week's baking, Zerelda stopped. "You wouldn't consider going off with them, would you?"

I bristled. "Of course not. I have Jamie to consider." I paused and smiled. "Maybe this is God's way of reminding me of my mission for Him."

When I had chosen to accompany Mary to Kansas, I'd tried to push from my mind all thoughts of going to China as a missionary. Now, I could think of nothing else. At bedtime, when I absent-mindedly put Jamie's nightshirt on backward, the little boy looked at me questioningly. I laughed and tousled his hair. In response, he threw his arms around my neck and clung with all his strength. Patting his back, I soothed, "It's all right, Jamie boy. I won't leave you until you don't need me anymore." I coaxed his arms from my neck, kissed his forehead, and adjusted his sheets. "Sleep, little one."

His worried eyes stared up at me; his mouth tightened with concern. A tear trickled down his cheek onto his pillowcase. "Would you feel better if I left your door open tonight? That way, you can see the light from my room." He nodded. After giving him a second kiss, I headed for my own room.

I set the lamp on the desk by the window. Pulling back the white ruffled curtain, I stared out at the gathering dusk. A lone chicken hawk circled lazily over the field, intent on finding a rodent for his supper. I watched the sky change from periwinkle to indigo.

My thoughts traveled to Mary and James in faraway Boston. If only I knew how long it would be before they returned to Kansas. I could make arrangements to join the Van Dorns in San Francisco and... I sighed and let the curtain fall back into place. Changing into my nightdress, I sat down at the desk to write a letter to Hattie. After scribbling out two sentences, I gave up, blew out the lamp, and slid between the sheets.

I rolled over and closed my eyes, enjoying the cool breeze wafting through the open window. Suddenly, I felt a light touch on my arm. My eyes flew open. I found myself staring into Jamie's ashen face. "Jamie, is something wrong?"

He bit his lip and nodded.

"Did you hear something? Are you sick?"

He shook his head no to each question.

I thought for a minute, then lifted one corner of my sheet. "Do you want to climb into my bed for a while?"

The child scrambled onto the bed and snuggled down beside me. Within seconds, I could hear the boy's soft, even breathing. Afraid to move for fear of waking Jamie, I stared into the darkness. Sure glad you can sleep. You aren't even playing fair. Streaks of vermilion filled the eastern sky before I finally dropped off to sleep.

The rest of the week dragged by in spite of my efforts to keep busy. Each morning after breakfast I took Jamie to see the goats. However, without Jake there to control Satan, Jamie had to be satisfied with petting them through the fence rails. One day, Jake put the does on the front lawn to graze. After watching Jamie and the three goats romp about the yard, I joined them in a game of tag. Both Jamie and the does caught on to the game quickly.

We played for hours. During that time I forgot about China, I forgot about Mary, I forgot about Saturday. I had just tagged Charity's rump and run in the opposite direction with the goat charging pell-mell after me, when I heard laughter. I stopped abruptly. The goat skidded into my leg, causing me to lose my balance. I landed with a thud on my stomach. Stunned, I struggled to catch my breath. Suddenly, four arms were lifting me to my feet.

"Are you all right, Miss Chloe?" Bo held onto my arm until he was certain I could stand. Darcy dusted off the hem of my skirt while Jake chased the frightened Charity about the lawn.

I rubbed at the grass stains on the bodice of my dress. "I'm fine, or at least, I would be fine if you hadn't shown up. What are you men doing here at this time of day?"

"At this time of day?" Darcy echoed. "What do you mean 'at this time of day'? We live here, remember?"

I glanced at the sky. The sun hovered above the horizon. Its light had already turned the world golden. I felt a blush scale my neck and face. "Oh, I guess I lost track of time, huh? Uh, how long were you watching?"

Darcy drawled, "Long enough."

"You should have seen yourself, Miss Chloe. I've never seen a girl run so fast in my life." Bo grinned and dipped his face.

"I'll have you know, mister, I could outrun all but the oldest of my brothers. I hopped a moving train, remember?"

Surprised at my vehemence, the shy farm hand gulped. "Yes, ma'am."

Gathering my skirts and my dignity about myself, I limped into the house and slammed the door behind me. Curious, I peeked out one of the parlor windows at the men still staring after me. I chuckled at the stunned expressions on their faces. I must have been quite a sight out there.

My chuckles turned to giggles, then to open laughter. Tears streamed down my face as I plopped onto the sofa, my laughter filling the empty room and echoing up the stairwell. I didn't hear Jamie enter. Suddenly he was there, snickering behind his hand.

"So you think that was funny, do ya?" I grabbed him in my arms and tickled his tummy. That's when I heard it again, the giggle. I resisted the momentary temptation to stop the roughhousing, and I continued the fun. In spite of himself, Jamie laughed out loud two more times before we crumbled to the floor, exhausted.

I leaned back against the front of the sofa and pulled him into my arms. "Oh, Jamie, I love you so much. Do you know how precious you are to me?"

The little boy grinned up into my face, then burrowed into my arms. How much he must miss his mother's tender loving. He must feel so confused. I thought of my own homesickness and pain. I understand a little how you feel, kiddo. We're both little lost lambs, aren't we?

Early Friday morning, I rushed about the kitchen cleaning up after breakfast while Sam hitched up the carriage. Jamie perched himself on the kitchen stool and watched me place the last clean bowl on the dish shelf, then close the door. "We're going to visit Aunt Bea today. Would you like to take your soldiers along to play with, or maybe your blocks?" I pointed at the leather valise sitting on the edge of the table. "I packed a change of clothing and a nightshirt for you as well as a few things for me."

When I touched his arm, he jerked away. His lower lip protruded threateningly. "Jamie, what's wrong? We're coming back to the ranch Sunday morning. I promise."

I heard the carriage pull up by the kitchen door. One look at Jamie, and I knew I hadn't eased his fears. Sighing, I closed the case. Sam bounded into the kitchen and picked up the valise. "This ready to go?"

I removed my apron and tossed it on the back of a chair. "I need to make one last check upstairs."

"You ready to go, champ?" Sam swept Jamie into one arm and held the valise with the other.

I raced through the house and up the stairs, grabbed my sunbonnet and shawl, then dashed down the stairs and out of the house. "Ready," I panted as I climbed into the carriage. "I'm ready."

Two miles outside of town, we pulled up behind Zerelda and her family. We waved as Sam guided the team and lighter carriage past the heavy farm wagon. "See you in town," she called.

I leaned forward and tapped Sam on the shoulder. "What is going on?"

He turned his head around toward me. "Visiting missionaries are as good a reason as any to get together. Should be a real circus in town by now."

"Where will they stay overnight? Not at Aunt Bea's, I hope."

Sam laughed. "They'll probably camp out in their wagons. Didn't they have revival camp meetings in Pennsylvania?"

I leaned out over the edge of the carriage to see the road behind us. "Well, yes, I guess."

By the time we reached the edge of town, we were part of a parade of wagons. It looked like every family in the county had decided to attend the meetings. As Sam eased the team out of the lineup in front of Aunt Bea's store, Zerelda waved her handkerchief and shouted, "See ya at the meeting tomorrow."

I waved back, then turned to find Aunt Bea standing in the doorway. Striding to the carriage, she instructed Sam to take the horses round back, then lifted Jamie out of the carriage to the ground. "You're getting mighty big, son. When your mama and daddy get back, they'll wonder what happened." The woman bent over and whispered in Jamie's ear. "There's a little something special for you in your room."

His eyes brightened. He looked to me for permission. When I nodded, he dashed into the building.

Then to me, she added, "Bout time you arrived. I've been looking for you all morning. Do you know that traffic started before breakfast this morning and hasn't let up since?"

I hopped down from the carriage and grabbed my bonnet and shawl. "It's good to see you too, Aunt Bea." I kissed the woman on the cheek and skipped toward the front door. "Isn't this an absolutely beautiful day?"

Aunt Bea tucked a stray lock of my hair up into the braid wound at the back of my neck. "It is now. I baked an apple pie this morning, and I've got a crock of Boston baked beans ready to take to the community picnic tomorrow. You've never tasted my Boston baked beans, have you? Genuine Back Bay, they are."

Early the next morning we set out in James's carriage for the Hays Community Church. By the time we got there, the lawn and sanctuary swarmed with people, many of whom had camped all night on the grassy field behind the church. Aunt Bea joined a circle of businesspeople debating how to bring new families into the area. Jamie and I strolled over to the steps and sat down.

Sam volunteered to take Jamie over to the grade-school playground. I entered the church, hoping to find a seat near the front of the sanctuary. Finding the sixth row unoccupied, I spread out my shawl in order to save spaces for Sam, Jamie, and Aunt Bea.

Suddenly, I heard a familiar voice - Mrs. Annabelle Van Dorn. As I expected, she was surrounded by a group of women. For a moment I considered approaching her immediately, then decided to wait until after the first meeting. Would she remember me? Would she once again make me feel like a foolish child? It didn't matter. I wasn't the same little girl she had met back in Shinglehouse, Pennsylvania. This time I wouldn't be put off quite so easily.

Mr. Victor Van Dorn strode into the room, leading an entourage of fans. The women surrounding Mrs. Van Dorn switched their homage to the dignified minister. I glanced at Mrs. Van Dorn and realized she, too, had deferred toward her husband.

The pews filled fast. I was glad when Aunt Bea arrived to help me save the seats. By narrowing her eyes and arching one eyebrow, Aunt Bea could quell even the most insistent bully. The room filled and overflowed into the church's side rooms, then out onto the steps. Some people drove their wagons up to the open windows in order to hear the man preach. Once Elder Van Dorn started speaking, I didn't notice the crowded conditions. I felt the same familiar stirrings in my soul.

"Americans have so much - too much. When my wife and I spoke in New York City, we were invited to stay at the homes of wealthy industrialists. I couldn't help compare their extravagant homes with the bamboo shacks of the people whom we serve." The man of God strode across the platform.

"We attended luncheons and benefit dinners in our honor. At one banquet, the food left on the plates would have fed a Chinese family of eight for a week. Everywhere we traveled, we've seen a country blessed abundantly by God."

His piercing gaze scanned the audience. "It is these very blessings that constrain us as Christians to help our Chinese brothers and sisters. They need a medical clinic where they can come for help. We need volunteers to staff the clinic."

After he kept us spellbound for more than an hour, Mrs. Van Dorn displayed the Chinese clothing and artifacts she'd shown the people in Shinglehouse. While she spoke, her eyes rested on me several times. I wondered if she could possibly remember me after all the presentations she'd made along the eastern seaboard.

I was surprised to discover that my desire to go to China had not diminished, but had intensified. I glanced at Jamie, sitting on the pew beside me, and realized that, while my feelings about China hadn't changed, my life had become more complicated. At the meeting in Shinglehouse, I hadn't understood loneliness, I hadn't understood commitment; now, I understood both.

I took advantage of the lunch break to approach Mrs. Van Dorn. Butterflies swirled in my stomach as I inched closer to the circle of women surrounding the celebrated missionary. When Amy saw me on the outer rim, she pulled me into the center. "Mrs. Van Dorn, I would like to introduce you to the newest member of our community, Miss Chloe Mae Spencer." Amy gently pushed me forward. Suddenly I found myself face to face with Mrs. Van Dorn once more.

"You probably don't remember me, but we met at the meeting you and your husband held in Shinglehouse, Pennsylvania, in June."

The woman studied my face, then shook her head. "I'm sorry. I've met so many people since then."

I smiled nervously. "Oh, that's all right. I didn't expect you to."

"So how did you get all the way out here to Kansas? Did your parents move West?"

I shook my head. "It's a complicated story. However, it is partly your fault that I'm here."

The woman's eyes widened. "I beg your pardon."

"Not really." I laughed. "However, it was at your meeting that I first decided God was calling me to China. I asked you how I could become a missionary to China. You advised me to find a husband who shared the same dream."

The pastor's wife reddened as the ladies about her murmured their disapproval. These pioneer women had fought and overcome incredible odds to survive on the Kansas prairie, many without the aid of a spouse. "Well, yes, I suppose I did tell you that."

I continued, "Well, my parents agreed with part of your advice anyway - the marrying part. When they tried to force me to marry a middle-aged farmer in the area, I ran away. And, here I am, on my way to China."

"I don't know whether I should commend you or spank you. You can't be much more than fifteen years old." The woman clicked her tongue in disapproval. "I'm sorry, but we need skilled people at the mission."

I straightened my back and tilted my chin. "First, I am seventeen, not fifteen. And I'm not without skills." I told her about my midwifery training and my experience caring for people with various diseases.

"Miss Spencer, you must talk with my husband after the afternoon meeting. And please forgive me for being so patronizing a few minutes ago." She took my hand in hers. "At every stop, young women ask to go back with us for a variety of reasons - some out of naive idealism, some to get away from their homes, and others because they've developed a schoolgirl crush on my husband."

After the meeting, Mr. Van Dorn walked down to the front pew, where I sat waiting. He asked me questions about my family, my training, and my present situation. Though I still detected a skeptical glint in his eye, I pressed my case.

"Mr. Van Dorn, I've already made it halfway across the continent. I'm healthy, bright, and trustworthy." I hurried on before he brought up the subject of my running away from home. "I have a ticket that will take me as far as San Francisco, where my brother lives. And, before I leave Hays, Mr. McCall has promised to pay me for my services these last few weeks. All I need is a sponsor."

Elder Van Dorn reached into his pocket and pulled out a business card. "All right, Miss Spencer, this is the address of the Chinese mission on Front Street by the wharf. If you make it to San Francisco before we sail, we'll take you with us."

My heart leapt into my throat. "Oh, thank you, Elder Van Dorn. You'll never be sorry, you'll see."

He wagged his finger in front of my face. "We sail for China on the thirtieth of September."

"I'll be there. Oh, yes, I'll be there."

"Remember, the thirtieth of September - or you'll have to wait until spring to sail."

I skipped out of the church into the late-afternoon sunlight and looked around for someone with whom to share my joy. I spied Aunt Bea's bonnet over by the parked carriages. She was talking with Zerelda and Amy. Sam stood behind the carriage, his back toward the crowd. Jamie squatted beside the carriage, watching a group of older boys play marbles in the dust.

I weaved my way through the lingering crowd. As I neared the carriage, Aunt Bea turned toward me, pain and sorrow distorting her usually tranquil face. Tears streamed down Zerelda's face. Amy, also in tears, rushed to me. "Oh, Chloe, I'm so, so sorry."

Baffled, I looked from one face to the next. "What? What has happened?"

Aunt Bea thrust a telegram in my hands. I gasped as I read the words on the yellow sheet of paper. "At 3:45 a.m. on August 30, my daughter-in-law, Mary McCall, passed away, stop. Services will be held at the Old North Church, Boston, Massachusetts, on September 2, stop. Take care of my grandson, Bea, stop. George P. McCall, esq."

I staggered back against one of the carriage wheels.

Amy grabbed my arm to steady me. "It's - it's not possible. James said she was doing better. Does Jamie know?"

The women averted their eyes. "We thought you should tell him, Chloe," Aunt Bea suggested.

I glanced at the people milling about. "Not here. It can wait until we get back to the ranch." I turned toward Sam. "Can we drive home this evening?"

He cleared his throat. "Yes, ma'am."

Aunt Bea stepped between us. "Wait just a minute. My brother-in-law asked me to take care of his grandson, did he not? I think it best you stay right here in town."

I closed my eyes and forced myself to breathe deeply. Not now, not in front of Jamie. "Aunt Bea, I respect you greatly, and we both know your wishes on this matter even before the telegram arrived. But don't you think our main concern right now should be what is best - "

"Excuse me, ladies." Sam held up one hand. "For that reason, let's move away from the carriage before continuing the discussion."

I glanced at Jamie. At the sound of our strong words, his attention had shifted to us. His worried gaze indicated he sensed trouble.

Sam led us over to a cluster of cottonwood trees beside the playground. "Forgive me, Mrs. McCall, but I must agree with Miss Chloe. The little tyke has suffered far more than any five-year-old should have to suffer. To tell him about his mother here would add to the cruelty."

Aunt Bea frowned, then glanced over her shoulder at the little boy waiting by the carriage, then back at me. "I don't know …"

"Please, Aunt Bea, I told you a few days ago that there have been a number of times recently when Jamie squealed. These were sounds of happiness, even though they were not words. Inside that little body is a hurt and confused child."

"I know you're right," the woman admitted. She uttered a deep, ragged sigh. "When I visited the ranch the other day, I could see the difference in him when he's there instead of here at my house. I'm just being selfish."

I touched her sleeve. "Thank you, for Jamie's sake."

Chapter 6

Hostage Heart

My fingers lingered on the nubby lace curtain in the hallway. Behind me I heard the grandfather clock at the foot of the stairs gong the half-hour. Mary's gone, really gone. I swallowed hard. My hand dropped, allowing the curtain to fall back into place.

Mary had become like a sister to me during the weeks we'd been together. I wanted to lock myself in my room and weep into my pillow. But Jamie needed to be fed. Jamie needed a bath. Jamie needed my help getting ready for bed. Jamie needs me more than ever.

On the way home from Hays, when I told the little boy of his mother's death, he stared questioningly into my eyes. "Do you understand what I'm saying, Jamie?"

He nodded, then climbed into my arms and buried his head in my shoulder. I waited for the tears, but none came, either from him or from me. When we reached home, Sam asked if there was anything he could do. I shook my head and led the child into the house. I moved through the motions of fixing him a bowl of leftover johnnycake and milk.

The sky behind the house had darkened by the time I tucked him into bed and kissed his forehead. "I'll stay here until you fall asleep." I sat down in the rocker beside his bed. He nodded and closed his eyes. I waited until his breath grew even, then slipped out of his room and into the hallway.

I stood by the window for some time. An icy hand gripped my heart. Death had intruded on my safe little world once more. First baby Agatha, now Mary. What if something happens to Pa before he forgives me? What if something happens to me? While I'd seen death sweep across the faces of Pa's patients, it had never before touched someone I loved or cared about.

Turning away from the window, I stumbled to my room and lighted the bedside lamp. Its soft glow helped push back the demons of despair. My stomach growled; I hadn't eaten since morning. I picked up the lamp and made my way to the kitchen. On the table was a jam sandwich and glass of milk that someone had left for me. I nibbled at the bread, but after the first few bites, I was no longer hungry. My appetite seemed buried somewhere beneath the rubble of my life.

I rinsed the dish and left it in the sink, then wandered aimlessly through the house, looking at rooms Mary would never get to enjoy. Pausing outside Mary's bedroom, I ached to open the door and see her sitting in the wing chair by the window. Tears welled up in my eyes when I peeked in on Jamie - he had no idea how much his life had changed that day.

I turned and entered my room at the end of the hall. One by one, I shed the layers of constricting clothing, then dropped a cotton nightdress over my head. I padded over to the dressing table, sat down in front of the mirror, and unbraided my hair. My mouth seemed pinched and drawn. Sighing, I picked up my hairbrush and counted to one hundred as I ran the brush through my hair.

When I finished, I glanced over at the packed valise sitting by the foot of the bed. I knew Mary's Bible was inside. With a bitterness I'd never felt before, I crawled into bed and blew out the lamp. I would not read about a God who allowed a young mother like Mary to die!

By morning, word of Mary's death brought visitors. The neighbor women began arriving with prepared food, and the neighboring farmers dropped by to volunteer their help bringing in the last of the crops for James. During the next week, someone from the community came each day to offer assistance. I was impressed, for I knew that, for farmers, it was the busiest time of the year.

When I commented to Zerelda on their generosity, she said, "Out here on the prairie, we either work together or die off."

Sam and Zerelda took over the daily chores, leaving Jamie to me. Instinct told me to keep him busy. And keeping a five-year-old busy took a lot of energy. We traipsed the meadow in search of groundhogs, waded in the stream, and spied on a family of swallows living under the eaves in the barn. We collected herbs and a few late flowers to dry in the pantry. I told Jamie stories about my brothers and sisters back in Pennsylvania. After I described the hideaway in my father's herb room, I suggested we make a special hideaway for us. We considered the tack room in the barn as well as a toolroom in one of the outbuildings, but we finally settled on the attic space directly over my bedroom. His mother's steamer trunk in the corner by the shuttered window decided it for us.

I helped Jamie cart his favorite picture books, a few pillows, and two extra quilts up the narrow staircase. All the while I wondered how much he understood about his parents' departure and his mother's death. In spite of my best efforts, the only time the little boy totally relaxed was when he was around the three nanny goats. Because they nudged the serious little boy into good humor, I made sure Jamie spent a part of every day with the playful creatures.

In the evenings after Jamie fell asleep, I found myself alone in the large, silent house. Rereading Hattie's letters made me homesick, but I read them anyway. The letters from Joe encouraged me with descriptions of life in San Francisco, helping me see past my present circumstances. I spent most evenings reading books I found in James's library.

Eager to leave Kansas and my pain behind, I wondered how long it would be before I heard from Jamie's father. I mourned the loss of Mary, of my family, of my thwarted plans, the pain in Jamie's eyes when he hid behind the metal-sided steamer trunk in the attic.

The warm summer evenings cooled to early autumn. Even cooler mornings followed. By the third week in September, the leaves on the trees along the stream turned yellow.

One day Aunt Bea delivered a letter from Jamie's grandfather, telling about Mary's funeral.

After the graveside ceremony, my son James left the graveyard. His mother and I haven't seen him since. We hope he is returning to Kansas. We wired Beatrice to be on the lookout for him.

Please know, Miss Spencer, James's mother and I appreciate all you did for our daughter-in-law and all you are doing for our grandson. James told us how you sacrificed your own plans in order to care for Jamie. Because we cannot presume upon your graciousness forever, Mary's sister, Miss Drucilla Bradley, left Boston for Kansas on September tenth. She will care for my grandson until other arrangements can be made. Also, I wired the news of Mary's death and James's disappearance to my older son, Ian, in Colorado. He should arrive in Hays soon.

I stared at the words swimming on the fine linen stationery. Why am I crying? Isn't this what I wanted? I will finally be able to get on with my dreams. True, I will miss sailing to China with the Van Dorns, but there will be other ships leaving for the Orient.

The next morning while Jamie played with the goats on the lawn, Zerelda and I cleaned the house from top to bottom. By four in the afternoon, sparkling clean sheets and pillowcases blew in the breeze on the line behind the house, the English sterling silver tea set in the dining room shone, and the mahogany furniture throughout the house glistened from being polished with linseed oil. Earlier that afternoon Sam and the men drove to town for supplies, leaving Bo behind to do the evening chores. Before they left, Jake returned the goats to their pen.

I stood on the front porch and waved goodbye to Zerelda as she left for home, then glanced about the yard. Jamie, where's Jamie?

I hadn't seen him since the men left for town. I looked up at the shuttered attic window and smiled. He probably fell asleep behind the trunk.

I ran inside the house and up the stairs, calling as I went. "Jamie? Jamie, are you up here? Jamie?" I climbed the narrow staircase to the attic and peered over the edge of the unstained floorboards, expecting to see a leg or a foot sticking out from behind the trunk. All I saw was the multicolored star quilt we'd left lying on the floor the night before. Panic rose inside me as I bounded down the stairs and out of the house, frantically calling his name.

I looked behind the house, then ran to the barn. As I passed the tackroom window, I could see Bo repairing a broken harness, but no Jamie.

The goats! I picked up my skirts and ran for the goat pen. The gate to the pen was open. Jamie cowered atop a haystack with Satan at the bottom, pawing the ground and butting the hay. The three nanny goats stood inside their pen, chewing their cud and watching. I didn't know whether the goat could do any serious damage to the child. When Jamie saw me, he started to scramble down the stack.

"No, Jamie, stay where you are!" I spied a worn-out broom leaning against the side of the barn and grabbed it with both hands. Holding it horizontally in front of me, I shouted, "Satan, you get out of here."

The goat swung his head my direction. A devilish gleam twinkled in his eyes. I inched closer. "I mean it, Satan. I'll use this broom on you if you come one step closer to Jamie or to me. Do you understand?"

Frantically, I searched my brain for the word Jake had used to make him stop. The goat lowered his head, ready to charge.

"Satan, stop! Halt! Cease!" No, that isn't it. Seeing the panic in the little boy's eyes, I changed tactics. In a calm, even voice I told him to slide down the back of the haystack and to go find Bo while I distracted the goat.

The goat, however, wasn't so easily distracted. He picked up Jamie's movement out of the corner of his eye, waiting until the child reached the base of the stack. Then Satan snorted, pawed the ground, and charged after the little boy.

Jamie's little legs had never moved faster. He tore around the side of the barn, with Satan in hot pursuit. As the goat raced by me, I lunged forward, falling face down in a wagon rut. Tears smarted my eyes as the gravel bit into the backs of my fingers crushed by the broom handle. I scrambled to my feet.

"Satan, stop! Stop, you old goat, you!" I couldn't think of anything nastier to say.

Bo heard my cries and stepped through the doorway in time to see me charge past, waving the broom over my head and screaming. He joined the chase.

The goat closed in on Jamie at the roadway. Jamie burst through the picket gate into the yard but didn't have time to latch it before Satan butted the gate wide open.

My mind raced with my feet, trying to remember the word that would stop the goat. Stop ... halt... owned by a congressman ... Yes, that's it!

"Veto, Satan! Veto!" I yelled. The goat skidded to a stop inches from the boy and swung his head my way. "Veto, you stupid creature!"

Jamie scrambled up the steps and into the house while Bo and I cautiously approached Satan. "Bad goat! Bad, bad goat!" I scolded, giving Bo time to slip a looped rawhide rope over the animal's head. I sighed with relief as I watched the young ranch hand lead the animal back to the pen.

Inside the house I found Jamie cowering behind the door. I sat in one of the kitchen chairs and called the little boy to me. Clasping his hands behind his back, the little boy hung his head and inched closer.

"Jamie, you opened the gate to the pen, didn't you?"

The boy studied the tops of his boots.

"Didn't Jake tell you never to go down to the goat pen without an adult along? You could have been hurt."

Jamie nodded. A giant tear slid down his cheek. A second followed. Suddenly, like the current bursting through a beaver dam, he threw his arms around my neck and sobbed onto my shoulder. Tears bottled up for weeks, perhaps months, flowed.

"It's all right, Jamie. You're safe now. It's all right." I carried him into the library and settled into the overstuffed chair beside the hearth. As he snuggled down into my arms, I realized I needed him almost as much as he needed me. Within minutes he'd fallen asleep in my lap.

The sound of horses approaching the house stirred me from my reverie. I smiled, relieved that Sam and the men had made it back from town. I carried Jamie over to the leather couch and covered him with a woolen afghan. On impulse, I picked up a Bible lying on the stand beside the sofa and tiptoed from the room.

Before I reached the dining room, I heard the tread of men's boots up the back steps and into the kitchen. I flung the hall door open. "Oh, Sam, I'm so glad you made it ho - "

My eyes bugged at the giant, foul-smelling, bearded stranger grinning into my face. "Howdy, ma'am. My name's Jedediah Lantry. These here are my buddies - Hitch, Boy, and Deadwood." He touched the tattered edge of his wide-brimmed felt hat, his other hand poised over a holstered Colt .45. Behind him three equally tough-looking men, with equally terrifying pistols, swaggered into the pantry.

I stared unblinking into his icy blue eyes. "Who are you? What are you doing in my kitchen?"

"Why, ma'am, we mean no harm. We're just hungry travelers hoping for a hot meal." He gripped my upper arm and thrust me toward the stove. "It would be right neighborly of you to fix us a little something, I reckon. You alone here?"

The instant he released my arm, I whirled about in fury. "Look, you hooligans, you have no right to burst into my kitchen and demand food. If you don't get out of here right now, I will call my ranch hand and make you leave."

The black-bearded leader threw his head back and guffawed. His associates did the same. "You mean you're gonna call that scrawny little runt we hogtied in the bunkhouse?"

"Bo!" I doubled up my fists and shook them in the stranger's face. "If you hurt him, I'll - "

The intruder grabbed my wrist. "You'll do what?" His eyes narrowed as we stood challenge to challenge. When I didn't cringe as he expected, he let me go. "Aw, shucks, ma'am, we don't want to hurt nobody. We're just hungry. You guys find anything?"

I could hear tins and baskets being shoved about in the pantry. I could only imagine the mess I'd have to clean up later. My first display of bravado came more from stupidity than strategy. When I saw how surprised the men were, I continued acting unafraid. I placed the Bible on the broad shelf and balled my fists to keep my hands from shaking. Remembering how my bravado could disarm my older brothers, I tilted my nose in the air and sniffed, "I thought the last of Kansas' riffraff disappeared fifteen years ago."

A loud thud from the pantry and a string of curses convinced me that I had to do more than toss out harmless insults. I set my jaw and pointed toward the pantry. "Call off your goons, and I'll fix you all a mess of blueberry flapjacks with honey on top. Oh, yes, and take off your hats, please!"

Slipping an apron over my head, I stirred the coals in the stove and added a log. When the tall, skinny one called Hitch started through the doorway into the dining room, I remembered the McCalls' silver tea set and flatware. "Mr. Lantry," I snapped, planting my hands on my hips. "I meant what I said. I'll feed you all you can eat, but you leash your dogs. If not," I unfastened my apron and lifted it over my head, "you're on your own."

The leader waved off my threat. "Tie up those apron strings, gal, we'll behave. Come on out, men, and set yourselves to the table for the lady."

I turned my back and smiled at the grudging respect I detected in his voice. I strode to the pantry and collected the ingredients I needed. "You gentlemen can each wash up over there in the sink. There's soft soap in the tin bucket under the sink on the right and fresh towels on the shelf behind the pantry door."

As I measured the flour into a large mixing bowl, I glanced out the window, hoping to see Sam and the men ride into the yard. The road stretched to the rise, empty. No cavalry coming to your rescue, sweetie. Looks like it's up to you.

I ignored the bemused smile on the leader's face and ordered the men around the kitchen. "Mr. Hitch, after you wash up, please get out the plates from that cupboard next to the pantry door. You'll find the knives and forks in the drawer behind you. Mr. Deadwood, I need a canning jar of blueberries from the pantry. Bring the open jar of blackberry jam and one of the unopened jars as well."

Sizing up my four adversaries, I turned slowly toward the one called Boy. Casting a smile as sweet as honey butter, I apologized, "I'm sorry, but I don't have any coffee right now, but if you men would like some fresh milk to drink with your flapjacks, perhaps Mr. Boy will go out to the goat pen and milk the goats."

Worry clouded the man's face. "Are they tame?"

I batted my eyelashes. "Like kittens."

"Well, then, I'd be glad to." The slack-jawed man preened himself and strutted out the kitchen door. I grabbed a half-gallon bucket next to the stove and ran to the door. "You might need this." I held out the bucket to him, then returned to the stove. The man who called himself Jedediah Lantry poked his face into the hallway. My wooden spoon stirred the batter more vigorously. The first dollup of batter splattered onto the hot griddle, followed by a second and a third. "If you could get the butter crock from the cold cellar out behind the house, Mr. Lantry."

"Hitch, get the butter!" the leader growled.

I flipped the flapjacks over. Oops, I guess he gives orders better than he takes them.

Suddenly my heart stopped at the sound of footsteps in the hallway. "Jamie - " I dashed toward the hallway door.

Before I could maneuver around the oak table in the middle of the room, the outlaw whipped out his gun and crashed against the swinging door. In jerking motions, he pointed the weapon straight ahead, then from side to side, searching for his victim. Bewildered, his gaze dropped to the wide-eyed child.

"Oh, dear Father," I whispered, "don't fail me now." I hurled myself past the bandit and scooped the frightened child into my arms. "Mr. Lantry, really! Is that necessary?" Caressing the back of Jamie's head, I whispered, "It's all right, Jamie. Everything's all right. Mr. Lantry and his friends are hungry, and I'm fixing them some flapjacks."

At the mention of the flapjacks, I sniffed the air. Smoke spiraled up from the iron skillet. Plopping the little boy down on the sideboard, I rushed to the stove. I tossed the three charred flapjacks into the garbage pail and started a new batch. "See what you made me do," I muttered under my breath.

Mr. Lantry shot me a warning glare. "Any more young-uns?"

"No. And no more old-uns either, that is, until Sam and the boys get back from town. They should be arriving any time now."

Hitch bounded into the kitchen and slammed the crock of butter in the middle of the table. Deadwood remained near the kitchen door. As for Mr. Lantry, he grunted and sat down at the head of the table.

I placed the platter of flapjacks in the center of the table. "Help yourselves, gentlemen."

In one motion, Mr. Lantry jabbed his fork into the stack of flapjacks and dumped them onto his place. Hitch didn't hesitate to join him. He swung one leg over the back of a chair and sat down. Deadwood glanced nervously out the kitchen window. "Shouldn't Boy be getting back soon with the milk?"

The outlaw leader slathered his stack of flapjacks with butter and scooped out a ladle of honey. "Go see what's keepin' 'im."

I shuddered when the man licked the honey ladle clean and dropped it back into the honey pot.

In the meantime, Hitch helped himself to the rest of the pancakes. I sighed. I'd made enough to feed the five ranch hands, plus Jamie and myself. Deciding there wasn't much else I could do, I whipped up another batch of batter.

Suddenly Deadwood burst through the kitchen door. "Come out here, boss. Ya gotta' see this."

"What? Did that sniveling kid break loose?" Mr. Lantry stuffed his mouth with pancakes and leapt from the table. "Don't try nothin', ya hear?"

The three intruders ran out of the house toward the barnyard. Helping Jamie down from the sideboard, I grabbed an apple from the wooden bowl in the center of the table. "Here, Jamie, take this apple to eat and run upstairs to the attic. Stay there until I tell you to come down. Do you understand?"

He nodded and immediately obeyed. Once I was certain he would be as safe as possible, I removed the frying pan from the stove, then dashed out of the house and across the yard to the barn. I was tempted to duck into the bunkhouse and untie Bo. Instead, I grabbed the barn broom and charged around the side of the barn.

Perched on top of the haystack sat Boy, his face pale, his gun drawn. Partway up the sides of the stack, Hitch and Deadwood waved their arms and shouted while Satan pawed the ground. When Hitch tried to break away from the stack, Satan lowered his head and charged, sending the frightened man scurrying back up the stack. The three does viewed the excitement from the far side of the pen beside a pail of spilled milk. Outside the fence, Mr. Lantry was clutching his sides and almost doubled over with laughter.

"Should I shoot 'im, boss?" Hitch shouted. "Should I shoot 'im?"

Shoot him? Shoot Satan? Indignant, I grasped the broom handle with both hands, lifted it over my head, and flew at the astonished Hitch. "Don't you dare hurt that goat! You big bully."

Satan, pleased to have one more victim to intimidate, shifted his attention toward me. I ignored him and headed straight for the cowering Hitch. "You put that gun away right this minute. You men and your vicious little toys!"

A cry from the top of the haystack halted our attempt to stare each other down. Boy pointed and shouted. I whirled about in time to see Satan's horns coming straight for me.

I shoved the broom at the goat shouting, "Satan, veto! Veto, Satan, veto!" He skidded to a halt, shook his head, and pawed the ground as if to charge again. I waved my arm toward the three does. "I said, veto, Satan. I mean it. Now, you get on back to the girls."

Out of the corner of my eye I could see Jedediah Lantry lean against the fence post. "I'd do what she says, Satan. She means it."

The goat squinted up at me. I waved the broom at him again. "Go on, get out of here!" The goat snorted, then lifted his head and sauntered over to the does as if to say, "I didn't intend to butt them anyway. I was just funning 'em."

Once the pathway cleared, the three men scrambled down the sides of the haystack and dashed for the open gate. My knees quivered like marmalade as I strode across the barnyard. Chloe Mae! You've convinced these men that you're tough, so don't faint now.

Latching the gate behind me, I leaned the broom against the side of the barn. "Let's head up to the house for those victuals, shall we?"

The men looked at me in disbelief, then at Mr. Lantry. He waved them forward. "You heard the lady."

The four men followed me up to the house and into the kitchen. Once there, I gathered the plates of cold flapjacks and set them in the warming oven while I griddled the rest of the batter. The men sat down around the table. Before placing the food on the table, I announced that I would say the blessing before they ate.

Smirking, they bowed their heads. I ignored the furtive glances they shot toward their leader. "Dear heavenly Father, thank You for the food You've given us and for Your abundant love and protection. Bless the guests at my table tonight. Fill them with Your love and Your peace. Amen."

Where did that come from? What ever inspired you to do such a thing? I placed the platter of flapjacks in the center of the table, then turned to fetch Mr. Lantry's plate from the warming oven. Boy, obviously famished after his encounter with Satan, dived for the platter, then leapt back, hissing a string of expletives like I'd never heard before.

I handed him a hot pad. "It's hot, Mr. Boy."

He glared at me and snarled. "I know that. And I'm not Mr. Boy. My name is - " A glare from the leader silenced him. "It's not important who I am. Just drop the mister."

"As you wish. Gentlemen, since we didn't do too well with the milk, would you like some herbal tea? Mint, perhaps?"

Mr. Lantry stared incredulously. "Mint tea? Like ladies of the garden club?"

"I do have some chamomile." I glanced about the table. Each of the men shook their heads, more out of fear of being laughed at by their leader than from personal taste.

The last rays of daylight illuminated the field of corn stubble to the east of the barn. Within minutes it would be dark. I lighted one of the kerosene lamps on the sideboard and set it in the center of the table. Thinking of Jamie alone in the attic, I lighted a second lamp, picked up the Bible, and headed toward the hallway door. "Help yourselves to the apples in the bowl. And now, unless there is something else you need, I'll just excuse myself."

Mr. Lantry leapt from the chair and drew his pistol. His mouth stuffed with flapjacks, he ordered, "You'll stay right here where I can see you."

Realizing I'd pushed my act of independence to its limit, I shrugged my shoulders in deference. "As you wish. Would you mind if I sit over there in the rocker until you finish eating?" I pointed to the rocker beside the stone fireplace.

He grunted and sat back down. My skirts swooshed against his chair as I passed. Without warning, an iron grip encircled my wrist. "Your man got any rotgut in the house?"

I looked at my wrist, then at my captor. "Excuse me?"

Like Satan's attitude as he retreated from the conflict, the bandit slowly released my wrist. His eyes told me he was only tolerating my arrogance. "I said does your man have any whiskey in the house?"

"Not to my knowledge." I sniffed, then strode to the chair and sat down. Opening the Bible to the ninety-first psalm, I tried to focus on the words. "He that dwelleth in the secret place of the most High shall abide ..."

I heard one of the chairs slide back from the table, but continued to read. "... under the shadow of the Almighty. I will say of the Lord, He is my refuge and my fortress: my God; in him will I trust. Surely he shall deliver thee from the snare of the fowler, and from the noisome pestilence. He shall cover thee ..."

Suddenly my every muscle froze as a calloused hand caressed the back of my neck. "Red, you sure are a purty little thing," Mr. Lantry whispered as he removed the hairpins from my hair. My braid dropped down the back of the rocker. "You must be all of eighteen."

In my mother's quiet, yet most authoritative voice, I said. "Mr. Lantry, you will please remove your hand from my person." I returned my attention to the words in front of me. I began reading aloud "... For he shall give his angels charge over thee, to keep thee in all thy ways."

With deliberate slowness, the intruder unbraided my hair, running his fingers through the rivulets, then draped the freed locks about my shoulders. Emmett Sawyer's leering face flashed across my mind. I'd faced down a cantankerous billy goat, I'd survived a twister, I'd hopped a speeding train, but the terror I felt deep inside warned of horrors I could only imagine. Taking a deep breath, I resisted the urge to bolt from the room.

His face moved closer to mine. "Hmm, hair and spirit like a raging fire! So what husband in his right mind would leave a saucy little filly like you unguarded? Surely not that pantywaist out there in the bunkhouse."

I looked toward the three men watching from the table, hoping one of them would speak up for me. As our eyes met, they turned away, stuffing their mouths with pancakes.

Mr. Lantry uttered a low, terrifying chuckle. "Don't expect them to help you. They know better." He circled one finger around a corkscrew curl near my face. "If you were my woman, I'd sure enough know how to keep you corralled."

In an effort to control the fear inside me, I silently counted to ten. "Mr. Lantry," I slowly turned and pushed his hand away from my neck, "I am not a possession; I am a person, a human being - not a filly."

Without looking up from his plate, Hitch chortled. "Looks like you got yourself a suffragette, boss."

Mr. Lantry clamped his hand around the back of my neck and squeezed. "Well, I'm man enough to tame even the mouthiest of women." Threading his fingers through my hair, he pulled my head backward toward him. "Ah, but you're not one of those man-hating females are you, Red? You're too unspoiled for that. You've got fire; you've got spunk. I like a woman with spunk."

I gulped, trying to swallow back the tears swimming in my eyes. In a matter-of-fact tone, I said, "You're hurting me, Mr. Lantry."

His eyes narrowed as he gazed down at me. He seemed uncertain about his next move. I took advantage of the short reprieve. O dear God, if You've ever answered my prayers before, if the words of this psalm are more than just poetry, do something now. I need to be rescued from this man's evil. You need to tread on this snake. Now, Lord, now!

Suddenly my attacker swung his head around at the sound of a chair scraping back from the table. Hitch stood and ambled around the far end of the table, one hand held up in a gesture of peace and the other idly resting on the butt of his pistol. "Ah, come on, boss. Leave her alone. She's been a good sport."

The other men at the table gasped at Hitch's words and leapt to their feet, their hands dropping to the guns in holsters at their sides. The instant Mr. Lantry loosened his hold on my neck, I sprang from the chair. Clutching the Bible to my chest, I whirled out of his reach.

Like two cocks in a hen yard, Hitch and Mr. Lantry faced off. Tension crackled throughout the room. The two other men sidled toward the sink. I glanced over my shoulder. I was less than two feet from the hallway door. I considered making a run for it. Think, stupid. Where would you run? To Pagets' place? To Amy's? They'd catch you before you were out the front gate.

"Ya know, boss," the man called Deadwood said casually, "we don't have time for this if we're going to make it to Hays by nightfall. The ladies at Dalton's Saloon are calling us. Nelly, remember Nelly?"

The leader paused, then nodded. "You're right, Deadwood. We can always come back for Red later, right?"

"Right!" His three sidekicks simultaneously heaved a sigh of relief.

Bless you, Deadwood, for giving his pride a way out. My knees went weak with relief. Swaggering over to the table, Mr. Lantry took the unopened jar of jam and stuffed it into the inside pocket of his coat. "You men grab a few of those flour sacks in the pantry and load 'em up with food. It's time we hit the trail."

You can say that again! I licked my parched lips. Take anything you want, just get out of here.

It felt like hours, but within a few minutes I was standing by the kitchen door watching Mr. Lantry swagger over to where the horses were tied. Deadwood and Boy followed.

"Thank you, Mr. Hitch," I whispered as the rangy outlaw passed.

He smiled and tipped his hat. "My pleasure, ma'am."

"Why did you risk so much for me?"

"Not for you. For my ma. When you sat by the fireplace reading the Bible, I saw her instead." He tipped his hat once more. "She was a redhead too, you know." He bounded down the stairs and mounted his horse. The bandits froze at the sound of approaching hoofbeats as the silhouette of Sam and the other ranch hands in the wagon cleared the rise. The horses pranced as the four outlaws argued about what to do.

When the ranch hands rounded the front lawn, the outlaw leader drew his gun. I had to do something. Without considering the consequences, I sailed down the back steps and shouted. "Well, Mr. Lantry, I hope you have enough provisions to last until you can get into town again. Tell that wife of yours not to be such a stranger, but to drop in any time. Kiss little Jed and Margaret for me."

Stunned, the outlaw looked at me, then at the men in the wagon. I ran pell-mell toward the incoming wagon, expecting to hear a bullet whiz by at any moment.

Skipping over to the farm wagon, I grabbed the horses' reins. The men's mouths gaped in surprise. I hopped up into the wagon, cupped the driver's grizzled face with my hands, and planted a kiss on his mouth.

"Oh, Darcy, dear, I'm so glad you made it back tonight. Did you remember to get that bolt of calico I ordered?" I whispered, "Act like you're my husband."

I snuggled next to Darcy's limp arm. "Oh, dear, where are my manners? Darcy, this is Jedediah Lantry and his men. They've hit some hard times, so I gave them a few provisions to tide them over. I hope you don't mind." With my free hand, I brushed back my wild and tangled curls, which then swished across Darcy's confused face.

As he pawed a few remaining strands of my hair from his mouth, he stuttered, "Uh, b-b-but of course not. Uh, bub, bub, ba, good to meet you. Mr. Lantry, was it?"

Sam rode his mount up beside the lead outlaw and narrowed his eyes. "Where did you say your spread was, Mr. Lantry?"

I knew Sam wasn't buying a word I said. So did Lantry. When I saw Lantry's hand drop to his pistol once more, I tossed my head from side to side and giggled. I'd seen my sister Myrtle use this technique to coax her husband Franklin into doing something he preferred not to do.

"I'm sure you men can chew the fat next time you come to visit, Mr. Lantry, but it's getting mighty close to dark. You wouldn't want one of your horses to step in a gopher hole or something on your way home. I think we can table the rules of etiquette this time, don't you, Darcy dear?"

Hitch signaled for Deadwood and Boy to follow him. "Come on, boss. She's right. We gotta be going. Them cows ain't going to milk themselves, you know."

"Right." Lantry stared at me for a minute, then flicked his reins. "Thank ya again, ma'am, and it was nice meeting your man. Goodbye, Mr. Darcy."

I stood up in the wagon and waved. " 'Bye, remember me to your wife."

Darcy grabbed my wrist and pulled me down in the seat beside him. "All right, Miss Chloe, what was that all about?"

"Ssh, wait!" I hissed, waving goodbye with my free hand. "Wait until they're out of hearing range."

Chapter 7

Strangers Abound

Sam leapt from his horse, hauled me off the wagon, and set me down on my feet with a thud. "All right, little lady, what was that all about?"

I looked up at him with as wide and innocent a stare as I could muster. "What? The neighbors coming calling?"

"Neighbors? Where's their ranch anyway?"

I waved my arm vaguely in a southwesterly direction. "Off there someplace, I reckon."

"Not likely! There's the Henderson spread, then the Buffords, and then the Czarnoffs' place."

I watched over my shoulder until the last of the riders disappeared over the rise. "Why don't we go inside the house? I'll make you a batch of biscuits and gravy and tell you all about it."

"Jake, take care of the horses. Darcy and Shorty, you men unload the wagon. Get Bo to help you. By the way, where is Bo?"

My eyes widened in horror, and my hand flew to my mouth. "Oh - no! He's, uh, in the bunkhouse, all tied up in his work."

Sam stared down at me. "He's what?"

I wrung my hands and cast a nervous glance toward the roadway, stalling for time. "Uh … oh, no, I left Jamie upstairs alone. I'd better go check on him."

Sam grabbed my arm. "Something's fishy around here. Darcy, leave the wagon to Shorty and go check on the boy. And, Jake, you'd better find out what's happened to Bo. As for you, Miss Chloe, you're staying with me." He led me by my arm toward the house. I struggled to keep up with his long, angry strides.

We climbed the back steps, and he held the screen door open for me but let it slam behind us. I paused and surveyed the messy kitchen. Dirty dishes covered the table, honey dripped down the sides of the jar and onto the table, flour and pancake batter decorated the stove. The chairs stood askew from the table. The abandoned Bible lay on the floor beside the rocker.

"What the - " Sam whistled. "Looks like we missed some party."

"I'd say." I groaned and began stacking the dinner plates to take to the sink and wash.

Suddenly a firm hand clapped over mine. "Leave 'em!" He took me by the shoulders, led me to the rocker, and sat me down. "Start talking, missy."

"I don't know where to start."

"Try the beginning."

"You mean where Jamie got chased by Satan or when those men arrived?"

"You're stalling, Miss Chloe. Let's hear it from when the men arrived."

I sighed and closed my eyes. I hoped Lantry and his men were far enough away so Sam and the boys wouldn't go after them. "I was rocking Jamie in the library when I heard footsteps up the back stairs and into the kitchen. Thinking you all had returned, I ran out to greet you. And these men were pillaging the larder."

My hands started shaking, and I bit my lip, trying unsuccessfully to keep back the tears. It didn't work.

Through a cascade of tears, I described the events of the evening. As I talked, Sam paced from one end of the kitchen to the other.

The heavy tread of boots bounded simultaneously up the back stairs and down the front. Bo, Shorty, and Jake charged in through the screen door, all talking at once, while Darcy burst through the hall door, carrying a frightened Jamie. When Jamie saw me, he squirmed out of Darcy's arms and into mine.

While Bo told his story, I nuzzled Jamie's neck and whispered, "It's all right, Jamie. They're gone now. You're safe."

"Honest, boss, I never heard 'em coming." Bo's pale blue eyes flashed with embarrassment and frustration. "I was in the tack room working on the harnesses, and suddenly two men were slapping me against the wall. They gagged me, then hogtied me to the workbench." He ran his hand through his disheveled hair. I could see bruises forming on his wrists. "What happened in here, Miss Chloe? I heard you go past the barn to the goat pen. I was hoping you'd come in and untie me."

"I couldn't. Did you hear the encounter they had with Satan?" I smiled in spite of the situation.

Bo chuckled. "I sure did. Jake, I'll never make fun of that old billy of yours again. He chased three of those hoodlums up the haystack."

When Sam glared at the young man, I hastened to explain. But even Sam allowed himself to smile when I told how the men dashed for the fence while I held Satan at bay with a broom. I told about feeding the men, but brushed over the worst moment - the confrontation between Mr. Lantry and his men over me. I couldn't make myself talk about it. Besides, I knew Sam was on the verge of chasing after the outlaws. If he did, someone would get hurt.

"So, after they'd eaten, they filled a number of flour sacks with food and planned to head out before dark. And that's when you arrived home." My eyes pleaded with Sam to understand. "Look, they all were armed and dangerous. That's why I pretended they were neighbors and you, Darcy, were my husband. I was hoping you men would be so baffled by my strange behavior that you'd let them ride out of here."

Sam turned toward Shorty. "Men, harness up the horses. Better get your rifles."

"Sam, no!" I pleaded. "It's already dark. You can't fight these guys in the dark."

Shorty lifted one bushy eyebrow. "She's right, boss. It would be suicide now. They'll be listening for us."

Sam narrowed his eyes up at the giant of a ranch hand. "I never took you for a coward."

Shorty's mouth hardened. "Boss, that ain't fair. You know better; you ain't thinkin' clearly."

I looked at the other men and saw the look of shock on their faces. Only Shorty could talk that straight to the no-nonsense foreman.

The foreman searched each man's face, then turned toward Bo.

"All right, we'll wait till morning; then you'll ride into the sheriff's office and make out a full report." Sam's attention fell on the loosened hair tumbling down my back and shoulders. He reached down and picked up the Bible and stared at the cover for a moment. "Something inside of me says you're not telling the whole story, Miss Chloe. Did those jackals hurt you in any way?"

I shook my head and swallowed hard. "No, sir. They scared me a whole lot, but they didn't hurt either Jamie or me." I held my breath as the foreman studied my face. "They scared me, that's all."

"Well, that settles it. It's too dangerous for a slip of a girl like you to be alone at the house for so many hours of the day. Mr. McCall would never forgive me if anything were to happen to either of you." Sam straightened and pounded his hat on his trouser thigh. "Pack up a week's supply of clothing for you and Jamie. Bo is taking you into Aunt Bea's tomorrow morning."

"What?" I leapt to my feet, setting Jamie down in the rocker. "I took care of myself nicely. And, I'll have you know, I am no younger than many of the farmer's wives in this county. And they do just fine."

"That may be true, but it doesn't change my decision. Mr. McCall put you and his son in my care. And until he returns, my word is law. Got that?"

I stood my ground for several seconds. When his eyes didn't flicker or his gaze soften, I knew I'd met a man as stubborn as Pa. One glance at Jamie convinced me that Sam was right - I didn't have the right to risk Jamie's safety. The memory of Mr. Lantry's hands on my neck and his fingers unbraiding my hair made me shiver. What if the bandits came back one day while Sam and the other men were out in the field? Jamie and I might not be so lucky next time. Yes, there was a difference between me and the other young women in the community. I was a single girl, left in charge of a child who was not my own. As I returned Sam's gaze, I could feel the tears surfacing once again. "Yes, sir, we'll be ready after breakfast."

Sam's eyes softened. He reached out to touch my shoulder. "Miss Chloe, I - " His hand fell to his side.

I dropped my head and turned toward Jamie. "Jamie, let's go upstairs and get ready for bed. Don't worry about this mess; I'll come down later to clean up. And, Sam, you are right."

It didn't take long for the emotionally exhausted child to fall asleep. As I studied his peaceful face in the lamplight, I wondered what secrets he kept locked inside that made him refuse to talk. I wondered how often he thought of his mother, of his father. I wondered how the day's adventures would affect him. I picked up the lamp and tiptoed from the room.

The kitchen was still in shambles, but I was thankful - I needed something to keep my hands busy. I had never understood when my mother had said there was nothing like soaking one's hands in a dishpan full of dirty dishes to wash away one's problems. As I stood at the sink, hands in hot, sudsy water, I understood.

Was it the sense of accomplishment a stack of sparkling clean dishes afforded women throughout history, the security found in performing a daily ritual, or, perhaps, a feeling of regaining control of one's life? The wash water had grown cold before I wiped the last dish and set it in the cupboard. I washed all traces of the intruders from the kitchen and pantry, then glanced slowly around the silent kitchen.

I'll miss playing house, but it was never mine. I hung up my apron, turned the lamp over the table low, and strolled out to the porch. Sitting on the top step, I rested my head against a pillar and looked up at the stars dotting the clear, moonless sky.

I'll miss all of this, God. I shuddered as I recalled the day's events. Thank You for being with me. I know You kept me safe from Lantry today. It wasn't dumb luck or quick wit; it was You.

I thought about Jamie and about his father, who'd seemingly deserted the little boy. I thought about my own father. I thought about my brother in California and about the Van Dorns, soon to board the boat to China. I wondered how soon Drucilla, Mary's sister, would arrive to care for Jamie.

As the autumn's chill seeped through my cotton dress, I thought of the copper bathtub upstairs and smiled to myself. I'll take a bath, then write a letter to Hattie. I rubbed my arms briskly and hurried inside. Of all the things I'm going to miss about this house, the heated copper bathtub is mighty high on the list.

The hot bath soothed the aches from my body and the sadness from my mind. By the time the water cooled and I dried off, all thoughts of letter writing had dissolved. All I wanted was a good night's sleep.

The next morning I packed my clothing in the steamer trunk Aunt Bea had lent me. Before closing the trunk, I picked up Mary's Bible from the bed table and wondered if I should take it with me. I can always send it back with Aunt Bea if I don't return to the ranch.

A look of consternation filled Jamie's eyes as he helped me haul a small footlocker down from the attic to his room and fill it with his clothing. We both turned toward the hallway when we heard the sound of Jake and Bo tromping up the stairs for the luggage.

"It's all right, Jamie. This is your home; you'll be back in no time. We're just going to Aunt Bea's for a short visit."

Bo carried the luggage to the carriage while Jake took Jamie out to the pen to say goodbye to the goats. I dropped the last of Jamie's favorite toys in a carpet bag and clasped it shut. Sam met me at the foot of the stairs and tipped his hat. "Are you ready, Miss Chloe?"

"Yes, I think so." As we walked to the waiting carriage, the foreman apologized once more. "You are one feisty and brave young lady; I admire you a lot. But I have to do what I think is best for the boy. You know that, don't you?"

I assured him I understood. "Thank you for your help and concern, Sam. I probably won't be back to the ranch. So I might not see you before I leave for California."

Jake, Shorty, and Darcy shook my hand and wished me well. Shorty asked for my recipe for buttermilk biscuits. I told him I'd write it out and send it back with Bo. Sam rolled and unrolled the brim of his hat until each of the men had said their goodbyes. Finally he stepped up to my side of the carriage. "I feel mighty bad for sending you to Mrs. McCall. Thank you, ma'am. Thank you for understanding."

I nodded and sniffed back the tears that had surfaced in my eyes. With a nod from Sam, Bo flicked the reins, and the horses trotted out of the driveway onto the main road. Holding onto my bonnet with one hand, I leaned over the side of the carriage and waved with the other until the carriage cleared the rise and the roof of the farmhouse disappeared.

The long ride to town passed too quickly. Neither Jamie nor I glanced toward the abandoned soddy as our carriage rolled by. When Aunt Bea's hardware store came into view, I heard Jamie utter a deep, ragged sigh. We would both miss the peace and solitude of the ranch. I gave him a quick squeeze, then adjusted my bonnet.

Bo drove the carriage up to the front door. While he tied the reins to the hitching post, I alighted from the carriage and lifted Jamie down. The door behind me burst open, and a smiling Aunt Bea wrapped her arms about Jamie.

"What a pleasant surprise! I am so glad you're both here." She eyed the trunks in the back of the carriage. "Will you be staying long?"

I shrugged my shoulders. "Uh, I'm not sure. It's a long story."

"Oh, good, I love stories." She slipped her arm in mine, and we strolled into the store with Jamie tagging behind. "Walter, just take the trunk up to the last room on the right. Jamie's can go in the small room across from Chloe's," she instructed Bo, who entered the store carrying Jamie's steamer trunk. "Jamie, would you like to have Walter take you to see the kittens in the barn?"

Jamie's eyes lighted up. He nodded enthusiastically. Aunt Bea turned to her young clerk. "Walter, would you mind?"

The freckled young man grinned. "No, ma'am." He took Jamie's hand and led him outside.

Aunt Bea led the way up to her second-floor parlor. Once there, she turned to face me. "Now, what has happened? I love having you here, but you were so definite about staying at the ranch. So why are you here?"

I reddened and sat down on the sofa. "Sam thought it best after what happened yesterday."

Before I could continue, Bo stuck his head inside the room. "I'm heading over to the sheriff's office to take care of that business Sam requested. I'll be back to say goodbye before heading for the ranch, if that's all right with you, Miss Chloe."

"The sheriff's office?" Aunt Bea gasped. "Whatever happened?"

I told her the entire story, from Jamie's encounter with Satan to Sam's reaction following the departure of the outlaws. "So, you see, I had to agree. I don't have the right to jeopardize Jamie's safety."

"Hmmph!" the woman snorted. "Leave it to men to think we women need their protection!"

"Excuse me?" I couldn't believe her reaction.

"I'm not minimizing the danger you were in, but danger is part of life on the prairie - and elsewhere. We women aren't fragile Georgia peaches to be cosseted.

You handled the situation well. Why should he complain?"

I shook my head in amazement. Of all people, I was certain Aunt Bea would support Sam's decision most enthusiastically.

"Don't get me wrong, I like men as much as the next woman. But if I've learned anything since coming west, the pampered lasses are the ones who either head east after one winter, languish in an early grave, or go stark-raving mad from cabin fever. Weak men haven't fared much better."

I smiled to myself. Obviously, Aunt Bea was off on one of her favorite topics. "Life is hard out here. It takes strong men and equally strong women to tame this land. Wasn't it Zebulon Pike, the man who first conquered Pike's Peak in Colorado, who said, 'Kansas is an alien land, fit for neither man nor beast'?"

The woman patted my hand. "Don't you let Sam's overcautious nature dampen your self-confidence. Now is not the time to weaken."

Aunt Bea stood and smoothed the wrinkles from her brown skirt. "Now that I've had my say," she added with a twinkle in her eye, "I'm sure glad Sam insisted that you stay in town."

I stood up and gave her a hug. "I think I'm going to enjoy it too."

"I put you in the same room as before. Just make yourself at home. I wish I could stay and chat, but I have a shipment of lumber coming in on the morning train."

We walked down the hall to my room, and I unlatched the trunk. "Fine. I was thinking of walking to town with Jamie after I unpack, if that's all right."

"That's a good idea. We'll spend some time together this evening. I want to hear what you thought of that Mark Twain book I brought to the ranch." Her eyes sparkled with excitement. "It's one of my favorites."

"Oh, Roughing It? I loved it, especially the part about the tarantula loose in the bunkhouse. Pa used to read it to us at night. It was fun reading it for myself."

She smiled as she touched my shoulder. "We're going to have such a good time together, Chloe." Then, as if embarrassed for revealing so much of her gentle side, Aunt Bea excused herself, calling as she retreated down the stairs, "Help yourself to whatever food you find in the kitchen. There's fresh apple butter in the cold cellar, and you'll find a tin of what the new German settlers call pretzels in the pantry. See you at suppertime."

I thought of Mary as I hung the dresses she'd given me in the wardrobe and placed her Bible on the night stand. When I leave for California, I'll have to give this to Aunt Bea to keep for Jamie until he's older. I closed my eyes against the thought of leaving Jamie behind.

The inkwell and pen reminded me that I owed Hattie a letter. After scribbling her a note about my first encounter with the "wild west," I addressed an envelope, then stuffed it, along with a few coins, into my skirt pocket and hurried across the hall to unpack Jamie's clothing.

I was in the kitchen slicing the bread for apple-butter sandwiches when Bo arrived, hat in hand. "Well, I guess I'd better be heading back, Miss Chloe."

Noticing him eye the stone crock of apple butter and the homemade bread I was slicing, I suggested, "Why don't you have a slice of bread with apple butter while you tell me what the sheriff said?" I slathered a slice of bread with the thick fruit sauce and handed it to him. He bit into the bread and smacked his lips. "Seems the Lantry gang is wanted several places - including down

Arkansas way for holding up a mercantile. He says you were lucky. Those boys usually play rough, especially their leader."

I filled a glass with milk from the cold cellar and handed it to him.

"Umm," he groaned, "I'd forgotten how good cow's milk can be."

"Cow's milk?" I grabbed an empty glass, filled it, and glugged down the deliciously cold liquid. "That was delicious! Don't tell Jake how much I enjoyed it."

Bo laughed and set his glass in the sink. "Well, goodbye, Miss Chloe. I'll sure miss you."

"I'll miss you too, Bo. You've been a good friend. Thank you."

He reddened and lowered his eyes. 'Well," he drawled, "you're mighty easy to be around, for a woman, I mean." I chuckled.

"I didn't mean that as it sounded. It's just that some women are - "

"It's fine, Bo. I think I understand what you are trying to say, and I appreciate it."

"Not entirely, ma'am," he mumbled. "Gotta go."

I walked out to the carriage and wished him well. As the carriage disappeared down the road in a cloud of dust, I smiled in spite of myself. I'd only be here in Hays for a short time; then I'd move on to the next phase of my life. I strolled toward the hen yard. I could hear Walter, talking with Jamie about the kittens.

The moment Jamie saw me round the corner of the henhouse, he ran to me and thrust a tiny bundle of silver-gray fluff into my hands. The grin the little boy gave me assured me he'd made the transition to Aunt Bea's house quite smoothly.

I held the tiny animal up near my face. "Ooh, he's so soft. You pretty baby, you. Isn't he beautiful, Jamie?"

Jamie nodded, his eyes alight with happiness. I handed the kitten to Walter. "Jamie, you must be getting hungry. I have some freshly baked bread with apple butter and some honest-to-goodness cow's milk waiting for you in the kitchen."

The child frowned, shook his head vigorously, and pointed toward the chicken house.

"We'll come back tomorrow, honey, I promise. After we eat, we'll walk to town together."

Again he shook his head and stamped one foot for emphasis. Startled, I glanced at Walter, then at Jamie. The child had never challenged me before. Since I had first met him, I couldn't remember him ever doing anything naughty. The boy folded his arms against his chest and swung his head from side to side.

"Jamie, you can't stay here alone." I knelt down on one knee and took his hands in mine. "Walter must get back to work in the store, and I am going to eat lunch. Now, as I see it, you have a choice - either walk back to the house with me, or Walter will carry you. Which would you prefer?"

Drawing his mouth into a pout, Jamie stood there a moment, then without warning, bolted toward the henhouse. In one swoop Walter scooped Jamie into his arms and strode back to the house. I hurried to keep up.

Walter set Jamie in a kitchen chair and shoved the chair up to the table. "Sorry, ma'am, but where I come from, when an adult speaks, children obey."

"You did the right thing, Walter! Thank you."

Walter tipped his head and strode out the door.

As I poured a glass of milk and set it in front of Jamie, I tried to decide whether this new facet of his personality was an improvement. Ignoring the milk and apple-butter sandwich in front of him, Jamie folded his arms across his chest and stared straight ahead.

"Look, Jamie, I know you're feeling angry, and I don't blame you. To you, it must seem like adults are always making you do things you don't wish to do, but I can't change things. I can't bring your mama back, and I can't hurry your daddy home - no matter how much I might want to."

He turned his face slowly toward mine. One tear trickled down his cheek. "Do you understand?"

He nodded slowly. I started when I thought I heard a tiny whimper. Knowing better than to draw attention to it, I stood up and pried open the tin of pretzels. "After you finish your sandwich, I have a surprise for you." I lifted one of the brown curlicues out of the container. "Aunt Bea calls these things pretzels."

Jamie took a bite from his sandwich as I nibbled on one of the crispy circles. "Umm, I like it. You want one?"

He nodded. I handed him three of the German treats. I cleaned up the kitchen, washed Jamie's face and hands, then told Aunt Bea we were leaving for town. "Is there anything you want me to pick up for you?"

She smiled and shook her head. "I got everything I needed this morning."

Leaving for town, Jamie and I detoured through the kitchen to fill our pockets with pretzels. We nibbled on them all the way to the train station, where I sent off my letter to Hattie.

"Oh, Miss Spencer, a letter from California came for you on this morning's eastbound." The master handed me an envelope.

I smiled down at my brother's messy scrawl, then tucked the envelope into my skirt pocket. "Jamie, how would you like to stop at Treat's Candy and Peanut stand for a licorice stick?"

He grinned and nodded eagerly. The sound of a train whistle caused us to stop and peer down the track toward the east. We could see the eye of the westbound Union Pacific bearing down on the town. Two passengers, a traveling salesman with his display case and a short, pinched-face businessman, stood by the edge of the wooden platform waiting to board. As Jamie and I walked past the men, I overheard the words Denver, Virginia City, San Francisco.

Three local farmers stood at the far end of the platform smoking their pipes and gossiping. The yardmen performed their tasks as the train eased into the station. The screech of brakes and a cloud of hissing steam brought the giant engine to a stop.

The faces of passengers staring out from behind the grimy windows appeared bored. For them, Hays was nothing more than an inconvenience somewhere between Kansas City and Denver. Before the conductor could set out the deboarding steps, a cowboy, his saddle and saddlebags in hand, leapt from the train and strode into the station.

With the steps in place, other passengers followed. A man in a black bowler hat and matching jacket emerged. A diamond stick pin held his gray silk cravat in place. He wore white kidskin spats over his black boots.

A voice behind me mumbled, "A real San Francisco dandy, there."

I turned and found myself face to face with the blond-haired mail boy. He had a large sack of mail slung over his shoulder. "I wonder if that stone is real?" he whispered.

A middle-aged couple emerged. The woman wore a gabardine traveling suit and a wide-brimmed hat stacked with feathers and flowers that defied gravity. "That's the Mortons. They go shopping once a year in Chicago. She always comes back wearing the latest finery."

I rolled my eyes heavenward. "She'd better hope the wind doesn't kick up before she gets home."

He laughed and pointed to a woman dressed in homespun crossing the platform to board. "Oh, look, Mrs. Saugus is going to visit her sister in Salt Lake City. Her sister Reba converted to Mormonism last year. Reba's the third of a wealthy Utah rancher's five wives."

I shuddered at the thought. That would never work for me! The day I share my husband with another woman … I hadn't finished my thought when a tall, muscular man with a full brown beard and mustache stepped from the train and surveyed the people on the platform. He glanced my way, tipped his hat, and grinned. I responded to the humor in his twinkling blue eyes with a smile.

The mail boy pushed his bag between us. By the time the mail boy moved past and deposited the bag onto the train, the stranger had disappeared into the depot.

Chapter 8

Relatives!

A wagon loaded with flour sacks rumbled by as Jamie and I crossed the dusty road in front of the station. Jamie waved at the driver, who tipped his hat to me and returned Jamie's greeting. We reached the other side of the street as two cowboys galloped toward the center of town. When Jamie tried to step up onto the wooden sidewalk, his short legs couldn't quite manage. I bent down to help him when, from nowhere, two strong hands lifted him onto the sidewalk, then offered to assist me. Startled, I glanced up into the eyes of the stranger I'd seen at the train station.

"Ma'am?" He touched the rim of his black, flat-rimmed felt hat.

"Thank you, but I..." He grasped one of my hands in his. With my free hand I gathered my skirts and allowed the stranger to assist me.

He held my hand for an instant longer than necessary. Flustered, I slipped it free. "Er, thank you again, sir."

"Ian McCall at your service, ma'am."

I blinked in surprise. "Oh! You must be James's older brother. I'm Chloe Spencer, Jamie's governess."

"Miss Spencer, my father has written many nice things about you. You're the lady who's on her way to China." I blushed under his scrutiny. "You're much younger than I imagined. I pictured you as a desiccated spinster."

"Spinster, maybe, but not yet desiccated." I chuckled at his apparent embarrassment. Stooping to Jamie's height, I said, "Jamie, I'm sure you remember your Uncle Ian. Say hello to him."

Jamie ducked behind me, but smiled shyly with recognition. The stranger peered around my skirts at the little boy. "I'm glad to see you again, Jamie. Do you know that you look much like your daddy when he was your age? Do you like to play with tin

112

soldiers like he did?" Jamie's eyes widened with surprise. "That's right. He fought the entire Battle of Gettysburg on our bedroom floor. One time I accidentally knocked General Pickett from his steed, breaking off the general's leg and his horse's tail."

Jamie giggled silently. Ian laughed with him, then ruffled the boy's hair. "I have just rented a carriage to take me to my Aunt Bea's place. Would you and Jamie care to join me, Miss Spencer?"

Jamie's pleading look told me he hadn't forgotten about the promised licorice stick. "I'd love to, Mr. McCall, but I promised Jamie a visit to the candy stand before returning to the house."

"That's Ian, if you please."

"Only if you'll call me Chloe."

He tipped his hat and bowed. "It would be a pleasure, Miss Chloe. And may I escort you to the store - or would Jamie prefer not sharing your company with his doddering old uncle?" He glanced down at Jamie, expecting a reply. Instead, Jamie hid behind me again.

"I am sure Jamie would enjoy your company, Mr., er, Ian."

"Shall we go, Jamie? Miss Chloe?" The man placed my hand on his arm. Jamie reached up and took my free hand possessively. I smiled to myself. I'd never seen the child act so protective of my attention.

We strolled along the boardwalk, nodding to the people we passed. At the dry goods store, Jamie tugged at my arm. We paused to allow him time to study the toy display in the window.

"Look." I pointed to a brightly painted wooden circus train. "Look, Jamie, look at the animals in the cages - an elephant, two tigers, a lion, a camel. Oh, see the monkeys."

The child pressed his nose and hands against the glass to get a better look. I resisted the urge to do the same. I glanced up at Ian. "I've never been to a circus, have you?"

"Yes, last spring a circus train came through when I was in Denver picking up mining supplies." Then to Jamie, he added, "That sure is a fine circus train - looks just like the one I saw. It sure does." Jamie looked up at his uncle, then back at the toy train. "Would you like to go inside where you can see it better?" his uncle asked.

"Maybe you'd better not encourage him further," I suggested.

The man brushed aside my caution and picked up Jamie in his arms. "Nonsense, we just want to get a good look at it, right?"

Jamie nodded enthusiastically.

"Women just don't understand these things, right, sport? We men know what we're doing." Ian winked over his shoulder at me as Jamie nodded once again.

After asking the proprietor's permission, Ian took Jamie over to the display and placed each piece in Jamie's hands. While pretending to be interested in a table of fabric bolts, I managed to stay within hearing distance as Ian spun wild tales about the circus performance he'd seen in Denver. "I liked the trapeze artists, swinging high above our heads, doing somersaults in the air and hanging from the swinging bar by their feet." I gave up pretending when Ian told about the lion tamer. "He put his head right in the lion's mouth and lived to tell about it!"

When Ian looked my way, I saw a pleased smile quivering at the corners of his mouth. To hide the color creeping up my neck, I cleared my throat and examined a bolt of green gabardine shipped from New York City. Wandering over to a hat display, I caught my reflection in one of the oval mirrors. High color still flooded my face. I sat down at the dressing table, slipped off my dimity-striped bonnet, and fluffed the hair back from my face while watching Ian and Jamie through the mirror. Reaching for a navy-blue creation topped with satin ribbons and clusters of red enamel strawberries, I placed it carefully on my head. I picked up the hand mirror to admire the hat. A bevy of ribbons cascaded down my back. I liked the way the dark blue contrasted with my hair's fiery highlights. One glance at the price tag, and I returned it to the pedestal. Three dollars for a hat?

After tying my own bonnet in place, I noticed Ian had left Jamie unattended in order to talk with the store owner. I hurried over to the boy's side, where he held up the wooden elephant for me to see.

"That's nice, Jamie, but we've got to get going if you're to get a licorice stick."

Eagerly Jamie took my hand and led me toward the door. His uncle caught up with us as we reached the candy store. One stick of licorice each, and we stepped out of the crowded store onto the boardwalk. Jamie and I decided to walk to Aunt Bea's instead of ride in the carriage, to Ian McCall's chagrin. As he drove away, I had the distinct impression Mr. McCall was not accustomed to being opposed.

That evening I smiled to myself as Aunt Bea blossomed in the warmth of Ian's unmistakable charm. I remembered my mother warning us girls of Irish blarney; now for the first time I saw it in action. After supper I insisted on doing the supper dishes so Aunt Bea and her nephew could talk in the parlor. Reluctantly Aunt Bea agreed. Jamie went with them.

I'd dried the last of the silverware when Jamie came running to me, his face wreathed with happiness. "Honey, what is it?" I asked.

He held up the engine from the circus train for me to see. Grabbing my hand, he dragged me into the parlor, where we found his Uncle Ian and Aunt Bea in the middle of the floor assembling the track for the train. Jamie dropped to the floor and dug into a large box containing the wooden animals.

Ian looked up and grinned. "The box on the sofa is for you, Miss Chloe."

I eyed the round box suspiciously. "Mr. McCall, I-I-I ..."

The man frowned. "Just open it, would you?"

I obeyed. As I lifted the cover and removed the tissue paper, I knew what I'd find - the navy-blue hat. "Mr. McCall, I cannot possibly accept this present from you. While it is proper for you to give your nephew the circus train, it is highly inappropriate for me to accept such a personal gift from you."

"Chloe," Aunt Bea interrupted, "Ian didn't mean any disrespect. He just wanted to be nice. See the shawl he bought me?" She held up a white woolen shawl dotted with pink embroidered rosebuds.

"I am sorry, but I can't accept it."

Ian walked over to where I sat on the couch and picked up the hat. "You've done so much for my brother and his family. I just wanted to say thank you."

I smiled, but remained firm. "A simple thank-you would suffice, I assure you. Your brother pays me well for caring for Jamie. Please return the hat."

He stared down at the hat for a moment. "I can't change your mind?"

I shook my head. "No."

A look of admiration entered his eyes. He clicked his tongue. "You're a hard woman to please, Miss Chloe."

I tipped my head to acknowledge his remark and turned my attention to Jamie, who thrust a wooden giraffe into my hands and tugged at my skirt. I sat on the floor and allowed him to show me each piece of the brightly painted train set. Although I was eager to escape from the parlor, I waited for Jamie to show signs of sleepiness.

The child didn't let me down. When he leaned his head against the front of the sofa, I suggested we put the toys away until morning. After getting him settled for the night, I slipped into my own room and spent the rest of the evening sitting in the oak rocker reading Mary's Bible.

I ran across the story of Abraham and wondered if I, too, would soon be traveling to a far country. As I rocked, I talked with God about China. Surely it wouldn't be long before I'd be on a train for California - and then?

The next afternoon I grabbed a Jules Verne book I'd been reading, as well as my bonnet. Questioned whether he'd like to take a walk to town, Jamie nodded enthusiastically. After alerting Aunt Bea to our plans, Jamie and I walked through the stubbled cornfield to the train station. I was hoping I'd have a letter from Hattie, and I was praying I'd have one from my father. His silence continued to disturb me. Having inherited his stubbornness, I'd returned the coin to him for what must have been the fifth time. At seventy-five cents a letter, I figured that soon, I would have more than paid in postage for my sins.

While I posted the letter, Jamie gazed down the empty track. I wondered what he might be thinking. Was he missing his mother and father? Was he hoping they'd be on the incoming train?

When I learned that there was no mail waiting for me, my face must have reflected my disappointment, for the postmaster added, "Sorry, miss, but the westbound is due any minute, you know."

"I'll be back." I smiled and turned away from the window. "Come on, Jamie, let's take a walk to the park. You can ride on the seesaw."

Jamie bounded ahead of me, around the corner of the railway station, and down the street toward the park beside the county courthouse.

"Wait for me, Jamie," I cried as I gathered my skirts in both hands and ran after the child. By the time I caught up with him, he lay across a wooden swing seat on his tummy, waiting for a boost. After I pushed him on the swing, he made the rounds to the slide and the seesaw, ending with the sandbox. At the sound of the train whistle, I glanced up from the sand mountain Jamie was building.

"Are you ready to head back to Aunt Bea's?"

He shook his head and packed another handful of sand onto the top of his mountain.

"When we get home, you can play with your circus train."

Jamie leapt to his feet and dusted the sand from his hands and knees.

"Last one to the sidewalk is a rotten egg," I shouted over my shoulder as I clutched the leather-bound volume in one hand, lifted my skirts above my ankles, and broke into a run. I reached the boardwalk seconds before the little boy. "You are getting to be quite a speedy sprinter, Jamie," I complimented the little boy.

On the way home, I stopped at the train station. Before I reached the window, the postmaster was calling my name. "Mail, Miss Spencer! Ya got mail from Pennsylvania." He thrust an envelope toward me.

I glanced at Hattie's familiar, carefully formed letters. "Thank you, Mr. Yancey." I stuffed it into my pocket to read later. I reached for Jamie's hand. "Jamie?"

He didn't hear me. He was too busy watching a girl of ten or so skip by. I guess he'd never seen anyone skip before.

"Come, Jamie, let's go home." Reluctantly, he took my hand, craning his neck to watch her until she rounded the corner of the station house.

"Would you like to learn how to skip?"

He stared up at me, uncomprehending. I executed several skips, then turned. "Come on, you can do it. See, it's easy." I demonstrated the art of skipping once more, and the little boy tried to copy me.

We leapt off the edge of the wooden platform onto the dusty ground. Taking his hand, I skipped down the pathway toward home. Within a few feet, he pulled free of my hand and skipped on ahead, his arms swinging in rhythm to his gait. Tears brimmed my eyes as I watched his obvious joy over a newfound skill. And I felt a tug at my heart for the mother who would never see this accomplishment or any of the hundreds that would follow.

The distance home seemed half as long as usual. I followed Jamie through the back door of the hardware store, where we found Walter counting carriage bolts.

Jamie bounded up the stairs while I stopped to talk with the young clerk.

Untying the ribbons on my bonnet, I asked, "Where's Aunt Bea?"

My question brought a euphoric smile to his face. His eyes glazed over; his gaze drifted upward. "She's upstairs with the lady."

I frowned. "Lady? What lady?"

His smile broadened into a foolish grin. "The one who came in on the afternoon express."

"She must be very pretty, this lady," I teased.

"Like the petal of a lily," he cooed. Suddenly he blushed and cleared his throat. "Well, Miss Spencer, she is mighty pretty."

"Hmm." I lifted an eyebrow and shook my head. Since I didn't want to interrupt Aunt Bea while she entertained a guest, I tiptoed up the stairs. But I couldn't help stealing a glance as I passed the parlor archway.

The visitor sat across from Aunt Bea and beside Ian on the sofa. A straw-and-lace hat lay on the seat between them. The younger woman's queenly pose gave her the air of holding court. Golden curls spiraled down the sides of her face, accentuating her wide cornflower-blue eyes and peachy complexion. Her delicate blue frock with white daisies embroidered on the bodice matched her eyes. Jamie sat at her feet, staring up into her face as she spoke.

Hearing my footsteps in the hallway, Aunt Bea called out, "Chloe, is that you? Come in here and meet Mary's sister, Drucilla."

My hand flew to my hair, disheveled from romping with Jamie in the park. Knowing there was no gracious means of escape, I squared my shoulders and stepped into the room. Ian rose to his feet and strode across the room. Taking my arm, he led me to the sofa as Aunt Bea introduced me.

"Chloe, this is Mary's sister, Drucilla - Drucilla Bradley. Drucilla has come to assume the care of Jamie until his father makes other arrangements." She turned toward the beautiful stranger. "And Drucilla, this is the remarkable Chloe Mae Spencer you've heard so much about. She's been a real lifesaver for James and for Mary. Jamie just adores her. I know you two girls will become fast friends."

One look into Drucilla's eyes, and I knew Aunt Bea would never be a prophet. The woman's gaze swept over me from the tips of my shoes to my frizzed-out hair. When those cornflower-blue eyes reached mine, they reminded me of blue ice on a winter pond. Her gaze returned to my dress - a yellow-and-pink calico Mary had given me before leaving with James for the hospital. I reddened at the look of suspicion I saw in her face. The muscles in Drucilla's face tightened into a brittle smile. She extended a kid-gloved hand toward me and simpered, "How very nice to meet you."

"Likewise I'm sure." I touched her hand and smiled. "Mary talked about you so much that I feel I already know you." What I said was true. Mary had adored her older sister. According to her, the only disagreement the two girls ever had was over which would marry James McCall. Personally, I could hardly imagine such harmony. As much as I loved Hattie, we'd been spatting since I uttered my first words. But then, Mary and I were so different, Mary, always so gentle and me, well -

I decided to meet Drucilla's unspoken accusations head on. "I notice you've been admiring my dress." I whirled about once, allowing the skirt to billow out around my feet. "Mary gave it to me after we arrived at the ranch. Your sister was so generous and so kind. I miss her terribly; I'm sure you do too."

A strained smile spread across her face beneath her shrouded gaze. "Yes, I do." She dabbed at her eyes with a lace-edged handkerchief that seemed to have appeared from nowhere. "Mary Elizabeth was such a child, so gullible and so naive. She never could read people." Again Drucilla glanced at my dress. "I understand why dear James acceded to her wishes by hiring you to care for darling Jamie. Of course, now that I'm here, you will be able to continue your journey west. China, isn't it?"

I bristled at her condescending tone and at her velvet-gloved innuendos. "Yes. Actually, I will probably stay with my brother in San Francisco until I can book passage to the Orient."

"How very interesting." She raised her gloved hand to cover her yawn and turned toward Aunt Bea. "Really, Aunt Beatrice, I am quite exhausted from my trip. Would you have Chloe bring a light lunch to my room in about an hour? I should feel a bit more refreshed by then."

My mouth dropped open in surprise, then snapped shut when I noted the wide-eyed, innocent look on her face. Phony! The sooner I get out of here, the better!

Aunt Bea must have seen my reaction, for she reached across and patted my hand. "Drucilla dear, I'm sure Chloe Mae will be busy with her own duties the rest of the afternoon. I'll be glad to bring you a light lunch when you waken from your rest."

Drucilla uttered her affected little laugh. "Oh, yes, of course, the boy. He must be quite a handful, being a mute and all."

If Mary's sister had been trying to raise my hackles before, now she'd succeeded beyond her greatest hopes. I pulled the surprised Jamie protectively to me. "Jamie is not a mute!"

I looked down at him. Bewilderment over my mood change filled his eyes. I ruffled his hair, then turned toward the blond stranger. "When Jamie is ready to talk, he will. Don't you worry!"

"Tsk! Yes, well ..." She smiled toward Ian. By the calf like expression in the man's eyes, I knew the entire exchange between Drucilla and me had flown ten feet over his head. "Ian, I'm having a terrible time with the latch on my Saratoga trunk. Would you be a dear and use those lovely biceps of yours to open it?" She fluttered her eyelashes and smiled.

I thought about what my mother would say. "That much jam on one slice of bread would make even a honeybee sick!" Swallowing hard to keep from laughing, I bent down and suggested to Jamie that we put the toys in the box and go to the barn, where his swing still hung. My fingers tightened around the giraffe's neck when Drucilla added, "Perhaps Miss Spencer will bring Jamie to my room later so that he and I may get acquainted?"

"You'll have to ask her yourself." Aunt Bea knelt down beside Jamie, picked up a wooden monkey, and placed it into the storage box. "She's a guest in this house, not my employee."

Thank you, Aunt Bea!

I cleared my throat. "I have a better idea. Why don't you come into the parlor and play with him and his train set. You'll get better acquainted that way."

She tilted her nose with disdain and stared at me as if I'd suggested she dance through a nest of vipers. "I did not ask you for advice on child rearing, Miss Spencer. Please, Ian, escort me to my room."

In silence, Aunt Bea and I watched her go. "Jamie," Aunt Bea suggested, "shall I ask Walter to take you out to the swing? I need to speak with Chloe for a few minutes."

Jamie's eyes lighted up. He nodded and Aunt Bea followed him from the room. When she returned, the older woman took my hands and led me to the sofa. "Here, sit." I obeyed.

She sat down beside me. "Please accept my apology for Drucilla's behavior. She's always been a frightful snob, I'm afraid." Aunt Bea shook her head slowly. "The Bradley girls always had too much of everything; spoiled rotten, if you ask me. For a while I was afraid James might marry Drucilla instead of Mary. She had her cap set for him, I can tell you."

Ian's rumbling bass voice and Drucilla's higher, crystallike voice drifted into the parlor. "And where does your nephew Ian fit in?"

"I'm not sure." She frowned. "Of course, he's older than James and the Bradley girls. My sister-in-law, his mother, told me that Ian was courting one of the Vanderhydens, from down Providence way, before he and James took it in their heads to move out West."

A head popped around the corner of the archway. "Did I hear my name?" Ian grinned, then strode over to his aunt. "What's going on here? Two old biddies gossiping the day away?"

Aunt Bea stood and straightened to her full five feet and eleven inches. "Young man, neither Chloe nor I are old biddies. And as to the gossiping, we were sharing pertinent information."

"Pertinent information? How pertinent can information regarding Cecilia Vanderhyden be?"

Aunt Bea reddened at his attack, then led an attack of her own. "Just how long were you eavesdropping, young man? Didn't your dear mother teach you better manners?"

Laughing, he threw up his hands in surrender. "I give, I give." He threw an arm about Aunt Bea's shoulders and gave her a squeeze. "Aunt Bea, you should have been a Back Bay, shyster lawyer." Toward me, he added, "Watch out for this one, Miss Chloe."

Aunt Bea patted her nephew's chest. "Look who's calling the kettle black! What is a genuine Harvard-trained lawyer doing prospecting for gold in Colorado anyway?"

Ian grinned. "You make it sound like I traipse into the back country with a pickax and a trusty mule. I'm as much a prospector as James is a Kansas dirt farmer. Besides, James and I jointly own both the mines and the ranch, dear heart."

She rolled her eyes at her nephew. "Well, that's what it looks like to me."

"Of all people, Aunt Bea, you should understand why James and I didn't want to settle into Boston society on Dad's money. You were our inspiration. Look how you and Chester set out for Kansas despite Grandma's claims that you'd be fodder for the worms before your wagon crossed the Hudson River."

"Aw, go on now." Despite her protest, I could tell Aunt Bea enjoyed the flattery. "I'll admit your grandmother wasn't too happy with either your uncle or with me, but she adjusted and is still the reigning baroness of Beacon Hill, if I can believe all she says in her letters." Aunt Bea's face clouded. "And to think, she outlived her son. The Kansas frontier doesn't play fair, does it?"

"Life doesn't play fair, Aunt Bea." Ian planted a kiss on the older woman's cheek. "I hear Fort Hays is worth seeing. I know you're busy doing inventory on the new shipment of farm tools that arrived this morning. Perhaps Miss Chloe would be willing to give me a short tour of the fort?"

Aunt Bea glanced my way expectantly. "I'll be glad to watch over Jamie until Drucilla is ready to spend sometime with him."

I looked at Aunt Bea, then at Ian.

"Don't act so enthusiastic," Ian teased. "Besides, I have a package to return to the dry-goods store. It's only fitting you should come along." Taking my silence for a yes, Ian strode from the room. "I'll have the carriage ready in ten minutes."

I stared after him. "Go on, get out of here; go have some fun. You've been on duty with Jamie twenty-four hours a day for weeks. You need a break." I felt Aunt Bea's arm slip about my waist. When I hesitated to reply, she read my mind. "Ian is a respectable young man, and you are almost family." As a clincher, she added, "It will frost Drucilla's cake to awaken and find the most eligible bachelor in the region is sightseeing with a pretty little thing like you."

I laughed nervously. I had never been any good playing these kinds of games against other girls. They always won. I had always been too much of a tomboy to be taken seriously. Boys preferred girls like Drucilla, who fluttered their eyelashes and simpered. I knew I was too direct. Except for the Chamberlain brothers and for Emmett, but then Emmett didn't count - for anything.

I hurried to my room and slipped into the green lawn dress I'd worn on the Chicago excursion with Cy. Quickly I brushed through my hair, rebraided it, and wrapped the braid about my head. Grabbing a white cotton poke bonnet, I ran down the stairs to meet the carriage.

In spite of my reservations, Ian proved to be a charming escort. The short tour of the fort ended much too quickly. We chatted amiably as the easy clop-clop of the horses' hooves took us toward home.

He glanced over at me. "You've never asked me why I arrived on the westbound train instead of the east."

I looked up at him in surprise. "I didn't think it was any of my business." "Then you did notice." "Of course."

"You are a strange woman indeed." He shook his head. "Actually my father's wire caught up with me in Kansas City. I had business there with the former owner of the mine, Gustave Bacon."

When I said nothing in response, Ian continued, "I'm going to hate to see you go, Miss Chloe. When do you think you'll be leaving?"

I glanced over at Ian in surprise. "Well, I, uh, guess I haven't thought much about it."

"Well, now that Miss Drucilla is here, I am sure she and I can handle one five-year-old boy. We're thinking of taking him back to Boston to his grandparents next Wednesday. Of course, I'll want to go out to the ranch to make arrangements with Sam and to pick up the rest of the boy's belongings."

My breath caught in my throat. What a fool you are, Chloe Mae. You've been duped. This entire afternoon was part of Drucilla's plan to get rid of you as quickly as possible.

I cleared my throat. "What does Aunt Bea have to say about this?"

"She knows it's for the best." Aunt Bea is in on this too? My stomach tightened as if I'd been kicked. "And I suppose Drucilla - why did I even ask."

He continued to avoid my gaze. "We will, of course, pay you generously for your faithful service. I myself would like to throw in a little extra to ensure your trip to the Orient. The family has appreciated all you've done, but we have no right to impose upon your kindness any longer."

"I hardly know what to say. This news has come so suddenly. What about Jamie? The change might ..."

"Surely you knew you'd have to leave him sooner or later. And besides, he's a child. He'll do as he's told."

"I'll need to go out to the ranch to collect the rest of my belongings."

"Of course. Tomorrow morning?"

I nodded. "Tomorrow morning."

He flicked the reins over the horses' backs, urging them on. "We should be back from the ranch in time for you to board the westbound express on Tuesday." With his business settled, Ian slipped back into the role of the debonair escort.

As we drove up in front of the hardware store, Walter burst out the door, his eyes wide with terror. "Did you see the boy run past here?"

"Jamie?" I leapt from the carriage. "What is going on?" I hurried inside the store and up the stairs toward the kitchen, where I could hear Drucilla screaming and Aunt Bea sputtering like a teakettle perched on hot coals.

"That child! That odious child!" Drucilla screamed. Aunt Bea dabbed helplessly at a bright burgundy splotch staining the entire front of Drucilla's white linen suit. "A London original ruined by that nasty little urchin!"

A telltale pot of beets spread across the wooden kitchen floor. "Drucilla and I were talking while I was boiling beets for pickling when Jamie ran through. I didn't hear him coming. I turned with the pot in my hand and, well, you can imagine the rest."

Drucilla held her skirt out from the petticoat. "That child needs a good licking! I am sure my camisole and petticoat are ruined also." She glared at me. "It's your fault, you know. You think I don't know what you're up to?"

"I beg your pardon?" I glanced at Aunt Bea and back to Drucilla, confused by her accusation.

"I know what you're trying to do. You might fool Mary Elizabeth and dear gullible James by worming your way into the child's life, but you don't fool me."

I looked toward Aunt Bea for help. She shrugged, picked up a dishrag, and began cleaning up the spilled beets. I felt my pressure rise with what Pa always called "my Irish." "What are you talking about? If you have something to say, say it!"

"I think I made myself clear. You have the audacity to ask me what I'm talking about, you standing there in one of my dear departed sister's favorite gowns? You got her clothes, her son. Were you planning to go for her husband as well?"

My face reddened in horror. When I looked toward Ian, who now stood in the doorway, he turned away in embarrassment. Aunt Bea stared first at me, then at Drucilla.

What was it my mother always said, "A soft answer turneth away wrath"? Right! How could Drucilla say such a thing? How could anyone think such a thing after all I'd done for the McCalls? I ached to scream in the woman's flawless face, to claw at her self-satisfied eyes, and to mess up her perfect golden curls. Then I remembered Jamie. If she'd screamed such fury at me, what had she done to him.

"Jamie! Where's Jamie? What did you do to Jamie?"

"Do? Do? When I get my hands on that little monster, I'll -" Suddenly Drucilla spied Ian. Instantly her anger dissolved into helpless tears. "Oh, Ian, I am so glad you're here. It has been so, so terrible. Where have you been? Oh ..." She fluttered her hand in front of her face and crumpled into the startled man's arms.

Without waiting for the next act in her melodrama, I bounded down the stairs and out of the store. "Jamie? Jamie!" I called. "Jamie, it's Miss Chloe. Where are you? It's all right. No one is going to hurt you."

I glanced about the empty yard, trying to think where the little boy might hide. I saw Walter searching over by the barn, so I headed in the opposite direction, toward the cornfield, calling Jamie's name as I searched.

Chapter 9

Deadly Attacks

People stared at me as I ran through town, dodging in and out of the stores, hoping to find Jamie at one of the spots we'd visited a few days before. I should never have left him. I should never have left him.

When I arrived at the empty playground, I collapsed on the lower end of the seesaw. There are hundreds of spots where a small boy could hide if he had a mind to.

"Dear Father, please protect that little boy. I love him so much." Where would I go if I were frightened and scared like Jamie? Home, I'd go home! Like a lightning bolt I tore out of the playground and down the rutted roadway. How far can one five-year-old run in such a short time? Short time? How long has it actually been since he tore out of the kitchen?

As I ran past the hardware store, Walter came out to meet me. He'd saddled up one of Aunt Bea's horses. "We haven't found him yet, Miss Chloe. I checked the storm cellar and the orchard. Mr. Ian rode into town to search for him and for you."

I paused to catch my breath while Walter continued his report. "Mrs. McCall is searching the storeroom. I don't know where the lady went."

The lady? Who cares? Boston would be a good place to start. For a moment I stared down the road leading toward the ranch. When a vision of the abandoned well at the sod house popped into my mind, I ripped the reins from Walter's hands and leapt onto the back of the surprised horse. When I squeezed my knees against the horse's side, she lunged forward. "I have an idea where he might have gone," I shouted.

A second nudge, and the horse tore down the road. I heard Walter calling after me, but I didn't look back. If my guess was right, Jamie could be in real danger. The jouncing gait loosened my braid until it beat a syncopated cadence against my back.

A mile or so from Aunt Bea's store, I spotted a bright red object in the grass beside the road. I climbed off the horse and picked up the caboose from the circus train. How could one little boy have gotten so far in such a short time?

When I arrived at the path leading to the abandoned soddy, I stood up in the stirrups, craning my neck to catch a glimpse of the little boy. I called to Jamie as I urged the horse onto the overgrown path. The tall grass brushed my skirt, and sticktights fastened themselves to the hem of my petticoat. The house cast long shadows on the rubble and prairie grass beyond. As the horse stepped into the clearing beside the house, I surveyed the area. No Jamie.

Sliding off the animal's back, I called Jamie's name again. Midstep, I heard a rustling in the grass. Instantly, I froze as I stared into the glistening eyes of a seven-foot rattlesnake, coiled and ready to strike. From the corner of my eye, I could see my horse nervously sidestep out of range.

I considered my options. If the rattler sinks its fangs into my skirts or my boot, I'll be fine. If its fangs hit my shin - well, I won't go down without a fight! Glancing about me for a long stick or a heavy rock, I felt a sharp object poke me in the side. I turned enough to catch sight of the sleeve of Jamie's wool plaid shirt. The last thing I need is to have to worry about Jamie's safety as well as my own.

"Move away from me, Jamie," I warned. "Step back."

He didn't move. Again the object poked me in the side. Only after my fingers encircled one end of a five-foot board did the little boy back off toward the storm cellar.

The snake and I moved simultaneously. Its fangs sank into my green lawn skirt. Before it could pull back to strike again, I shoved the board into the snake's back, but the soft earth gave with the pressure. I heard the delicate fabric of my favorite gown rip, as I stared in horror at the snake writhing at my feet. I could neither leap away from the creature nor deliver a second, deadlier blow to its head.

The impasse ended when a good-sized rock crashed down on the snake's head. I swung around in time to see Jamie dust off his hands. Lifting the child into my arms, I alternately scolded and praised him for his bravery as I set him on the horse and climbed up behind him. Once on the main road, I said, "Running away wasn't a smart thing to do, you know. It never settles anything."

How ironic, telling him not to run away from his problems. Of all people ...

A tear trickling down his grimy cheek, Jamie looked up into my eyes. "Don't go," he said.

Stunned, I stared down at the little boy.

"Don't go," he said again.

Incredulous laughter escaped my lips, and I hugged him to me. "Jamie, you talked!"

The boy wriggled from my grasp and faced me again. His upper lip engulfed his lower one. "Aunt Drucilla said you were going far, far away and never coming back. You aren't, are you?"

"You're talking!"

Impatient with my answer, Jamie drew his mouth into a pout.

"Uh, well, I don't know. I had thought I'd stay until your father returned, but ..."

"He's not ever coming back. Neither is my mama. They went away with my little sister and left me here."

Furious at Drucilla's insensitive remark, I drew Jamie protectively into my arms. "No, Jamie, that's not right. Your baby sister died before your mama left, remember? And your daddy took your mama to see a special doctor in Boston, remember?"

He shook his head. "Daddy's not coming back. Neither is my mama. And now, Aunt Drucilla says you're leaving me too."

"Jamie, if I promise to stay with you until your daddy returns, will that make you happy?"

The little boy shrugged his shoulders and settled his head against me for the rest of the ride to Aunt Bea's.

Night filled the sky by the time the horse slowed to a stop outside the darkened feed store. Lights glowed from Aunt Bea's second-story living quarters. Ian and Aunt Bea burst from the house. The anxious woman lifted Jamie from my arms while Ian helped me dismount. I glanced up toward a second-story window in time to see a curtain flutter back into place. Ian caught the direction of my gaze. "Drucilla was so upset, she went to lie down."

"Yes," I said grimly, "I'm sure she was."

When Aunt Bea offered to take Jamie inside for his evening bath, he pulled away from her and wrapped his arms about my legs. She started toward him, but I waved her away. "I'll settle him in bed tonight, Aunt Bea. Thank you." I glanced at the woman and at Ian. "In the morning, we need to talk."

I stayed with Jamie throughout the evening. He begged me not to tell anyone he'd spoken. When he finally fell asleep, I tiptoed to my room. As I crossed the hall, I heard Ian, Aunt Bea, and Drucilla discussing my fate. I closed the door behind me and leaned against the doorjamb. How can I keep my promise not to leave without revealing his secret?

Tears welled up in my eyes as I ran my fingers over the tear in my favorite dress, the dress that held such special memories for me. Carefully, I laid it across the trunk at the foot of my bed, promising to examine it more closely in the morning. I washed in the cool water in the washbasin and dried off with a scratchy Turkish towel. As my lightweight flannel nightgown fell down over my head and shoulders, I decided to escape the day's troubles in the pages of one of the good books Aunt Bea had lent me.

I picked up Moby Dick, by Herman Melville, and settled into the rocker by the window. A knock sounded on my bedroom door. "Who's there?"

Before I could answer it, the door flew open, and Drucilla stepped into my room. "Excuse me, Miss Spencer, but I think it is important that we talk without the presence of either my dear Aunt Beatrice or Mr. McCall."

I folded my hands in my lap and watched as the woman gazed about my room. When I didn't speak, she sniffed and elevated her nose slightly. "May I come in?"

I clenched my hands in my lap as the muscles in my face tightened. I knew the signs; I could almost hear my father's chuckle as my Irish rose. "As you can see, I've already retired for the night, Miss Drucilla."

She sauntered into the room. "This will not take long." With the thoroughness of a housewife bent on spring cleaning, Drucilla's gaze swept the room. She eyed the torn dress for a moment, then walked over to the open wardrobe. With slow deliberation, she fingered each of the dresses Mary had given me. "I know your game, Miss Spencer, if that's your name. I've dealt with con women much more adept than you, though I have to say, your wide-eyed, innocent look is good."

My eyes widened; my mouth dropped open. "I-I-I don't know what..."

Her lips parted into a lazy smile. "Hmm, quite good, actually, for someone so young." She continued her perusal of my sleeping quarters. Her fingers lingered on the night stand. "I wonder what else of dear, departed Mary Elizabeth's I would find in here? Perhaps her jewelry? No, you'd be more discreet than that, wouldn't you?"

"I'm sorry, but I don't understand," I whispered, watching the woman pick up something lying on the stand. I couldn't remember what had been lying there. My head was unaccountably filled with buzzing.

She crossed the braided rug by the foot of the bed and stood so close to the rocker that I could smell the light scent of gardenia she wore. Her eyes focused on Mary's Bible on the desk beside me. "How brazen, even Mary Elizabeth's Bible."

I looked up at her in surprise. "I beg your pardon."

"My sister's Bible." She snatched the book from the desktop. "If you don't mind."

Embarrassed, I stumbled over myself to explain. "Mary left it here for me to use until she returned. She enjoyed having me read to her."

"My dear Miss Spencer," the woman hissed. The buzzing in my head grew louder. Her smile widened. "And this?" She dropped Pa's twenty-dollar gold piece into my lap. "I suppose you have no idea where this might have come from?"

I stared at the coin as if it were the mate to the rattler Jamie had killed earlier. "I-I, know exactly where it came from. This was my father's, my grandfather's, in fact."

My accuser uttered a disbelieving chuckle, clicked her tongue, then sauntered over to the armchair beside the wardrobe. "My, my, I would have expected a more creative answer than that."

"But it s the truth."

"Come, come. I've heard your incredibly tender melodrama, running away from a cruel father and loveless engagement, delivering my sister's baby, attaching yourself to Mary Elizabeth." She paused beside the chair. "At first I wondered why you hung around after Mary Elizabeth reached Kansas."

With well-practiced dignity, Drucilla drew the chair to the edge of the halo of light produced by the kerosene lamp on the desk next to me. She sat down, her face partially hidden in the shadows. "Why didn't the devoted and saintly missionary to China bid the handsome young farmer and his desperately ill wife farewell immediately?" The icy tinkle in her laugh sent shivers of fear throughout my body. I leaned forward in the rocker. Moby Dick thumped to the floor at my feet.

"Miss Drucilla, I do not wish to hear - "

She leaned forward, quiet and intense. "You will listen if you do not want me to bring charges of theft and embezzlement against you."

"Theft!" I screeched. The shock of her words forced the breath from my body.

A cynical smile formed at the corner of her mouth. "Look, let's be reasonable. You recognized a good thing when you saw it, and you stayed around for the pickings. You figured that the least you'd get were my sister's belongings and the most - well, James McCall is quite a catch, wealthy, good-looking, and now, the grieving widower with a young son to raise alone. A young son, I might add, who worships the ground you walk on."

"Ma'am," I cleared my throat, "you have it all wrong. Aunt Bea will tell you - "

"Ah, yes, dear, befuddled Aunt Bea. If she had her way, you'd be canonized by the Roman Catholic Church."

My fear turned to anger. I loved and respected Beatrice McCall, no matter what this impudent woman had to say. "Miss Drucilla, you may think what you like, but I have done nothing wrong. Also, you can be certain that I have no designs, whatsoever, on Jamie's father! Mary was my friend."

With a fluid motion Drucilla rose to her feet and turned to face me. "So noble, so noble."

I choked back the tears that insisted upon forming. "Why are you doing this? Why are you saying all these hateful things?"

She lifted one eyebrow. "Tsk! Tsk! Does the truth bother you?"

Unable to contain my irritation any longer, I opened the bedroom door and pointed toward the hallway. "I believe our conversation is at an end. If you'll excuse me, I wish to retire now."

As she swept past, she murmured, "I won't let you get away with your scheme, Miss Spencer."

Closing the door behind her, I glanced across the room to where the Bible had lain. I thought of Mary and wondered how two girls so different from one another could have come from the same family. My promise to Jamie echoed in my mind. How will I keep that promise, Lord, now that Drucilla has made it clear I am not welcome here? I thought I'd been letting You lead me. What went wrong?

After a restless night, I made a decision. Since I was not in Ian's or Drucilla's employ, I would continue to care for Jamie until either James McCall himself returned or Aunt Bea ordered me to leave.

I awakened at dawn to a nippy breeze blowing through the partially opened window beside my bed. Hearing the sound of metal clanging against metal, I peered toward the barn where Aunt Bea kept a small herd of milkers. Walter was walking toward the barn, two milk pails in each hand. When he glanced up toward the window, I drew back into the shadows.

Considering the announcement I was about to make, I chose to wear the brown calico dress I'd run away from home in. After brushing the snarls from my hair, I drew it back into the tightest, most severe knot I could manage. There! That should add a good ten years to my age!

I hurried downstairs to fix breakfast. I cored five large apples and filled each with brown sugar, cinnamon, and a dollop of butter. After placing them on a cookie sheet, I put them in the oven. Within minutes the warm, mellow aroma of baking apples filled the room.

I'd just whipped up a batch of biscuits when Aunt Bea entered the room. "My, you are up early this morning. I take it you slept well?"

I smiled and asked if she'd like me to scramble some eggs.

"Sounds good. Chloe, let me open the store, and I'll be back to set the table."

By the time she returned, Walter had brought in a pitcher of fresh milk for the breakfast table. Ian and Jamie soon sat down at the table. We ate in silence. After the last bite of my baked apple, I could keep my peace no longer. "Mr. Ian, I've decided that since Jamie's father was the one who hired me to look after his son, he should be the one to dismiss me."

Ian's fork clattered onto the plate in front of him. Obviously he knew about Drucilla's visit to my room. Before he could reply, Aunt Bea spoke, "That makes sense to me. If I were James, I'd expect Chloe to remain at her post until I returned."

I smiled gratefully at Aunt Bea, then winked at Jamie. He grinned through a wide milk mustache.

"I'm not sure how Drucilla will take your decision," Ian mumbled.

I think you have a good idea how she'll take it.

Aunt Bea collected the dirty plates as she spoke. "Speaking of Drucilla, when she awakens, please tell her to fix whatever she wants for breakfast. I have an unusually busy day ahead of me in the store."

I took the plates from Aunt Bea's hands. "I'll take care of the dishes. You go ahead and do whatever you have to do."

"Thank you, Chloe. I appreciate you. Then, if you'll excuse me?" She strode from the room.

Ian pushed his chair back from the table. "Perhaps I should see if Drucilla needs anything."

Taking his glass, I turned toward the sink. "Yes, perhaps you should."

"Chloe, I had nothing to do - never mind." He turned and left the kitchen.

I heard Jamie's chair scrape and felt his arms encircle my legs. "I love you, Miss Chloe."

"I love you too, you little scamp."

To say that Drucilla was upset over my decision was an understatement. I could hear her response from the opposite end of the house. I wondered if Ian was surprised to learn how the sweet crystallike voice she always used when in the presence of men could become so harsh and grating when her will was thwarted. I finished the dishes as quickly as possible. As I placed the last clean bowl on the shelf, I looked at Jamie and whispered, "Ya wanna go for a walk this morning?"

We escaped the house before the woman emerged from her room and spent the next half-hour leaping from tie to tie on the railroad tracks. The brisk exercise warmed us before we sat down on a grassy knoll to wait for the eastbound train.

"Jamie, why do you refuse to talk to people?"

The little boy shrugged his shoulders.

"What happened that made you decide not to speak anymore?"

Again he shrugged.

"Well, if you ever want to talk about it, I'll be glad to listen."

He nodded.

"I'm glad you talked to me yesterday." I picked a strand of prairie grass and nibbled on one end. "Why did you decide to talk then?"

His sad brown eyes looked up into mine, then down at the grass. "You were going to leave me."

I stared down the tracks, my eyes tracing their path across the rolling prairie. "It's not because I want to. Sooner or later, I'll have to leave you."

He jerked his head up. "You promised. You promised!"

I placed my hand on his arm. "Jamie, I promise to stay with you until your father comes. After that, we'll just have to wait and see."

"You promised!" Jamie twisted away from me. The faint sound of a whistle drifted to us from the west.

"Let's try to get the engineer to blow the whistle again." I showed Jamie how to signal the engineer, and he allowed himself to be led closer to the tracks.

As the morning train roared into view, a familiar chill of excitement coursed through me as the monster approached. The engineer responded to our signal with two long blasts. We ran along the gentle slope beside the track, waving at the passengers, some of whom returned our greeting. The railroad man in the caboose waved a big red hanky at us.

After the train had passed, I tackled Jamie. We tumbled laughing down the slope. When we stopped rolling, we lay in the grass, watching a flock of geese heading south.

Jamie jumped up and began running in circles, flapping his arms and honking like the geese. Catching the spirit, I joined him. As my skirts twisted about my ankles, I lost my footing and flopped to the ground in a heap of calico. Jamie collapsed beside me, tears of laughter streaming down his face. "You look so funny, Miss Chloe."

"Funny? You think I look funny? How about you?" I tickled his side.

Laughing, he pointed to the back of my head. I discovered that part of the knot I'd wrapped so tightly in place had sprung loose and bobbed about like a giant doughnut. I readjusted the pins still holding my hair in place. "There, is that better?"

He nodded.

"I can't hear you, Jamie."

"Yes." He hid his grin behind both hands.

"I heard you that time. Now that the train has passed, would you like to walk the tracks into town and see if there's any mail for us today?"

"Umhum. Race ya." The little boy leapt to his feet and scrambled up the gravel shoulder to the track. Dancing a jig on the wooden ties, he shouted, "Beat ya. I beat ya, Miss Chloe."

I stood up and charged after him, crying, "Unfair! Unfair! You got a head start."

He giggled and hopped from tie to tie toward town.

As we passed the hardware store, Walter waved vigorously to us. Thinking he was just being friendly, we waved back. But when he ran toward us and continued to gesture, we stopped and waited.

"Miss Drucilla is looking all over for you two. She's got a bee in her bonnet to go out to the ranch this morning."

I sighed. "Thanks, Walter." I glanced down at Jamie, whose grin had melted into a pout. "I guess we'd better go back to the house, huh?"

As we entered the farm yard behind the store, Jamie whispered, "Don't tell." I winked and assured him I would keep our secret.

We found Drucilla looming over us from the back steps. Instinctively, Jamie grabbed my hand.

"Where have you been?" Drucilla stormed down the steps toward us. "Ian has had the carriage ready to take us to the ranch for over an hour."

"If you had told me, I - "

"Tsk!" She clicked her tongue in disgust. Without another word, she climbed the steps and entered the house.

I hurried toward the stairs with Jamie in tow. "I'll be out in a minute. Jamie will need a sweater."

"The child isn't going with us," she called over her shoulder. "I've arranged for Aunt Beatrice to care for him for the day. So if you would please hurry, I would like to be back before dusk."

Jamie squeezed my hand tighter. Knowing Aunt Bea had enough to do without having to care for Jamie, I considered refusing. But if Drucilla were going to the ranch to find evidence against me, I wanted to be there to defend myself. I glanced down at the frightened child, "I'll be back Jamie, I promise. You be a good boy for Aunt Bea, ya hear?"

Chapter 10

Standing Accused

Somehow I survived the silent carriage ride to the ranch and was pleasantly relieved to find Zerelda at the house. Drucilla treated the kind and generous neighbor with the air reserved for servants. As Drucilla moved through the house inspecting the rooms, Ian mumbled something about taking care of the horses and finding Sam, then disappeared out the back door.

Drucilla saved the kitchen for last. As she bustled across the dining room and through the kitchen door, Zerelda tugged at my elbow, causing us to drop back out of hearing range.

"What's with her? The lady of the manor?" Zerelda hissed.

I giggled, then caught myself. "She thinks she is anyway."

Zerelda narrowed her eyes. "Well, if you ask me, the thought has crossed her mind. There's no doubt that the woman's got her cap set for James."

I shook my head incredulously. "Where did you get an idea like that?"

My friend patted my arm. "You innocent child. Didn't you see the greed in her eyes as she fondled the silver tea set? And the way her eyes danced when she counted the pieces of English china - obscene!"

"I don't thi - "

"Zerelda!" The kitchen door swung open, and Drucilla's voice boomed throughout the dining room. "Zerelda! I was speaking with you about the provisions for winter. I would like to see them, please."

Zerelda cast her eyes heavenward, cleared her throat, and turned to face the woman. "Yes, Miss Bradley, I'll take you to the storm cellar immediately."

I heard the back door slam shut. I walked out the front door onto the porch, where I'd spent so many quiet summer afternoons with Jamie and many balmy evenings alone. The world on both sides of the white picket fence had drastically changed. Jamie's swing hung limp and abandoned. Of the myriad of brightly colored flower beds bordering the house, only a few zinnias and marigolds still blossomed. One limp rambling rose dangled from the trellis at the far end of the porch.

I leaned over the railing and inhaled deeply; it seemed I could almost smell the coming snows of winter. Emotions played tag in my heart. Though I wanted to keep my word to Jamie and to resist Drucilla's attempts to dismiss me, I also longed to head West, to reach California before the snows closed the passes through the Rockies. The brisk breeze fanning my face might have swept down from one of those far mountains that stood between me and my dreams.

Engulfed in my thoughts, I failed to hear Ian round the corner of the house and climb the porch steps until he spoke. "Miss Chloe?"

I jumped and gasped.

"I'm sorry. I didn't mean to startle you." He sat on the railing beside me. Tightening my arms about myself, I edged a few steps away. He moved closer. "I'm glad I caught you alone for a minute."

"Oh?" I lifted one eyebrow.

"You must know that Drucilla intends to get rid of you one way or another. Wouldn't it be a bit silly to oppose her when you yourself would prefer to complete your trip to San Francisco? She's a very determined woman."

I turned my face away. "That's true, she is." "Then why make it difficult for yourself? Stubbornness?"

I smiled. "Partly. I don't like to be bullied. More important, though, is the fact I gave my word to your brother that I would stay with Jamie until he returned. I see no reason to break that promise."

Ian chuckled under his breath. "I see a very good reason. Five-foot, two inches of blond fury. As long as I've known her, Drucilla has been a willful person. Don't underestimate her; she'll eat you alive."

I frowned and continued to study the horizon. "Why are you telling me this? To scare me off?"

He chuckled again. "Partly."

In frustration, I whirled about. "I don't understand it. You seem to be a strong, purposeful man. Yet this diminuitive blond woman has you wrapped around her pinkie."

He shrugged. "We go back a long way."

"But," I thought about Zerelda's observations, "it seems like Drucilla has her eyes on your brother now that he's widowed. And didn't she try to break up Mary and James before they were married? Where do you fit into all this?"

Ian scratched the side of his head, then shrugged his shoulders. "You're probably right." He folded his arms across his chest. "Drucilla is an expert horsewoman. She has entered and won dozens of equestrian competitions in the Northeast. And Mary was always there in the stands, cheering her on. You might say James is the only prize Drucilla ever lost."

The longing in his voice caused me to turn to face him. Knowing that I might be overstepping my position, I asked anyway, "You love her yourself, don't you?"

He reddened. "I tried not to. She's the main reason I headed West to Colorado."

Drucilla's accusations niggled at the back of my mind. "Do you believe I tried to steal Mary's belongings or that I am hoping to become Mrs. James McCall?"

His gaze shifted to the porch floor, then toward me. "Uh, no, not really." A look of fear and warning filled his eyes. "But don't depend on my support, Miss Chloe. I may appear strong, but where Drucilla is concerned - "

A voice behind us called, "Did I hear my name mentioned?"

We whipped about to find Drucilla and Zerelda standing at the foot of the porch steps. Instantly, Ian's manner changed to one of solicitous Eastern gentry. "My dear, have you finished your tour of the place? Did you find your sister's heirloom jewelry?"

Lifting her skirts about her slim ankles, Drucilla climbed the steps. "No, but I didn't expect I would, did I, Miss Chloe? Did you speak with Sam, the foreman?"

Ian shook his head. "No, he's not here right now. He's due back at any time though."

She pursed her lips in irritation. "Well, would you take me on a tour of the farm buildings, please?"

A smile broke out across his face. "I'd be glad to." He took her arm and led her back down the stairs. Zerelda hurried up the steps to where I stood.

A sudden image of Satan and the does in the pasture behind the barn flashed across my mind. "Oh, be careful of the —"

A sudden jab in the ribs caused me to catch my breath. I looked at Zerelda in surprise as she finished my statement. "...mud in the barnyard. It may soil that lovely dress of yours, Miss Bradley."

"I wasn't going to say that," I hissed, glaring at the woman who'd drawn me to her side.

A wide, impish grin filled Zerelda's face as she waved at the departing couple. "See you in a few minutes."

"Zerelda! I was trying to warn them of Satan."

Maintaining her smile, she aimed me toward the front door. "I know what you were trying to do, but I couldn't resist."

She pulled the door open and propelled me across the threshold. I shook my arm free of her grasp. "Zerelda, I've got to warn them. It would be wrong not to."

Nodding, her eyes danced with deviltry as she mocked my expression of reprimand. "Yes, wouldn't it?"

I pushed the door back open and stepped onto the porch in time to hear a shrill scream. I bounded across the yard and through the open gate into the barnyard, Zerelda a couple steps behind me. Behind us we heard the clop of approaching horses, and in front of us, we heard Ian's shouts as well as Drucilla's terrified cries.

The sight that met us proved equal to our imaginations. Satan stood over Drucilla, who was covered with mud from the toes of her white kidskin boots to the tip of her nose. The three does stood over by their shed while Ian circled Satan and his prey, an extended pitchfork in hand. The goat eyed Ian as the man tried to lure him away from Drucilla, but whenever the man crossed an invisible line in the mud, Satan lowered his head and glared, causing Ian to retreat.

I charged into the pen, shouting and waving my hands in the air. "Stop, Satan, stop. Arrest! No, uh, um," I couldn't remember the command that the congressman had taught the goat. I glanced over my shoulder. Zerelda stood outside the fence, tears of laughter flowing down her face. The ranch hands with rifles in hand rounded the corner with Jake in the lead. The armed cowboy dashed past me. "Veto! Veto! Satan! Veto!"

The goat, reluctant to retreat, lowered his head and turned toward the stocky, balding man. "I said Veto!"

Shaking his head violently, the goat turned and ambled to the far end of the enclosure. Ian tossed the pitchfork toward the haystack and rushed to Drucilla. He and Jake lifted her from the mud. I swallowed hard to keep from laughing at the sight.

"Are you all right?" I gasped, trying to brush the thick clay from her skirt and bodice.

"All right? Do I look all right?" she snarled. "Of course I'm not all right. Ian, that animal should be shot."

"Now, Drucilla," he demurred.

"I mean it. Shoot it!"

"Now, ma'am," Jake pushed back his wide-brimmed hat. "Satan didn't mean no harm. He was just playin' around."

"Is that your beast? Get rid of it now if you want to keep your job here at the ranch," she snapped and yanked the rifle from the astonished man's hand. Her eyes narrowed as she aimed the weapon at him. "Either you do it, or I will!"

"Just wait a minute here." Sam ambled over to Drucilla and gently removed the gun from her hands. "There'll be no shootin' on my land, do you hear?"

"Your land?" she screeched.

Sam glanced over his shoulder at me. "Miss Chloe, just who are these strangers? By the way, it's good to see ya again."

I walked over to Sam. "Sam, I'd like to introduce you to Miss Drucilla Bradley, Mrs. McCall's sister from Massachusetts, and Mr. Ian McCall, James's brother from Colorado. And this is Sam Johnson, the McCall ranch foreman."

Drucilla yanked at her skirts and glared at the black man standing before her. "You, sir, are the former foreman of the McCall ranch. Get your gear together and get out. Is that clear?" When the man didn't budge, she turned toward Ian. "Tell him, Ian."

Ian moved reluctantly to her side and started to speak. One look into Sam's malevolent stare, and Ian turned toward Drucilla. "Now, dear, don't be hasty. Why don't you go up to the house and tidy up a bit while we men discuss the fate of the goat?"

Sam squared his shoulders and planted his hands firmly on his hips, then narrowed his eyes at Drucilla. Though she tilted her nose defiantly, I saw her lower lip quiver.

In a low rumble, he said, "I am foreman of this ranch until Mr. James McCall tells me to go, or one of us is poking up daisies, whichever comes first. And the goat stays too! Is that clear?"

Flipping what was left of her cascade of golden curls about her shoulders, she whirled about and stomped through the barnyard toward the house.

Sam directed his gaze at Ian. "Do you have anything to add?"

Ian didn't meet Sam's gaze. "No, sir, can't say as I do."

"Fine, then let me introduce you to the boys."

Zerelda chattered all the way to the house. "I couldn't help it. I've never seen such a funny sight in my entire life." I had to admit that I couldn't help but laugh also. "So when do you leave for California?"

I shook my head. "I honestly don't know. If she had had her way," I rolled my eyes toward the ceiling. "I would have been on the afternoon train. But I can't abandon Jamie. In his eyes, that's what his mother and father did."

"Poor little tyke."

I smiled. "I'm seeing signs of improvement, which, of course, makes it harder for me to leave right now."

She eyed me thoughtfully. "Mary Ellen Conners could sure have used your midwife skills last Friday evening. The Conners' baby was born breech. Both the mother and the child died."

"Oh, I'm so sorry. Why didn't you come and get me? I would have been happy to help."

"The women around here are waiting to see if you're gonna stay. But I'll remember that next time. Will you remain at the ranch?"

I shrugged my shoulders. "I doubt it. I'm not sure I can hold out against Drucilla."

Zerelda's face hardened. "You'd better!"

I laughed and promised to visit her before leaving for California. We spent the rest of the afternoon chatting while we baked a batch of bread and pared vegetables for a hearty stew for supper.

By the time Drucilla came downstairs, Zerelda's carriage was pulling away from the house. She found me in the kitchen, scrubbing flour off the tabletop. Four apple pies baked in the hot oven behind me. I glanced up as she entered, then walked to the sink to rinse my dishcloth in the dishpan. Her muddied gown had been replaced with one of Mary's. For a moment I felt as irritated with her for wearing Mary's clothing as she must have felt with me.

She strolled over to the stove and peeked under the tea towel where I had fresh bread cooling. "I've looked everywhere for Mary's jewelry pouch. You know, the green velvet one with the diamond clasp. I know she left Boston with it, so it should be here." She paused, waiting for me to speak. When I didn't, she continued. "I've looked everywhere. I don't suppose you might know where it is?"

I scraped at a mound of moistened flour, then ran the dishcloth across the residue. "Somewhere in either Denver or Chicago, I would imagine."

She emitted a low chuckle and started to speak, when the tread of heavy boots caused us to turn toward the back door. Ian strolled in and sniffed the air. "Hmm, apple pie, my favorite."

Drucilla simpered up into the man's face. "We thought you'd enjoy a little treat this evening." The quick glare she gave me dared me to challenge her.

He peered under the tea towels covering the loaves of cooling bread. "It looks like you two ladies have been busy all afternoon."

Drucilla heaved a ragged sigh and fanned her perfectly manicured hands before her face. "Homemaking is exhausting."

I disappeared into the pantry in order to hide my irritation. Catching sight of my reflection in the small window behind the door, I couldn't resist the urge to imitate her exaggerated gestures. "Homemaking is exhausting!" I turned in time to see Ian watching me, amusement written on his face. I slipped behind the partition and caught my breath.

Ian's voice drifted into the pantry. "So, Drucilla dear, have you decided to spend the night here at the ranch, or have you completed your, uh, inspection?"

"Ian," she simpered, "I'm just taking care of my dear departed sister's affairs as she would have me do."

I heard him cross the room and open a cupboard door. "Did you find the jewelry?"

"No." A bitter edge entered her voice. "Not that I expected to after all this time. I had hoped Miss Spencer would be more helpful, though." She sniffed as if brought to tears. "I did so treasure my dear granny's emerald brooch."

"The matching earrings too?" I couldn't miss the sarcasm in his voice.

Unable to linger in the pantry any longer, I decided to face my attacker head on. "Mr. McCall, Miss Bradley believes that I stole her sister's jewelry. It was stolen, but not by me. The wet nurse whom Mary hired to accompany her and the baby to Kansas ran off with it the night the baby died."

The lift of Drucilla's eyebrow negated the need for any comment.

Ian frowned. "Then it is missing."

"Oh, yes. And if either of you has any doubts, you can check the records at the Union Pacific regional offices. Your sister did file a complaint, and a search was made of the train, including all of my belongings, I might add." I picked up two oven pads. "If you'll excuse me, I need to check the pies to see if they're done. We wouldn't want Miss Bradley's pies to burn, would we?"

I ignored Drucilla's glare and opened the oven door. "Another five minutes, wouldn't you say, Miss Bradley?"

Ian urged the furious Drucilla from the kitchen. "We'll leave everything in your competent hands, Miss Spencer. Miss Bradley and I have important business to discuss in the library."

I closed the oven door and stepped out onto the back porch. A chill breeze fanned my flushed cheeks as I stared at the barn and fallow fields beyond. I can't take this, Lord. I love Jamie dearly, but I cannot abide that woman. She won't be happy until she's forced me out of here.

Looking up to the sky, I gazed at a flock of geese heading south. And how do I know that James is coming back? What if he's met with an accident? Been killed? How long am I obliged to keep my promise to him or to his son ? Feeling calmer, I returned to the empty kitchen and removed the pies from the oven. Closing the oven door, I placed the hot pads on the table next to the bubbling pies.

I studied the rough, whitewashed walls and the big stone fireplace. Another woman's kitchen, yet, for a time, it had been mine. I glanced at the rockers beside the fireplace and imagined my mother sitting there crocheting another baby's afghan. "Chloe, some memories always stay with a woman, no matter how long she lives - her first love, her first child, and her first kitchen."

My first kitchen - I was a part of it and it, of me. I thought of the coming winter and realized that spring would be a long time coming. In a very short while, I had put down more roots in the rich prairie soil than I ever had intended - roots that would have to be dug up or cut off. Stop being so dramatic, Chloe Mae! I thought of Jamie, and in my heart I knew Drucilla was right about one thing - the sooner I left Kansas, the better.

That evening Drucilla called me into the library after I had finished the supper dishes. "Mr. McCall and I wish to speak with you regarding your stay."

I took a detour up to my room and collected the notebook in which I'd kept a log of every cent James had left to cover Jamie's and my expenses while he was gone. The moment I entered my room, I knew someone had searched it. Reluctantly, I went back down the stairs to the library. As I entered the room, Drucilla motioned me toward the straight chair beside the desk while she crossed to the leather couch and made herself comfortable. When I saw Sam leaning against a windowsill, I nodded and smiled. So this is judgment day for both of us.

Ian sat at James's oak roll-top desk, where papers covered the surface. He swiveled the desk chair around to face me. "Miss Chloe, I have been reviewing my brother's ledgers regarding your employ. It seems he valued your service greatly. At least, he's been very generous."

I eyed the man warily. "Yes, Mr. McCall has been most generous." I handed him the notebook and an envelope containing coins and bills. "In addition to my salary and a train ticket to San Francisco, as Mary promised when I agreed to travel with her, Mr. McCall entrusted me with a household allowance to cover any expenses Jamie and I might incur during his absence."

As Ian studied the entries in my log, I glanced over at Sam. He grinned and winked. His strength and encouragement buoyed my flagging spirits. The change clattered onto the desktop. Drucilla craned her neck to glimpse the money passing through Ian's fingers as he counted. "Hmm," Ian muttered, "looks like everything's accounted for." A sigh of relief escaped his lips; an expression of disappointment crossed Drucilla's face.

"From what I can see, both you and Sam have been good stewards of my brother's property. I am sure that if he were here, he'd be pleased. However, with James's disappearance, some changes will have to be made." Ian cleared his throat and looked down at a stack of papers on the desk. "Mr. Johnson, we will, of course, keep you and the other hands on until we find a buyer."

Sam bristled. "A buyer? You would sell the ranch out from under your grieving brother?"

"Sam, I may call you Sam?" Ian rested his arms on the wooden arms of the chair. "No one knows where my brother is, if he is still alive. He may never return. I can't wait until the place is overrun with buffalo grass before I take action. As for you, Miss Chi - , er, Miss Spencer, I will honor my brother's agreement with you as he outlined in his papers."

Drucilla strolled over to the desk and placed her hand possessively on Ian's shoulder. "Since I will be accompanying Jamie to his grandparents' home in Boston, you are free to leave for San Francisco at any time." The woman batted her eyelashes at me and flashed me a brilliant smile. "Are there any questions?"

I clenched my hands by my sides, aching to slap the self-satisfied look off her face. "Yes, I'd like to know if the decision for me to leave was made before or after you searched my room?" Drucilla's face clouded with fury.

Ian leaned forward, then glanced up at Drucilla. "Searched your room?"

"Yes, is that not so, Miss Bradley?"

Drucilla protested, "I had to be certain she didn't have the jewels stashed away somewhere."

Ian arose and took my hand. "I am so sorry for Drucilla's indiscretion. Please accept my apology."

I slipped my hand out of his and stared into his eyes. "I understood the reason for today's excursion to the ranch before we left Aunt Bea's place this morning. Did Aunt Bea know you intended to dismiss me?"

"Of course." Drucilla insinuated herself between Ian and me. "It was her idea, you know." When I looked to Ian for verification, he averted his eyes.

With long, angry steps, Sam strode to my side. "Mr. McCall, I'm smellin' something rotten here. I know James McCall, and he'll be back. Mark my words." His dark eyes narrowed. "And I know Beatrice McCall. She wouldn't hurt this little gal for anything."

Ian straightened. "Mr. Johnson, I believe our business is completed for this evening. You may leave. And Miss Chloe." He opened the bottom drawer on the desk, hauled out a steel cash box, and opened it. Removing a yellow envelope from the box, he handed it to me. "I believe this should more than compensate you for your services. As a gesture of gratitude, I have added an additional six weeks' payment."

Drucilla opened her mouth to object, but Ian continued, "I believe that concludes our business. So, if you will excuse me, I intend to retire for the night. Miss Drucilla, may I escort you to your room?" The woman pursed her lips but allowed herself to be led from the room.

I looked at Sam and he at me. "I don't know whether to be sorry or relieved."

"Mr. James won't be relieved, I'll tell you that. He's gonna be one irate rooster when he finds out what those two have been up to."

I shrugged my shoulders. "What can we do about it? As Miss Bradley said, we're only hired help."

Sam shook his head in disgust. "That woman reminds me of 'the lady of the manor' where my pa sharecropped after the war." The man's shoulders sagged as he walked toward the door. "I guess I'd better tell the boys the news. I hope James high-tails it back here before Ian finds a buyer. As for you, little lady, I will be sorry to see you go."

I walked over to Sam and kissed his cheek. "I'll miss you too - and the rest of the ranch hands." He nodded and left.

I strolled out to the porch for one last look at the brilliant stars blanketing the prairie from horizon to horizon. After a few minutes, I climbed the stairs to my room. With no one to talk to, I decided to pour my emotions out in a letter to Hattie.

My thoughts flowed from my pen as never before.... I know Mary's sister truly believes I stole the jewelry. And I don't know how to convince her that I'm innocent. Innocent, a strange word for me to use as I stare down at Pa's twenty-dollar gold piece. I've prayed, and I know God forgives me, but Pa ...

And then there's Jamie. I must break my promise to a little boy whose short life has been filled with broken dreams and promises. Will he revert to his cocoon of silence and never again emerge? Pray for me, dear sister and for this torn-apart family.

Your sister, Chloe Mae Spencer

The next morning, Drucilla appeared much earlier than usual. The ranch hands and I had just sat down to a breakfast of scrambled eggs and grits when she breezed through the door.

"Good morning, gentlemen. Isn't it a lovely day? A bit chilly for the season, though, don't you think?" Her perky remarks were met with stony silence. Even Darcy, the Southern gentleman who never could resist a woman's charms, suddenly found his bowl of grits intriguing.

The woman tossed her blond curls about her shoulders and sat down next to Bo. She flashed the young cowboy a radiant smile. He reddened and turned away.

"Well, Miss Chloe, what are we having this morning?"

Before I could answer, Sam drawled, "We're having grits and eggs. Help yourself." He pointed to the stove. His eyes dared me to offer to serve her. I settled back in my chair.

Surprise flooded Drucilla's face as she realized I wasn't moving from my seat. I chewed and swallowed a mouthful of egg, then pointed toward the cupboard. "You'll find the dishes in there and the silver in the drawer on the left."

Ian entered the kitchen just as Drucilla slid the chair from the table and stormed past him to the cupboard. "Oh, grits! I love 'em. Will you get me a bowl, too, Drucilla?"

"Get it yourself," she snarled.

Ian stared in surprise, then ambled over to the cupboard for a bowl and plate. Behind us, the clanking utensils punctuated Drucilla's anger. Sam grinned and lifted his glass of goat's milk in a toast to me. Yeah, Satan! Goat's milk had never tasted so good.

Chapter 11

Tears of Regret

The men waved their hats and shouted goodbye until our carriage crested the rise, and the two-story farmhouse disappeared from sight. That the ranch crew obviously liked and would miss me irked Drucilla. She wrapped herself in a pout and refused to speak. After a few tries at conversation with her and then with me, Ian concentrated on the road ahead of the carriage.

When we passed the abandoned soddy, I thought of Jamie. He'd changed so much since that day when I found him curled up in the corner of the seat, terrified by his mother's cries of pain. I wondered again what lay ahead for him once I left. Will he revert into his cocoon of silence? If only I can get him to open up to another person, then maybe …

As our carriage pulled in behind the store, Jamie bounded out the door, his face wreathed with smiles. My heart lurched as he flung his arms about my legs.

"I missed you," I whispered, squeezing his hand tightly.

"I missed you too," he whispered.

When we reached my room, he hopped up on the edge of my bed while I took off my bonnet and cape. "Are we still keeping your talking a secret?"

He nodded and grinned.

I knelt down in front of him. "Aunt Bea doesn't know?"

He shook his head slowly. "When do you plan to tell her?" He shrugged and rolled his eyes. "Don't you think she deserves to know?" He shrugged again.

I adjusted the collar of his shirt. "She's been so nice to you. Think how happy she'd be if you shared our secret with her."

The child gave his head a determined shake. I sighed and gave him a hug. "What am I going to do with you, you little scamp?"

He laughed and hopped off the bed. Grabbing me by the hand, he dragged me into the parlor, where he had the circus train set up in the middle of the floor. "Walter helped me put it together," he confided. "See? See, this is the monkey car, and this is the one the lions and tigers ride in."

He reached down and picked up a brown camel. "Oops, the lions would eat him if he rode with them, huh?"

Out of the corner of my eye I saw a shadow pass by the archway leading into the hall. "They sure would." I laughed.

Jamie dropped the camel into another freight car. "Zebras don't eat camels, do they?"

I shook my head. "I don't think so."

Suddenly Jamie's eyes lighted up. "Oh! I forgot to tell you about the kittens. Muffin had six babies while you were gone."

"She did? Well, aren't you going to show them to me?" He leapt up and raced for the stairs. "Come on," he called.

I gathered my skirts in my hands and hurried after him. As I stepped into the hallway, I came face to face with Drucilla. The slow nod of her head and the self-congratulatory smile on her face told me she'd heard Jamie's every word. Sorry, kiddo, our secret's no secret any longer.

With Aunt Bea busy in the store and Ian in town on business, Jamie and I kept out of Drucilla's way for the rest of the morning. At lunch, Drucilla insisted on taking Jamie for a ride in the carriage. Welcoming the opportunity to get away by myself for a few hours, I found a book in Aunt Bea's library to read. Back in my room, I curled up on my bed for a couple hours of good reading. In the middle of the Town-ho's story, I started at the sound of Drucilla's angry voice outside my room.

"James Edward McCall, you straighten up this minute, do you hear? When I speak to you, I expect you to reply with a yes, ma'am, or a no, ma'am, do you understand? I won't tolerate your defiance."

I scrambled off the bed, then paused from indecision. Maybe I should keep my nose out of this. Before I could decide, I heard the sound of a child's running feet followed by the determined click of a woman's heels, then a door slam. The shouts continued from outside Jamie's bedroom door.

Silence was the main course at the supper table that evening. Drucilla glared from me to Jamie and back again, Jamie nibbled at his food and pouted, Ian avoided eye contact with everyone, and Aunt Bea seemed preoccupied. At the end of the meal, Aunt Bea suggested Drucilla help with the supper dishes while I put Jamie to bed.

When I tried to question Jamie about the afternoon, he responded by squinting his eyes accusingly and extending his lower lip, but he refused to talk. With my finger I tilted his head up toward me. "Jamie, if you think I told Aunt Drucilla your secret, you're wrong. She heard us talking today, when we were in the parlor, remember?"

He jerked his head away, scrambled into his bed, and pulled the covers up under his chin. I walked over to the bed to kiss him on his forehead. "Do you want me to pray with you tonight?"

His brown eyes snapped with fury, and he turned to face the wall. I sighed and knelt down beside his bed.

"Dear Jesus, Jamie is angry with me right now, and I'm sorry. Please help him to forgive me. And help him to have a good night's sleep. Amen." Kissing the tip of his ear, I stood up and tiptoed from the room.

As I stepped out into the hallway, Ian was waiting. He asked me to join him, Drucilla, and Aunt Bea in the parlor. By the look of sadness in Aunt Bea's eyes, I knew Drucilla had spread her poison.

"Chloe," Aunt Bea patted the place beside her on the sofa, "please come and sit down beside me." I obeyed.

"Chloe, Drucilla gave me some distressing news this afternoon. I don't quite know what to make of it. She claims she overheard Jamie talking with you." The woman took a deep breath. "Is that so?"

"Yes, but - "

Her frown silenced me. "How long have you known Jamie could speak? How long have you been keeping this from us, his family? Didn't you think we had the right to know?"

I reddened. I hadn't thought of it that way. I swallowed the lump forming in my throat. "I'm sorry. I've known since the day he ran away to the abandoned soddy."

She placed her hand gently on mine and gazed into my eyes. "Why didn't you tell us right away?"

"Because I promised him I wouldn't." My heart pleaded for her to understand.

Her lips tightened. "That was not your promise to make. You have an obligation to us as well as to the child. With both of his parents gone, we are forced to make decisions that will affect the rest of his life."

Drucilla added her sarcasm. "Were you planning to tell us before you left for California, or were you hoping we would keep you on as long as he remained mute?"

"Yes. No!" My gaze leapt to her face, then to Aunt Bea's. I straightened imaginary wrinkles from my skirt. "I'm sorry, I thought I was doing what was best - for him. I thought I could coax him into revealing his secret himself."

Drucilla continued, "Really, you are such a wonder. My only wonder is how long it's going to take you, Aunt Bea, to see this miracle woman for the manipulator she is." Drucilla held up her hand and inspected her carefully manicured nails. "She's after all she can get, and if the child gets hurt because of it, so what!"

Anger and pain seared my senses. "That's not true. Jamie is the only reason I am still here. If it weren't for him, I would have been on my way to China right now!"

"Tsk! Tsk! Save it for the stage, Miss Chloe." Drucilla chuckled. "They tell me community theater is big in San Francisco."

I looked at Ian, then at Aunt Bea. "Is, is that what you think?"

She shook her head and glanced toward the floor. "No, of course not…" Her voice drifted off uncertainly. Both Aunt Bea and Ian avoided my gaze.

When Drucilla caught my eye, she pretended to hide the tiny smile forming at the corners of her mouth.

Finally Ian spoke. "Is this really necessary, Drucilla, since you plan to leave with the boy for Boston tomorrow?"

"Tomorrow?" I gasped.

Aunt Bea placed her hand on my wrist. "Yes, we think it's best to get the child back with his people as quickly as possible. It will make the loss of his parents much easier for him to handle." She patted my hand gently. "You are welcome to stay as long as you wish."

"I, I wish to leave as soon as possible. Oh, no, I did promise to say goodbye to Zerelda."

Ian rushed to my side. "I would be glad to take you to the Paget place tomorrow morning. It would be a pleasure for me to drive you, Miss Chloe."

After catching a glimpse of the irritation on Drucilla's face, I allowed him to help me to my feet and to hold my hand a second or two longer than necessary. "Why, Mr. McCall, how nice of you. After breakfast, I'll explain to Jamie what is happening and say my goodbyes, then leave. Now, if you'll excuse me, I have some packing to do."

Aunt Bea's hand brushed my sleeve as I passed by. "Chloe, I …"

My tears started flowing the instant I stepped into the hallway. Fearing I would give Drucilla the satisfaction she craved, I hurried to my room and closed the door. The moment had come. I was leaving Kansas. By the end of the week I would be in San Francisco. I'd dreamed of this moment for months, but not this way. Everything had turned out wrong, so very wrong!

I opened the wardrobe and gazed unseeing at the clothing within. What do I take with me? The clothes Mary gave me? The dresses and books Aunt Bea insisted on buying for me?

Should I use Mary's valise or buy a cheap case at the general store?

I opened the drawer in the night stand. The white leather change purse Mary had given me lay on top of my railway ticket. The purse bulged with the coins and bills James had given me as wages. When I spied Pa's twenty-dollar gold piece next to the ticket, I crumpled in a heap on the floor beside the bed. Is God punishing me for running away from home or for stealing Pa's money? Is Jamie going to suffer for my sins?

Why God, why? I thought You were leading me. No matter what I do it turns out wrong. Is this my punishment? You said I was forgiven. I buried my face in the blue-and-yellow quilt. It's not fair to take out my mistakes on Jamie. He can't possibly understand.

I arose to my feet and stumbled to the desk. I needed answers, so I turned to the only source I knew, Mary's Bible. Then I remembered - Drucilla had taken the Book with her the night of her unexpected visit. A new flood of tears fell. I sat down heavily in the desk chair and buried my head in my arms on the desktop. Outside the window, heavy storm clouds shrouded the moon and the stars. I shivered from the cool nip in the bedroom air and blew out the lamp. Slipping into my nightclothes, I sank into the down mattress and pulled the bedding up around my chin, certain I would not be able to sleep.

A gray light filled the room when I finally awoke from my dreamless sleep. A light blanket of white covered the field beyond the barn. Shivering, I hurried over to the washstand, broke the crystal-thin layer of ice on the water in the pitcher, and poured it in the basin.

After washing and dressing, I hauled the valise from the wardrobe shelf. One glance at the dresses Mary had given me, and I stuffed them in the case. Leaving them behind would be admitting I'd stolen them, as far as Drucilla was concerned. I chose to wear two of the heaviest dresses for warmth. By the time I finished packing, the case's latches strained; the sides bulged. I laid my shawl and cape across the case, placed my purse under my bonnet, and headed down the stairs for breakfast. I had one thought on my mind - leave as quickly as possible!

Only Jamie and Ian were in the kitchen when I arrived. Aunt Bea had already gone downstairs to the store. We ate in silence. Even Jamie sensed the tension. Ian took his dishes to the sink and mumbled something about hitching up the horses.

When we were alone, I told Jamie the news. He stared at me, his lips narrowed in anger.

"You'll be able to see your grandfather and grandmother again. Won't that be nice? I'm sorry, Jamie, but it really is for the best."

He continued to stare wordlessly.

"When your daddy comes back, Aunt Bea will tell him where to find you."

"My daddy's never coming back, is he? He's dead."

I shook my head. "No, Jamie. Where did you get an idea like that?"

Jamie's lower lip quivered. "Uncle Ian told Aunt Bea that last night. That's why they're sending you away."

"Uncle Ian doesn't know where your daddy is right now. But I know that your daddy will come for you as soon as he can."

He shook his head slowly and tightened his lips. I reached to kiss him, but he pulled away and glared at me accusingly.

"Please try to understand. There's nothing I can do."

With slow deliberate movements, the child walked from the room. I heard the carriage pull up outside the back door and then Ian's footsteps on the stairs and down the hall. "All set. Are your bags packed?"

I nodded. "In my room. I've got to go to Jamie."

I headed down the hall, expecting to hear the sound of crying coming from Jamie's room. I paused at the door and listened. Silence. I knocked gently. "Jamie, may I come in?" I listened, then knocked again.

Opening the door, I peeked inside. Jamie sat cross-legged in the middle of his bed, his arms folded across his chest, staring straight ahead. "Jamie, I'm here to say goodbye."

I bent down and kissed his dry cheek. He didn't move. "I'll write to you from California. I'll send you pretty postcards of palm trees. Have you ever seen a palm tree?"

He refused to respond.

"And when I get to China, I'll write and tell you all about the Chinese sampans. Will you write to me and tell me about Boston? I've never been to Boston." I blotted my tears on the sleeve of my dress. When I realized that nothing I could say would produce a response, I kissed him once more and walked to the door. "Be a good boy for your Aunt Drucilla and Uncle Ian. I love you, and I'll miss you." I lifted my hand and gave a tiny wave, but he continued to stare straight ahead.

Defeated, I hurried downstairs. I paused in the doorway of the store and called to Aunt Bea.

"I'm leaving now. If I don't see you again, thank you for everything. And, please, forgive me. I thought I was ..." Before she could reply, I turned and ran out the back door to the waiting carriage.

Zerelda welcomed me with arms wide open and let me cry myself dry. She neither championed my cause nor condemned me. She led me into her kitchen and fixed me a cup of piping-hot mint tea. Once I'd spent my fury, she insisted I take a nap.

I awoke to the warm glow of a kerosene lamp. Zerelda sat on the small settee by the window, reading her Bible. When I stirred, she closed the book. "I marked a few texts that may help you. Why don't you freshen up a bit and come downstairs for supper? My husband David will finish his evening chores any minute and be hungry enough to eat the entire poundcake I baked this morning if I let him."

I waited until she left the room, then dragged my body from the bed and padded across the room to the settee. Opening the book to where my friend had inserted a crocheted bookmarker, I read the words she'd underlined in Psalm 27. "When my father and my mother forsake me, then the Lord will take me up. Teach me thy way, O Lord, and lead me in a plain path, because of mine enemies. Deliver me not over unto the will of mine enemies: for false witnesses are risen up against me, and such as breathe out cruelty…. Wait on the Lord: be of good courage, and he shall strengthen thine heart: wait, I say, on the Lord."

My eyes scanned the next text she'd underlined, Psalm 32:1. "Blessed is he whose transgression is forgiven, whose sin is covered." In the margin, Zerelda had penned, "You are forgiven. All sin is gone."

In my heart, I knew my sins had been forgiven. I'd asked for God's forgiveness when I first began studying the Bible with Zerelda and Mary. Yet, like a dog digging up old bones, my mind wouldn't let the past go, and I couldn't stop believing that my problems were direct punishment for my sins. Idly, I turned the worn page until my eyes rested on another passage Zerelda had marked, Psalm 36:7. "How excellent is thy loving-kindness, O God! therefore the children of men put their trust under the shadow of thy wings."

The next marked passage took my breath away. "Commit thy way unto the Lord; trust also in him; and he shall bring it to pass."

I dropped to my knees in front of the settee. Heavenly Father, forgive me for not trusting that You are kind and loving enough to forgive my sins. Help me to forgive myself. And if I was wrong for not telling Aunt Bea about Jamie's ability to speak, forgive me for that too.

If I commit my way to You and trust in You, You have promised to … Fear and self-pity played monkey in the middle with my reason. My eyes misted. This committing business isn't easy, is it, Lord? Neither is the trusting.

I put my elbows on the settee and my head in my hands. All right, dear Lord, it's Yours - I'm Yours. I've messed up enough of my life, thinking I have all the answers. If You want me in Kansas or California or China or who knows where, it's fine with me. I, I… The words froze in my mind, yet I knew I had to say them.... will even go back to Pennsylvania, if You wish. Amen.

I couldn't believe I'd prayed those words. Going back to Pennsylvania, to my father's house, had to be my worst nightmare - or my most frequent dream. I brushed my hair, then hurried downstairs to help my friend prepare supper.

That evening, when Mr. Paget opened his Bible to read to the twins, he read about the kind Shepherd searching for his lost sheep. I hope the Shepherd knows His way around the Kansas prairie, I thought. The picture of Jesus searching Kansas for me stayed with me throughout the night. For the first time since Ian and Drucilla had arrived in Hays, I slept peacefully.

The next morning I read to the twins while Zerelda straightened the house. In the afternoon, we decided to dry pumpkin strings for winter use. While I peeled, Zerelda cut the pumpkins into three-inch strips, then strung them on strong twine with a large darning needle.

After examining one completed string, she attached one end of the twine to a hook on her porch roof support and stretched it out in the sunlight, fastening the string to a hook on the next porch roof post. The kitchen door slammed behind her as she stepped back inside. "Brr! Looks like another storm is brewing in the west, maybe snow. I should have gotten to this earlier."

She bustled over to the sink, filled a teakettle with water, and carried it to the cookstove. "I waited because the secret to good-tasting pumpkin is well-ripened fruit and well-ventilated bags, of course." After stoking the fire, she placed the kettle on the burner. "I make my bags out of cheesecloth, then hang them in the storm cellar until I'm ready to use them."

The warmth of the friendly yellow-and-white kitchen filled me with peace. I sliced the last pumpkin in half and scooped out the seeds. "My ma always did this after we kids were back in school in the fall. Later, she'd grind up the seeds to stretch our supply of wheat flour. With so many kids in the family, nothing was ever wasted."

Zerelda chuckled. "That's the law of the prairie, too, you know. There's a practical use for every — " She paused and listened. "Someone's coming. A carriage." She wiped her hands on her apron and hurried to the door.

Rinsing my hands in the sink, I dried them on a handtowel and followed her out onto the porch. Her husband must have heard the carriage also, for he stood by the hitching post with his hands jammed into the back pockets of his overalls.

I shielded my eyes from the late-afternoon sun as I watched the carriage approaching the farmhouse. As the driver slowed the horses to a stop, Mr. Paget called out, "Well, my goodness. James McCall. You are a sight for sore eyes!"

The man leapt from the carriage and tied the reins to the post. I froze and stared at the man I'd come to believe was dead. His gray woolen business suit, silver stickpin, and derby hat appeared incongruous in the surroundings. The full mustache was gone. As he shook his neighbor's hand, James looked up at me. "I've come to fetch Miss Spencer."

Before I could find my tongue, Zerelda bounded down the stairs to her husband's side. Grabbing James's hand, she pumped it enthusiastically. "James McCall, as I live and breathe, what are you doing here?"

He laughed. "I rolled into Hays this afternoon on the westbound. I haven't had time to get out of this city suit and into real clothes yet."

Zerelda stepped back and looked the man over like an approving mama. "Well, you sure do look mighty spiffy for a Kansas farmer. What do you think, Chloe Mae?" The three of them looked up at me.

A gust of wind whipped a cluster of stray curls across my eyes and nose. I lifted my arm to brush the curls aside. "I, I have a hard time believing that you are here."

"Why?" James strode over to the porch and paused at the foot of the steps. "In my letter, I told you when I'd be back."

"Letter? What letter?"

He climbed the stairs slowly as he spoke. "The one I wrote to you before leaving Boston. I gave it to my sister-in-law to post the morning I left for New York City."

"I'm sorry, but I never received a letter from you." A flicker of doubt appeared in his eyes. He turned toward David and Zerelda. "Imagine, getting home to find that your brother is trying to sell your farm out from under you, your governess has fled, and your sister-in-law is on her way to Boston with your son."

I bit my lip and turned my head.

The Pagets climbed the steps. Zerelda admitted, "We did wonder what had happened to you - disappearing like you did."

"Hmmph! So you know, I didn't just disappear. The day before the funeral, my father and I had a bitter argument over my son's future, and after the interment, I left. But Drucilla knew where I was going and how long I'd be gone. She herself volunteered to come ahead to care for Jamie."

At the mention of Drucilla's name, the memory of her hateful accusations came back. I could hear her New England accent accusing, "You're staying around, hoping to catch a wealthy widower." I could feel a rush of heat flooding my neck and face.

I realized that James was still talking. "I had business to complete in New York City before coming home. By the way, I took it upon myself to stop off at your home in Shinglehouse. I met your mother and your sister Hattie."

My eyes widened in shock. "You what? My mother? Hattie? Why?"

David put his hand on James's shoulder. "Look, you two have a lot to discuss, and I have chores to finish. Why don't you go into the parlor while Zerelda brews a pot of tea." He thumped James on the back. "It's good to have you back, old friend."

James shook his friend's hand. "It's good to be back."

Eagerly, I preceded James into the parlor. I couldn't believe he'd actually talked with my mother and my sister. I sat down on Zerelda's horsehair sofa. James sat down beside me.

"So, tell me, did you see my little sister Dorothy or my little brothers? How is my mother? She must be seven months pregnant by now."

He smiled and waved his hands in defense. "One question at a time. Yes, I saw the younger children. They send their love. Your little brother Worley wanted to know if you had fought any Indians yet. I assured him you hadn't. He seemed disappointed." James's eyes twinkled. "I waited around while Hattie wrote you a long letter. She also sent you a box of stationery, I suppose to encourage you to write more often."

"My mother? Does she look well?"

James frowned. "She seemed tired, but she was delighted to learn that you are doing well. She sent a trunk of your belongings along with me, as well as a sampling of your father's herbal concoctions."

"And Pa, did you see Pa?"

James studied his hands for a moment. "No, he wasn't there."

I leaned toward James. "Did, did Ma say anything about my father?"

He nodded and said gently, "She told me to tell you to give him time, that, sooner or later, he'd come around."

I sighed and turned away.

"Look, we'll talk more about your family on the way back to town, but right now, I need some information. Aunt Bea told me about Drucilla and your, er, problems."

I straightened my shoulders and stared at the intricate pattern on the wood stove on the other side of the room.

"Don't worry about my sister-in-law." He chuckled. "She's the only person I know who could make Mary Elizabeth livid with anger. I am, however, concerned about Jamie's speech problems."

I turned to face him. My eyes pleaded for understanding as I related the breakthrough Jamie had made during our last few days together. "Your aunt was right, and I was wrong. I had no right to keep the news from her, promise or not."

James shrugged to dismiss my apology. "Then he was talking. Clearly? In complete sentences?"

"Yes, as distinctly as you and I are speaking."

A grin swept across his face. "Praise God! I'd about decided my father was right that Jamie should be placed in a school for retarded children or at least in a children's hospital, where he could get help. Of course, Mary was dead set against that." His face clouded. "The last thing she wanted was for Jamie to grow up away from his family. That's one of the reasons we moved West."

"Speaking of Mary …"

He stared at his hands for a few seconds. His voice rasped with emotion when he finally spoke. "Mary Elizabeth died in her sleep from an allergic reaction to one of the drugs the doctor prescribed. Miss Chloe, you will never know how much she valued your friendship. And that's one reason why I'm here today."

I lifted one eyebrow. "I, I don't under …"

"Here." He reached in his inside coat pocket and handed me an envelope. "She wrote a letter to you. They found it in the bedside table after she died. I decided to deliver it personally."

Mary's delicate scroll rolled across the page - "Miss Chloe Mae Spencer." The light aroma of violets, her favorite perfume, accosted my senses. Removing the seal, I opened the envelope and withdrew the letter.

Dearest Chloe,

I wanted to write a few lines to let you know all is as well as can be expected here, though I do miss the taste of those quaint teas you encouraged me to drink. I have to admit that some of them did ease the pressure in my lungs for a time. I want to say thank you for being my friend, one of the only true friends I've ever had - with the exception of James, of course. And thank you for being so willing to set aside your dreams in order to care for my boy…. I don't know when I'll be home. Sometimes I wonder if I'll ever … Oh, well, as Zerelda said so often, "That's in God's hands" …

My tears fell on the parchment, splattering the ink. I swiped my sleeve at my eyes and continued reading.

I am writing this propped up in my hospital bed. Beside me is a window looking out onto a green lawn. A young woman is chasing a small boy across the grass. The child's laughter echoes off the drab gray stone walls of the hospital.

It reminds me of the times I watched from my bedroom window as you pushed my son on the swing or chased butterflies together in the field across the road from the house. Thank you, dear friend, for everything. Regardless of what happens to me, I can rest knowing my son is safe in your loving hands. With love and devotion, Mary E.

As I groped blindly in my pocket for a handkerchief, James offered a folded white linen one. "Here."

Gratefully, I sniffed into the man-sized cloth then dabbed at my eyes. I held the letter out toward James. "Would you like to read it?"

"I did, before I sealed it," he mumbled, pushing the letter away. For a few minutes, we sat silently dealing with our grief. Finally he spoke. "I'm not asking you to devote the rest of your life to my son, but if you could help us through the next few months, get us over the hump - I'm sorry, I'm making a mess of this."

"I, I, I'm not too sure." I remembered the text I'd read earlier about committing my way to the Lord and letting Him lead. "Will you give me till tomorrow morning to decide?"

"All right." He rose to his feet and offered me his hand. As he helped me to my feet, he said, "Come back to Aunt Bea's with me this evening. If you decide to leave, I'll see that you're on tomorrow's train. If you choose to stay, we'll be ready to drive to the ranch as soon as Jamie arrives."

"Wait! This is all moving too fast. What about your sister-in-law and your brother?"

"What about them?" He caught my hand, placed it in the crook of his arm, and led me to the base of the stairs. "Will you need help with your luggage?"

"Yes, but give me a few minutes to pack." Gathering my skirts in my hands, I ran up the stairs. A minute later Zerelda burst into the room.

"What is going on? James said that you are going back to Aunt Bea's. Is that what you want?"

"I don't know what I want," I wailed, plopping myself down on the edge of the bed. "I just don't know!"

Chapter 12

Change of Plans

An awkward silence hung between us as the carriage joggled over the dusty ruts to Aunt Bea's feed and hardware store. My gaze rested on James's woolen trousers and polished leather boots. Except for the missing mustache, he looked like the James who had left for Boston a couple months earlier. I remembered his anxious face and Mary's pale, drawn face the morning they boarded the train. Never would I have imagined the events that followed.

My thoughts shifted to the present, to my abrupt change in plans. That morning I was planning to leave for California and by evening I was again considering staying in Kansas to care for a small child who needed me. The thought of facing Beatrice McCall again filled me with anxiety. I feared that I had let her down by not keeping her informed of Jamie's progress. My mistake made Drucilla's lies plausible in her eyes, and I wondered what other stories Drucilla had fed the older woman.

As Aunt Bea's store came into view, James glanced my way. "I cleared up the misunderstanding about the missing jewelry and the family Bible with Aunt Bea, you know."

He'd read my mind. I cast him a smile of relief. "I'm glad," I sighed.

"And don't worry about Drucilla. I've known her since we were kids." He chuckled to himself. "I understand her churlish nature. Why do you think I chose to marry Mary Elizabeth?"

Not knowing if I should laugh or frown at his audacity, I stared straight ahead at the two-story building looming up in front of us. The carriage rolled past a farm wagon onto which Walter was loading bags of feed. James waved and urged the horses around to the back of the feed store.

Halting the horses by the back door, James turned to face me, his eyes holding a tinge of warning. "You need to understand, Miss Chloe. I will never marry again. So don't stay in Kansas for the wrong reasons."

I sputtered in surprise. "Excuse me, Mr. McCall. You don't seem to take my goal to travel as a missionary to China seriously. I assure you, you'll remarry long before I will even consider marrying for the first time!"

A smile tugged at the corners of his mouth. "Hmm, I wouldn't put too big a wager on that prophecy."

"If I were a betting woman - " I sputtered, hopping down from the carriage before he could come to my assistance.

I heard him chuckle behind me. "If I were a gamblin' man - "

I hurried into the feed store. Of all the audacity! He's as bad as Drucilla. It would take more than an eligible widower to keep me in Kansas.

I was still sputtering over James's ridiculous comment when Aunt Bea rushed up and threw her arms about me. "Oh, Chloe, I'm so thankful James caught you in time and convinced you to stay. I was afraid you might have already left for California." She held me at arm's length and searched my eyes. "Forgive me for not trusting you and my own instincts more."

"Forgive me," I replied, biting my lip between phrases, "for making and keeping a promise that I had no right either to keep or make."

Helping me out of my cape, she continued, "Forgive me for forgetting that you are barely more than a child yourself. Seventeen years old! It's from making mistakes at seventeen that you learn to be a wise old bird like me." I laughed and gave her a hug.

"I have a surprise for you upstairs, my dear - as a peace offering. I want our friendship to return to what it was before Drucilla poisoned it."

"That really isn't - "

"Now, don't spoil my surprise." She led me up the stairs to my old room, drew me into the room, and pointed to a box on the bed. "Open it," she urged.

I picked up the box and lifted the lid. "A brand-new Bible? For me?"

"Look inside on the first page."

I obeyed. My eyes filled with tears as I read the message aloud. "To Chloe Mae Spencer. If I had a daughter, I would want her to be just like you. With love, Aunt Bea."

I threw my arms around the woman's shoulders. "Thank you. Thank you so much."

That evening, James excused himself and retired to his room early, leaving Aunt Bea and me to talk into the night. As I sat across from her at the kitchen table, drinking hot chocolate and eating Scottish shortbread, I realized how much I'd come to depend on the strong, loving woman and how much I would miss her friendship when the time finally came for me to leave.

It wasn't until her wall clock in the parlor gonged twelve that we headed for bed. When I finally reached the privacy of my room, I opened Ma's trunk. My heart leapt to my throat as I recognized the garment folded so carefully on top. There lay the yellow gingham dress she'd made for me, along with the rust-colored satin sash and the matching bonnet. I held it up in front of me and gazed into the mirror. Visions of Emmett and the Fourth of July celebration danced before my eyes. I forced the troubling thought from my mind and concentrated on the pride I'd seen in my mother's eyes as she had handed the dress to me that morning. Carefully, I hung the dress in the wardrobe, then returned to the trunk.

Next was a garment I didn't recognize. I unfolded a soft white dress and held it up to get a better view. As the folds of the skirt tumbled down in front of me, I noticed rows upon rows of hand-embroidered daisies stitched along the hem. A note was pinned to the bodice.

"When the day comes, I will not be with you on your wedding day, my daughter. This dress represents my prayers for your happiness and my love for you. Each daisy was stitched with a special prayer." Beside the delicately embroidered dress was a long, white infant dress of the same fabric. I ran my fingers over the soft cotton lawn and the shiny silk threads in the cutwork. The note attached to the infant dress read, "I made this for your first child. Chloe Mae, you will make a wonderful mother someday."

I wiped at the tears sliding down my cheeks before they spattered on the delicate white fabric. For the first time I realized the extent of my one hasty decision. Not only would I suffer the consequences, but so would all who loved me.

Mama, I love you too. If only we could have shown our love to one another while we were together. Why did we have to wait until we were separated by so much distance and pain ?

It was like Christmas as I removed the other items she'd packed: my everyday dresses, three new aprons, my black patent-leather dress boots, my favorite sunbonnet. Ma attached a note to my heavy woolen dresses.

"I understand Midwestern winters can be fierce. I'm sure you'll need these, as well as the long woolen underwear I packed in the bottom of the trunk." I laughed through a new rush of tears. I remembered all the arguments we'd had over my wearing those hated long johns to school. To make her think I was wearing them, on washday, I'd crumple them and rub them on my bedroom floor before putting them in the stack of dirty clothes. Ma, you always did get the last word.

I paused when I discovered that beneath the two pair of itchy underwear was a tin of her homemade oatmeal cookies and my well-worn copy of Little Women. Protruding from the pages, I found one of my mother's lavender-and-white crocheted bookmarks.

As I removed the rest of the clothing, some old, some new, I found letters from my brothers and sisters tucked along the walls of the trunk. Even Myrtle had sent a letter, filled with news of my nephew's latest accomplishments. I fought back tears as I read my mother's letter. It made me feel so close, yet so far from her side. She told me her time was drawing near for the new baby to be born and how she wished I were there to help her. Suddenly I wished I could be also.

I pawed through the trunk, hoping to find the one letter most important to me - the one from my father. Finally, admitting defeat, I reached for my new Bible and opened it to Psalm 37:5. "Commit thy way …"

The flickering lamp reminded me that it was almost out of fuel. Reluctantly, I closed the Bible and dressed for bed. As I slid beneath the covers, I caressed the soft flannel sleeves of the nightgown that still smelled of my Pennsylvania home.

In a dream I was running in the apple orchard with Patches when the first rooster crowed. I dressed and repacked the trunk. After breakfast, I walked into town to window-shop. On impulse, I bought myself a new camisole and a baseball for Jamie. That afternoon, James loaded our luggage into the back of Aunt Bea's carriage. A little before four, James and I drove her team to the station to welcome the westbound train.

As the steam engine hissed and screeched to a stop, James stepped into the shadows of the depot's awning while I ran along the cars, scanning the windows for Jamie's familiar grin. As I reached the last set of steps, Jamie burst from the train, dashed past the startled porter, and flew into my arms.

"Miss Chloe, Miss Chloe!" he squealed. "I thought you were gone forever. I thought I'd never see you again."

With the child in my arms, I laughed and whirled about in circles. My skirts billowed in the breeze. A shadow fell across us. We stopped, face to face with James.

The man held out his arms to his son. "Jamie?"

Jamie's laughter died. I held my breath while the child stared into his father's eyes. Slowly, the boy released my neck and reached for James. "I-I-I thought you wouldn't come back, Daddy." As Jamie burrowed his face into his father's neck, the man squeezed his eyes shut, his face suffused with pain. When a tear slid down the man's cheek, I turned away, pretending not to see.

Ian and Drucilla disembarked from the train, matching scowls on their faces. When Drucilla glanced my way, her frown deepened. She said something to Ian, then, with a flutter of her gloved hands, she hurried to James. Ian trailed behind.

"Oh, James, I am so sorry. If we had only known you were returning." Her voice dripped with syrup. "How very fortunate that you caught Miss Spencer before she departed for San Francisco. She was so eager to leave." Drucilla flashed her most captivating smile at James.

My mouth dropped open. "Eager ..." I gasped, then clamped my lips shut. I will not allow you to pull me down to your level!

At the sound of the woman's voice, Jamie's eyes filled with fear. Clutching his father's jacket lapels, the boy again buried his face in the man's soft suede coat. James hugged the child tighter and turned to Drucilla. "Drucilla, you seem to be upsetting my son. Please, back away."

"Ba ...?" She fluttered her lashes in distress. "Ian and I were only trying to do what we believed was best for the child. I hope you understand. I couldn't bear to have you upset with me, James."

The man ignored Drucilla's protests. "Miss Chloe, I'll take you and Jamie to the carriage. On the way I'll grab Jamie's luggage. I would like to leave for the ranch immediately."

"Leave for the ranch?" Drucilla's voice rose dangerously high.

"What about Ian and me? Aunt Beatrice is expecting us to dine with her this evening."

Calling over his shoulder, James strode across the wooden platform. "Do whatever you wish, Drucilla. I have business to attend to at the ranch this evening. And Jamie and Miss Spencer are coming with me."

Running to keep up with James's long strides, I glanced quickly at his face. His lips formed a thin, determined line that matched his eyebrows. The only other time I'd heard him speak so forcefully was the day

I requested that he purchase my ticket to California immediately.

Without a word, he strode to the waiting carriage. He set Jamie in the front seat of the carriage and assisted me into the seat beside the child. Turning, he called to his stunned relatives, "Will you two be needing a ride back to the feed store?"

Ian led the speechless Drucilla to the carriage. "What about our luggage?" Ian asked his brother.

"Aunt Bea can send Walter for it later." James rounded the carriage and hopped into the front seat beside Jamie. "Well?"

Ian helped Drucilla into the back seat, then climbed aboard himself. He'd barely sat down before the horses lunged forward. James drove the team with such a vengeance that I held onto my bonnet with one hand and to Jamie with the other as the vehicle bounced over the rutted street.

When we reached the feed store, Aunt Bea came out to meet the carriage, and James leapt down and strode over to her. All four of us remained in the carriage while Aunt Bea and James appeared to be arguing. Then James turned abruptly and returned to the carriage.

"Aunt Bea, I'll send a couple of the boys back with your rig by nightfall. And thank you, dear heart. I know you did the best you could under the circumstances."

"James, don't you think you should give the child a chance to rest a bit before making the trip to the ranch? The last two days have been extremely tiring for him."

James turned to his son. "Do you need to stay here for a while?"

Jamie's eyes twinkled as he shook his head. "I want to go home," he whispered.

The father's eyes glistened with tears at the sound of his son's voice. James glanced at me and lifted a questioning eyebrow. I grinned. "I'm ready to go."

"Then let's head home, son." Ruffling the boy's hair with his free hand, James picked up the reins and called, "Ian? Drucilla? You heard the boy. Unless you plan to come along to the ranch minus your luggage, you'd better hop down."

Ian leapt from the carriage and helped Drucilla to the ground. I turned in time to see the startled looks on Ian's and Drucilla's faces and a knowing smile form on Aunt Bea's lips. James drove at a saner pace after we left the edge of town. He seemed to be inhaling the freshness of the prairie as we rode. Within a few miles, the cold, brisk wind had penetrated Jamie's and my coats. James drew a red woolen blanket from under the front seat and tossed it to me. "Here, you two, wrap up in this."

I shook the blanket open and wrapped it around Jamie's and my shoulders. "There's plenty more blanket here."

He started at the suggestion. "No! I'm fine."

As the carriage passed the abandoned soddy, Jamie stood up and pointed. "Look, there's the sod house where I killed the snake."

James shot me a surprised glance. "Killed a snake?"

"Yes," Jamie continued, "while you were gone, I ran away, and Miss Chloe came looking for me." The story tumbled out of the small boy like feed spilling from a new sack of grain. Once he started talking, Jamie couldn't stop. He reported every detail that had occurred since James and Mary headed East. He told about the gunmen showing up at the ranch.

James looked over at me. "You two are lucky to be alive."

Jamie laughed. "Oh, no, Miss Chloe made 'em behave. I just wish I got to see old Satan chase them up the haystack."

His father looked first at Jamie, then at me. "Up the haystack?"

I shrugged. "It was rather funny, sir."

"I can imagine. Aunt Bea said that Satan did the same thing to your Aunt Drucilla."

Jamie turned toward me accusingly. "He did? No one told me about it." Folding his hands, the child nodded his head defiantly. "I'm glad. Aunt Drucilla is not a very nice person."

James cleared his throat and glanced down at the child's intense face. "Well, son, Aunt Drucilla is your mommy's sister, you know. And your mommy would want you to be nice to her."

The boy's shoulders drooped. "I know. Uncle Ian says I should show her proper re-re-spect." He looked up into his father's face. "I do try, honest."

James paused for a moment. "Was your Uncle Ian nice to you?"

"Oh, yes. Wait until you see the circus train he bought me. He bought Miss Chloe a bonnet, too, but she made him take it back." The boy looked at me quizzically. "Why did you make him take the hat back?"

I felt my face redden. "Well, I thought it was …"

"Inappropriate for a gentleman to purchase a piece of clothing for a lady, son," James interrupted.

Jamie's brow knitted. "Was it in-ina-a-prop-riate for me to keep the train?"

James laughed. "No, son, he's family. That makes it all right."

Jamie's frown deepened. "But isn't Miss Chloe family too?"

James cleared his throat and flicked the reins. "No, son, Miss Chloe is a friend, not family."

We rode in silence for a time as the child mulled over his father's words. Finally he spoke. "Daddy, what do we have to do to make Miss Chloe family?"

To keep from smiling, I bit my lip and studied the fading prairie grass.

James spoke slowly. "Well, son, I'm afraid, when it comes to family, we don't have a lot of choice. We're born with 'em. But when it comes to friends, ah, we have all the choice in the world. That makes friends special, huh?"

The boy nodded. I could tell we hadn't heard the last of his questions. A few minutes passed. "Was Mommy family?"

"Of course," James replied. "Mommy and your grandpas and grandmas, your aunts and uncles back in Boston."

Jamie sank into silence once again. My gaze swept the countryside. We had less than two miles to go before reaching the ranch.

"Daddy?" Jamie peered up into his father's face. "Can someone be both family and a friend?"

"Yes, I guess they can."

"Good." Jamie took my hand in his and smiled up into my face. "I like having you as my friend." Then he frowned. "But I don't know if I'd like it if you became my mommy. I don't want a new mommy. Aunt Drucilla said she'd die before she'd allow you to become my mommy."

I gulped and choked. My face blazed with color. I couldn't make myself look toward James as I tried to think of what to say. "Jamie," I traced imaginary lines on the child's hand, "your mommy will always be your mommy. No one else can ever fill her place in your heart." I tapped his chest with my finger. "Never, ever forget that. She was a very special lady."

"Good!" Jamie huffed. "Then Aunt Drucilla can't be my mommy either, can she?"

"No, son," James interjected, "that isn't likely to happen." The child heaved a heavy sigh, then folded his arms and settled back against the seat, his questions answered.

I glanced at James out of the corner of my eye and saw the corner of his mouth twitch and the muscle in his jaw tighten and relax a number of times. For a moment, James McCall reminded me of my pa, Joseph Riley Spencer, and I shook my head to remove the thought. James halted the team at the edge of the McCall spread.

"Isn't it the most beautiful spot in the entire world?" A few months before I would have strongly disagreed. But on that evening, I too, saw beauty in the golden fields of buffalo grass, in the stubble fields of grain, and in the treeless plain that swept east to meet the sky.

"Look, son," James pointed toward the ranch. "We're home."

A smile spread across the child's face. He turned toward me. "My swing. I can see my swing."

James shook the reins, and the team bounded forward. "Sam has a surprise for you, son. I brought it all the way from Abilene."

"A surprise? What is it, Daddy? A pony?"

James grinned at me behind the child's back. "You'll just have to wait till we get there to find out."

As the carriage pulled into the yard, Sam and the other hands met us. The team stopped beside the corral fence. Beyond the fence stood a jet-black, two-year-old gelding. Jamie jumped up and down with excitement. "My pony. That's my pony, isn't it, Daddy?"

"Well, not exactly. Cookie's a colt, not a pony. And he's not broken to the saddle yet." He placed his arm around the child's shoulder. "By the time Bo teaches you to ride, Cookie will be trained as well." Glancing over his shoulder, James asked,

"Do you ride, Miss Spencer?"

Jamie didn't hang around for the answer. He leapt from the carriage and scrambled up the side of the rail fence to examine Cookie at closer range.

I demurred, "After a fashion. I used to ride the workhorses on our farm back East."

"Wonderful. Then you'll have to help Jamie learn. I know Mary had a couple riding outfits you can wear if you wish." He paused a moment, then continued in a quieter tone. "In fact, after I've gone through her belongings to pack away things I think Jamie might appreciate later or get rid of clothing I might find it hard to see another woman wearing, you are welcome to keep anything of hers."

"Oh, I don't know if..."

"Nonsense, a Scotsman would never agree to perfectly good clothing going unused." Before he could turn around to help me from the carriage, Sam rounded the vehicle and offered me his arm. When my feet hit the ground, I thanked the foreman.

Sam tipped his hat and grinned. "We're sure glad to see you, Miss Chloe. We thought we'd seen the last of you when you left."

I nodded and grinned. "I thought so too."

James asked Bo to water and feed the horses before making the return trip to Aunt Bea's. Behind us, Sam grabbed James's valise and Jamie's case. Darcy and Jake hauled my trunk from the back of the carriage and carried it up to my room. Shorty hefted James's Saratoga trunk on his shoulders and took it to the master bedroom. Within minutes, Bo and Darcy left for town, one driving Aunt Bea's team and the other, the farm wagon.

In the kitchen, Sam and I rustled up a batch of scrambled eggs and hot buttered toast for supper. As we all sat around the heavy oak table swapping the previous week's adventures, I sipped a glass of cool goat's milk. I had to admit to Jake that the goat's milk tasted almost palatable.

The talk continued until the last of the eggs was cleaned from the platter, the toast had grown cold, and Jamie had fallen asleep with his head on the table. Rising to his feet, James suggested we call it a day. "We'll have an early start in the morning, Sam. I want a complete report. We should go over the books, too, before my brother arrives tomorrow morning." He scooped the child into his arms and carried him from the room.

I followed them into the hall. "I'll be right up to put him to bed."

James called over his shoulder. "Don't bother. I can do it, Miss Chloe."

I turned back to the kitchen to find Sam and Jake stacking the dishes in the sink. "I'll take care of those, gentlemen. You have to get up earlier than I to do morning chores."

They thanked me and headed out the back door. Sam stopped in the doorway. "It sure is nice to have you back, Miss Chloe. I hope you plan to stay for a long while."

"Thanks, Mr. Sam. It's nice to be back."

Then hesitantly, he asked, "Do you think the other lady will be returning too?"

I frowned. "I wouldn't be at all surprised."

"Hmm! Too bad." He donned his hat and turned to go. "Well, good night."

"Good night." As I pumped the water to fill the kettle, I mumbled under my breath, "You can sure say that again."

I stoked the fire and placed the kettle on the stove. While the water heated, I carried the lamp over to the pantry and peered in. Everything looked the same. The bottles of elixir I'd made lined the top shelf. Next to them, bags of dried herbs and teas rested side by side. Drying herbs hung from the rafters over my head. I inhaled the familiar aroma of mint, thyme, and rosemary. It felt good to be back home.

The teakettle's whistle drew me back to the kitchen. Pouring the hot water into the basin, I added a dash of cold and picked up the dishcloth. I began to sing as I washed the supper dishes. "Amazing grace! how sweet the sound, That saved a wretch like me ..." The next words to the hymn escaped me.

"I once was lost, but now am found ..."

I turned at the sound of a rich baritone voice behind me. James picked up a dishtowel and continued to sing as he dried a platter.

"... Was blind, but now I see. Through many dangers, toils, and snares ..."

I reached for the platter. "I can do that, James."

"I have already come ..." Ignoring me, James set the platter on the table and reached for a dinner plate. "... 'Tis grace hath brought me safe thus far, and grace will lead me home."

I finished washing the rest of the dishes as he sang the last verse of the hymn. He folded the wet towel and placed it on the oven door handle. "It feels so good to be home, Miss Chloe. So good."

"I imagine it does, sir." I stacked the plates and carried them over to the dish cupboard.

"Where does this go?" I turned to find James holding the heavy iron skillet.

I pointed. "On the hook behind the stove."

I took off my apron. "It's been a long, tiring day. I think I'll just go up to my room and start unpacking before going to sleep."

He nodded. "Good night, Miss Chloe. Thank you again for agreeing to help me with Jamie."

Up in my room, I unpacked the trunk and put my belongings into the wardrobe. After hanging the last dress in the closet, I dropped into bed and instantly fell asleep.

We'd barely finished eating breakfast when we heard the farm wagon return. I hopped up from the table and peered out of the window over the wet sink. A groan escaped my throat before I realized it. Squeezed on the driver's seat were three people, two men and a woman. A third man sat in the wagon bed with the luggage. From the frothy dress the female wore, I knew Drucilla had arrived.

Shorty, Sam, and James got up from the table and strode out onto the porch. Jamie followed. When the child saw who the passengers were, he bolted into the house and up the stairs. Alone at the table, Jake slathered a second helping of corn bread with Amy's blackberry jam.

I walked out onto the porch. "James, what rooms would you like prepared for your brother and sister-in-law?"

He shrugged and waved me aside. 'Whatever rooms they stayed in before, I suppose."

"Miss Drucilla slept in your room, sir."

At that revelation, he cleared his throat. "Oh, well, uh, put her in the bedroom above the dining room, the one next to Jamie's."

I raised my eyebrows. As I turned to go back into the house, I wondered how the elegant Miss Bradley would appreciate her room assignment. I only hoped Zerelda had been maintaining the seldom-used room.

"Miss Chloe." James turned around to face me. "Keep in mind that you are hired to care for Jamie, not to wait on Miss Drucilla. If you choose to help with any of the housework or the cooking, it is not a part of your employment."

Out of the corner of my eye I saw Sam help Drucilla down from the wagon. As James started down the stairs, I called to him. "James, I don't want to be forward, but you and I need to work out the details of my job. While Zerelda does a fine job, a big house like this needs daily attention."

His steps slowed as he considered my words. "You are right. We'll talk in the library after supper tonight."

I hurried into the house and up the stairs to check on the guest rooms. On the way by the linen closet, I chose two sets of embroidered sheets and the matching pillowcases.

Running into Ian's room, I glanced about. The dark mahogany wood glistened, evidence of recent care. I threw open the window and stripped the bed. A few minutes of airing, and the place will be springtime fresh.

Leaving a set of sheets on the bed, I hurried down the hall to what would be Drucilla's room. It, too, showed signs of loving care. Again I opened the window and threw back the covers. I shook open a fresh sheet and quickly tucked in the edges.

After shaking a second sheet free, I smoothed and straightened it on top of the first. As I tucked the last corner under the mattress, Shorty lumbered into the room and dropped Drucilla's trunk in the only empty corner. Drucilla stepped in the room behind him. Shorty, a giant of a man, shot a nervous glance toward the door.

"Excuse me, miss." He squeezed by Drucilla and disappeared into the hall.

Drucilla glanced about the small, carefully appointed room, her upper lip curled into a snarl. "Well, isn't this lovely?"

I tugged the quilts into place. "I'll be done here in a moment." After plumping the pillows, I turned to leave. As I edged past the woman, she pointed to the washstand. "I'll be needing fresh water in the pitcher."

"Oh, of course." I smiled and arched an eyebrow. "The bathroom is right down the hall, the door beyond Jamie's room."

I hurried down the hall before she had a chance to recover and knocked on Jamie's door but received no answer. Carefully, I opened the door and peeked in. The little boy was nowhere to be seen. A thump overhead bought a smile to my face. Ah, you little scamp!

He'd retreated to his hideaway in the attic. I decided to let him stay hidden while I went downstairs to clear the breakfast dishes. In spite of what James had said about my being hired only to care for Jamie, there were chores to be done to keep a big house like his running smoothly.

That evening, after Jamie was in bed, I met with James in the library. Holding an ivory letter opener in his hand, James motioned me to the leather chair beside the desk.

"As you pointed out this morning, a large house like this needs an overseer. So, while she's here, Drucilla has volunteered to keep the house running smoothly. She'll work with Zerelda to do so." He tapped out a rhythm on the desk with the letter opener as he spoke. "I have talked with Drucilla regarding your status here. She understands that your main responsibility is Jamie. However, should you wish to volunteer your help, I am sure she'd appreciate it."

I swallowed hard and nodded. If I thought my mother was a hard taskmaster, I could only imagine what this woman would be like.

Zerelda's comments about my doctoring in the area when necessary came to mind.

"James, as you know, I am a trained midwife. If I'm needed, I'll be glad to help deliver babies. Would that be all right with you?"

"Of course, and any other way you can help our neighbors is fine too, as long as Jamie is not neglected."

I brightened. "Wonderful. Then you don't mind my little stash of herbs and elixirs I've stored in the pantry?"

"Why should I? I saw how your medicines eased my wife's pain ..." He stared at the elephant carving on the instrument in his hand.

When he finally spoke, I could barely hear his words. "Nothing ever turns out like we imagine, does it?"

"No, I suppose not."

He continued as if he didn't hear my reply. "For so many months I pictured Mary as queen of our little castle. When I'd see Zerelda polishing the silver, I pictured Mary's tiny hands caressing the shiny surfaces. When I'd see you flipping pancakes for the boys or pushing Jamie on the swing, I saw Mary doing those things." He glanced about the shelf-lined room. "She would have loved this room. She appreciated having you and Zerelda study the Bible with her. I was never much of a Bible-reading man before Mary took sick. But during our last days together, I could see the strength Mary received studying the Word."

Not knowing what to say, I remained silent, staring down at my hands.

"When she first died, I was furious with God. Then I took my anger out on my parents, especially my father. That's when I left for New York." He reached in the center drawer of the desk. "By the way, it seems Drucilla forgot to give you this when she arrived." He handed me an envelope addressed to me. "It's the letter I sent, telling you of my traveling plans. I gave it to her to post. She chose to keep it for some reason."

I slipped the letter into the pocket of my skirt. "James, if it's any consolation, I miss Mary too. It's like we discovered God together, at a time we both needed Him."

James nodded and leaned back in his desk chair. "I appreciate being able to talk with you about her. Everyone else shuts me off when I mention her name. It's like they want to forget she ever existed."

I remembered the varying ways Pa's patients handled their losses. "People react to death in different ways."

"I suppose so."

I leaned forward. "Any time you want to talk about Mary, I'll be glad to listen."

"Thank you, Miss Chloe. You've been a true friend to Mary - and to me.

"By the way," he continued, "Jamie's sixth birthday is in two weeks. I'd like to do something special for him. Do you have any ideas?"

I thought for a moment, then smiled. "I think what he would enjoy most is getting to know you again. The two of you have been apart for so long."

"You might have something there. Thank you, you've given me an idea. Would you see if Zerelda will make him a birthday cake?"

"Uh, may I make it instead?"

"Sure, he'd like that." James rose to his feet. "If you need any ingredients, let me know before the next trip to town."

"Thank you. And please know, for Jamie's sake, and for yours, I'll do my best to get along with Miss Drucilla."

While his face remained stoic, the man's eyes twinkled. "I'm sure you will, Miss Chloe."

Chapter 13

Learning to Wait

After two days, I understood what my mother meant when she said, "No kitchen is big enough for two women." The first to go were my herbs and elixirs. Before lunch the first day, Drucilla declared that she could not abide my "smelly concoctions" in her pantry. Rather than argue, I carried my precious potions up to the attic. Jamie silently watched as I lined them up on an unused bureau.

Poor Jake felt the brunt of her second attack. No noxious goat's milk would be served in her kitchen. Though James refused to force Jake to get rid of his goats, James appeased her by promising to buy two milking cows for home use. Silently I rejoiced in this decision.

"While you're at it, James, I need a flock of laying hens if I'm going to operate this kitchen properly." Up to this point, Zerelda had been bringing a dozen eggs with her when she came to clean the house. Before the end of the first week, we were enjoying creamy cow's milk with our meals, and a small flock of chickens adjusted to the henhouse that had been standing empty.

Drucilla's first task was to inventory, clean, and rearrange the kitchen and pantry. I don't know why it bothered me so much to have her take over the kitchen.

I wouldn't have minded her reorganizing the library or the linen closets, but the kitchen - by nightfall, I wondered why I'd ever been so foolish as to volunteer to help her.

Like an army commander, she assigned each of us a list of duties, from James to the ranch hands, down to Ian, Jamie, and me. I was in charge of breakfasts, which suited me fine.

In spite of my ill feelings toward the woman, I had to grudgingly admit that she knew how to run a household. In little over a week, she had the place operating smoother than I'd imagined possible. When I told her so, she smiled gratefully.

188

On Jamie's sixth birthday, I was surprised when, at breakfast, Drucilla volunteered her mother's recipe for fresh apple cake without demanding that she make it herself. Since it was Zerelda's day to bake bread, we decided to work together. Immediately after James and Jamie left for town, Zerelda arranged the ingredients for her bread on one end of the table, and I assembled what I would need for Jamie's cake at the other end.

The biting wind howling and the heavy gray clouds outside made the cheery farm kitchen a cozy place to spend the day. While Zerelda told me about Abigail Hostetter, the wife of the new Congregational minister who had moved to Hays, I peeled apples for the cake.

"Wait until you meet her," Zerelda confided. "She is the most charming person I've met in a long time. Intelligent too. She's already making a difference in the Ladies' Literary Soc - "

"Who's intelligent?" Behind me, Drucilla pushed the dining-room door open and walked into the room.

Zerelda looked at Drucilla, then mumbled, "I need to get the bread starter from the pantry."

Pretending to have missed the snub, Drucilla sat down in the rocker next to the fireplace. "I didn't realize a hamlet like Hays had a literary society."

I smiled. "Hays is much bigger than you might think. Aunt Bea tells me that there are almost a thousand people living in the area. And now that the U.S. government might turn the fort over to the state, more will be moving in all the time."

Drucilla inspected her nails. "I was president of the Beacon Hill Ladies' Literary Society."

I arched my brow in surprise. I'd never seen her reading any books. "Really? How interesting. Perhaps you should get involved with the local club while you are here."

Zerelda returned to the kitchen carrying the crock of starter dough. "They meet at two o'clock every Tuesday at the library."

Drucilla cast a wary glance toward me. "Would you be willing to go with me, Chloe? I don't know anybody here."

Immediately I thought of Jamie. "If it's all right with James." I glanced toward Zerelda. She shrugged.

Drucilla brushed away my concern. "I'll make sure of it. If nothing else, I'll arrange for Aunt Bea and Walter to watch him for an hour or two on Tuesday afternoons. It will be fun."

While I'd never thought of an afternoon with Drucilla Bradley as fun, the enthusiasm in her voice proved contagious. "Yes, I think it might be fun at that."

Drucilla didn't change overnight, but, I have to admit, she tried to fit in. I came to enjoy the formal dinners the five of us ate around the mahogany dining-room table. Before the first month was out, I decided that I could learn to appreciate eating from imported china and drinking out of lead crystal. The woman could teach me a lot if I would open my mind enough to learn.

A few batches of cookies and other special treats for the ranch hands, and the men decided they could tolerate her. Ian and James thought of her as their childhood friend and so accepted her as one of the family. Only Jamie stubbornly resisted her friendly overtures. Whenever she was around, he resorted to his old weapon - silence.

One night, after Jamie refused to answer a question Drucilla asked him at the dinner table, his father sent the boy to bed without dessert. When I excused myself in order to follow the child to his room, James signaled for me to sit down. "He can manage by himself."

Ian rescued the mood by telling about his first attempt to help Darcy string barbed wire. We were laughing by the time we finished the apple cobbler Drucilla had prepared that afternoon. When she asked to speak with James in the library after supper, I volunteered to do the evening dishes. Ever the courteous gentleman, Ian helped me clear the table, then stuck around to help dry the dinnerware.

With slow, deliberate strokes, Ian ran the dishtowel over the china platter. "You know, Drucilla has her cap set for James."

I glanced over my shoulder. He averted his eyes. "I suppose so."

He cleared his throat. "She usually gets what she wants."

"Yes, she does." I scraped at a chunk of burned-on cobbler crust with a paring knife.

Ian took the platter to the dining room, then returned. "Doesn't that bother you?"

I scraped at the last piece of scorched crust. "What?"

"Her wanting to marry James."

"Why?"

"Well, for some reason, I thought you - "

Why is everyone always trying to marry me off? I whirled about, fighting to control my ire. "Where did you ever get such an idea in your head?"

Taken back by the force of my attack, he struggled to defend himself. "I don't know. I just thought - "

"Well, you can stop thinking." I squeezed the water out of the dishcloth. "I have no intention of spending the rest of my life on the Kansas prairie. China is my goal."

Ian threw his hands up in defense. "Sorry, it's just that you two spend a lot of time talking with one another."

"We have a lot to talk about - mainly his son." I licked my suddenly dry lips and heaved a disgusted sigh. My fingers clenched the baking dish with a death grip. "I'm a good listener, I guess."

The man eased the dish from my hands. "Hey, I'm sorry. I shouldn't unload my frustrations on you."

A wave of regret washed over me as I read the misery in his eyes. "I'm sorry too, Ian. Does Drucilla know how much you care for her?"

He stared down at the ceramic plate in his hands. "One evening her parents threw a dinner party. In the course of the evening, I followed her to the gazebo and declared my love for her." He paused. "She laughed at me and pointed toward the lake. James and Mary Elizabeth were strolling hand in hand on the dock. 'That's the man I plan to marry,' she said."

I placed my hand on his wrist. "Oh, Ian, I'm sorry. You must have been devastated."

Wistfully he smiled down at me. "Why can't I fall in love with a woman like you?"

I arched one eyebrow. "A woman like me? And what kind of woman is that?"

"Someone who hasn't already promised her heart to another, I guess."

The back door flew open. Sam burst inside. "Where's James? It looks like a blizzard is blowing in. We've got to round up the cattle in the back pasture."

"I'll get him." Ian glanced down at his crisp trousers and suede vest. "Saddle up the horses while we change clothes." Ian bolted from the room.

I turned toward Sam. "Is there anything I can do?"

"Yes." Sam nodded. "Have a pot of hot stew simmering on the stove for us when we get back."

I followed him out onto the back porch. Tiny white flakes pelted my face as I rounded the edge of the house. Hunching into his coat collar, Sam waved and shouted, "And don't wait up."

I shivered and ran toward the kitchen door, smack into James. The unexpected impact sent me flying, landing full force on the slippery porch floor.

His concerned face loomed over me, and his gloved hands reached out toward me. "I'm so sorry. Are you all right?"

I nodded. Before I could gather my wits about me, he lifted me to my feet and steadied me. "Are you sure you're not hurt?"

"Yes, I'm sure." I tried to wriggle free from his grasp, but he held on.

"Good, then listen to me. A prairie blizzard can last as long as three days. If we aren't back by morning, the cows will need milking. Can you handle that?"

"I-I-I think so." Even though I'd never done it myself, I had watched my brother milk Pa's cows many times.

"Good, because I doubt Drucilla has any idea how to milk a cow. See this rope? It could save your life." He held up a coil of rawhide in one hand. "I'm going to tie one end to the porch railing and the other to the handle of the barn door. When you go out to the barn and back, don't let go of the rope. I've heard of people getting disorientated and freezing to death less than ten feet from their own back doors."

I looked up at the tiny driving snowflakes. "Do you think this storm will be that bad?"

"I don't know. But don't worry about us if we don't get back tonight. We'll wait out the storm in one of the line shacks."

Bundled so only his eyes and nose appeared above the heavy leather jacket, Ian bounded out of the house. "Ready to go?"

"Ready." James clambered down the porch steps after Ian.

"I'll be praying for you all," I called into the howling wind.

"Thanks." The two brothers called and waved.

I hurried back inside, where Drucilla waited. I noted a strange sadness in her eyes. Reaching for an apron on the peg inside the pantry door, I said, "Sam asked if we could have a hot stew simmering when the men return."

She thought a moment. "I soaked a pot of beans, planning to use them for Boston baked beans tomorrow. However, a bean soup would go a lot farther."

We worked side by side, preparing the ingredients for the soup. As the liquid bubbled in the pot on the stove, we looked at one another and smiled.

"I guess there's not much to do now but go to bed," I said.

She nodded and sighed. After lighting a second lamp, I took one of the lamps and headed for the hallway door. "How did you do it?"

I paused in the doorway. "How did I do what?"

"How did you convince James to marry you instead of me?"

Shock bolted through me. I tried to speak, but my words came out in a stutter. "I be-be-beg your par-don?"

"How did you do it? I was sure that once Mary Elizabeth was gone from his life, James could learn to love me." A cloud of pain dulled her usually brilliant blue eyes. "I didn't mean that how it sounded. I wasn't waiting around for her to die or anything."

"I honestly do not know what you're talking about, Drucilla." I steadied myself on the edge of the broad shelf. "James doesn't love me. For that matter, he once told me he'd never allow himself to fall in love again."

"Really?"

"Really."

She made her way over to the rocker and sat down. "But I thought that was the reason you stayed in Kansas - to marry James and his money."

"This may surprise you, but I have no intentions of marrying anyone, any time in the near future. I'm in Kansas for four reasons." I relaxed a bit and sat down in the nearest kitchen chair. "First, I genuinely loved Mary Elizabeth as a sister, and second, I adore her son. Third, ships heading for China won't sail until next spring, so why not stay and help with Jamie as long as I can? And fourth," I felt a little silly mentioning the fourth reason, "and probably most important, I ran ahead of God once before ..." My voice grew husky, and I finished my statement in a whisper. "... and have suffered for it. I don't want to do it again."

"I guess I don't understand your last reason." Drucilla picked up the iron poker and stirred the coals in the fireplace. "I've never thought about what God might or might not want me to do. I've just always done what I wanted."

"Me too," I whispered, "until now."

While the wind howled and the snow obliterated the world beyond the farmhouse, we shared stories of our childhood. Drucilla described what it was like growing up in a well-to-do Boston family, always having to do the right thing, say the right thing, wear the right thing.

She chuckled. "At times I wanted to hike my skirts halfway up my pantaloons and slide down the bannister like my older brothers did. Other times I wanted to rip the blue satin bow from my curls and do somersaults on the front lawn."

I laughed, surprised to find us so similar. "Well, I was Ma's burden child. From the time I turned twelve years old, she was after me to be more ladylike. Either I laughed too loud or I walked like a boy or I made the mistake of saying exactly what I thought." I told Drucilla about Pa and about hopping a train West. We giggled ourselves into tears after I strutted across the kitchen floor imitating the pompous Emmett.

At the end of my performance, I turned slowly to face her. "In some ways, I wish I'd listened more when she tried to train me properly. You've helped me see the benefit of knowing proper etiquette."

"Really?" Drucilla smiled through misty eyes. "Thank you, Chloe, for saying that. Not counting my sister, I've never had a female friend." The woman studied her hands for a moment. "Mary Elizabeth was always the popular one. She had friends galore."

"Your sister was a very special person."

"I know." Drucilla lifted her gaze to meet mine. I could see a wariness beneath the surface. "Do you know what it's like to have your little sister marry the man you love? I'm twenty-six years old. By society's standards, I'm considered long in the tooth' for marriage."

I didn't know what to say. This woman was one of the prettiest, most delicate creatures I'd ever met. Her every pore oozed with confidence. Yet, in the back of my mind I could hear my mother and the ladies at grange meetings gossiping about Clayton, the barber, courting a twenty-four-year-old spinster over Coudersport way. A teasing smile quivered at the edges of my mouth. "I know one man who idolizes you."

She drummed her fingers on the tabletop. "Yes, I know." We studied the embers in the fireplace without speaking. I marveled at how a late-night atmosphere and the intimacy of a fireplace drew people together. Drucilla must have been thinking the same thing. For in a quiet, hesitant voice, she said, "Do you think you and I could ever become friends?"

I glanced over at her and smiled. "I'm willing to try, if you are."

Her face broke into a smile. "Oh, I'd like that very much."

When the hall clock gonged midnight, we looked at each other in surprise. I stood and stretched. "You know, sitting here won't bring the men back any sooner. We might as well get a few hours' sleep if we can."

"You're right. Let's call it a day." After she set the soup pot on a back burner, we each took a lantern and padded upstairs to our bedrooms. She paused as I opened the door to my room. "Chloe, I honestly did believe that you stole my sister's jewelry and were out to marry James for his money."

"I know."

She took a deep breath. "And if you want the Bible back that Mary Elizabeth gave you, you may have it."

I shook my head. "No, Aunt Bea gave me one of my own to use."

Drucilla lingered as I stepped inside my room and placed the lantern on the desk by the window. "I notice that you and Zerelda always spend a few minutes together after the work is done to read the Bible together. Do you think Zerelda would mind if I joined you two once in a while?"

I unpinned my braids and shook them free. "I think she'd like that."

Drucilla eyes sparkled at my reply. "Good. Well, good night."

"Good night."

She closed the door behind her as she left. I thought about the strange turn of events as I dressed for bed. I'd never known a woman like her. The closest was Mrs. Chamberlain - and I'd only observed her from a distance. And Drucilla Bradley made Isabelle Chamberlain seem common in comparison.

Before hopping into bed, I picked up a copy of the Montgomery Ward catalog Aunt Bea sent with Jake the last time the men went into town. With Christmas coming, I decided to compile a list of gifts to get for my family in Pennsylvania, for Joe in California, and for my friends here in Kansas. My leather change purse bulged with coins and bills. Since I had nowhere to spend it, the money had accumulated. I didn't know how far my money would go, but I figured it wouldn't hurt to dream.

When the fuel in the lamp dwindled, and the wick threatened to sputter out, I turned it off and snuggled down to sleep. Once again I thought of Drucilla and our strange conversation. Remembering what James had said about Drucilla's nature, I allowed my suspicious nature to take over. Can I trust her? I'd watched her cast her spell over others. Is that what she's doing to me?

I awoke with a start as the gray morning light seeped through my bedroom window. The cows! It's time to milk the cows. Oh, Chloe, you really did it this time.

Milk two cows? Why didn't you tell James that you've never milked a cow in your life?

I sat up and slid my feet over the edge of the bed. As they hit the cold floor, I shrugged off the memory of the warm spot in the center of the bed that I'd just abandoned. Knowing I was late, I dug into the bottom drawer of the oak dresser and located my brother's trousers and hauled them on. Pa's shirt, a pair of heavy socks Ma had packed in the trunk, my everyday boots, and I was ready to do morning chores.

As I passed the wall mirror, I caught a glimpse of my uncombed hair. Not wanting to waste time braiding it, I tied it back into a tail at the nape of my neck, then bounded down the stairs. I grabbed one of James's heavy jackets from the hall closet, buttoning it as I ran.

A gust of arctic wind hit me as I opened the kitchen door. The barn was only a gray silhouette through the pelting snowflakes. I burrowed deep into the coat collar and half-slid, half-tramped down the porch steps.

Holding on to the rope James had strung the night before, I struggled through the knee-deep snow toward the barn. I'd never felt so cold in my life. As my knuckles stiffened, I realized I'd forgotten to wear a pair of gloves. By the time I reached the barn, my face stung and ice coated my lashes. A cloying warmth hit my face as I opened the barn door and eased inside. After shaking the snow off James's jacket, I lighted a lantern. Shining the light around the still-dim interior, I wondered where to start. The two milk cows stared at me from their stall.

A stool. I need a stool - and a pail. Where will I find a pail? I tried to picture my brothers as they milked Pa's cows. Did Joe milk on the left or the right side?

I grabbed a large armful of hay and walked over to the first stall. The animal eyed me suspiciously. "I don't blame you, baby. I wouldn't trust me either. But if we work together, maybe we can both survive this experiment." I put the hay in the manger.

Behind me I heard the barn door creak. Good. Drucilla heard me leave and came out to help.

I bent down to take a closer look at the business section of the cow. "Have you ever milked one of these beasts?" I shouted.

"Many times," a familiar male voice answered. "How about you?"

I straightened and turned to find myself staring into James's amused face. "That beast, as you call poor Pansy, would have become indignant if you tried to milk her a second time in one morning."

"When did you get back? I didn't hear you come in."

"Good, then we succeeded." He folded his arms and leaned against the railing. "Of course, if you had checked your soup pot, you would have discovered that it was empty. It was delicious, I might add."

My face blazed with color as I followed his gaze to his jacket, to my brother's trousers, then to my frizzled hair. His grin infuriated me.

"I couldn't very well wear a taffeta traveling gown to milk cows, now could I?" I pursed my lips in a prim bow, which broadened his smile even further.

"Did I say anything?"

I glared. "You were thinking it! That's enough." Thinking only of wiping the grin from his face, I threw a handful of hay at him, then pushed past him out of the pen.

Without warning, I felt a handful of hay being forced down the neck of my shirt. I whipped about in surprise. "Of all the …"A shower of hay hit my face.

James stood in a half-crouch, grinning, and beckoning me. "Come on. You want to have a hay battle, I'll give you a hay battle."

Never one to dodge a challenge, I scooped up another handful of hay and tossed it at his face. Whirling about, I dashed for the barn door and threw myself against it to open it, and struggled though the deep snow toward the house. Wind and new snow had almost obliterated the tracks I'd made earlier.

I glanced over my shoulder in time to see James burst through the door, lose his footing, and fall into the freshly fallen snow. I doubled over with laughter.

As he rose to his feet, he lowered his head and glared. "So you think that was funny, do you?"

"Hilarious!" I plunged back into the drifting snow. A snowball zinged past my head. Though my hands burned from the cold, I grabbed a handful of snow, formed a ball, and aimed for James's forehead.

Wham! The snowball found its mark. I laughed and tried to run. A second, then a third snowball flew past me. However, in trying to dodge the fourth one, I slipped and fell face first into a drift.

I came up in a sputter of snow, hair, and indignation only to find James looming over me, holding a giant, mixing bowl - size snowball. "Give?"

"Never!" I cried, lunging forward into his knees. Stunned by my sudden attack, he fell backward into another snowdrift. Before he could recover, I scrambled up the porch steps. He bounded up the steps behind me.

Laughing, I struggled to catch my breath. "I guess that will teach you to challenge a Spencer."

"Pure luck. And mercy on my part. Next time, beware."

I grabbed a broom from behind the door and swept the snow off my boots and trousers. Stepping behind him, I brushed the snow off his coat and pant legs as well. "Any time, anyplace!"

We stomped our feet on the dry porch and went inside.

"Big talk." He helped me remove the jacket, then laid both of our coats to dry over the back of the rocker by the fireplace. Tossing a log on the fire, he reached for the poker. "I haven't had a good snowball fight since I was a kid."

I inched closer to the hearth. The dancing flames soothed my stiff red fingers. "My brothers and sisters and I could whip all the other kids in school. Between battles, we built up ammunition depots in our snow forts."

He grinned and leaned against the mantle. "Ten little terrors of Shinglehouse, Pennsylvania?"

"Five, actually." I smiled at him and offered, "I'll make hot chocolate if you'll fetch the milk from the cold cellar."

Minutes later the sweet aroma of steaming hot chocolate filled the kitchen. I handed him a cup, then filled mine. I cozied my fingers around the hot mug and ambled over to the kitchen window, peering out into the forbidding new day. Larger, lazier flakes had replaced the finer, pelting ones that had fallen earlier.

I gazed on the hushed white world and sighed.

I sensed instead of heard James come to stand behind me. "There's something about the silence of freshly fallen snow. It's like we're all alone, the only people in the entire world."

Only half-hearing his comments, I was startled when he strode across the kitchen and slammed his cup down in the sink. "If you'll excuse me, I have some paperwork to do in the library." His brisk tone lacked the warmth he'd demonstrated moments earlier. "I told the men to sleep in late, so don't bother with breakfast. You might want to get a little more sleep yourself before my son wakens." He marched to the hallway door and pushed it open.

Puzzled by his abrupt change in attitude, I watched the door swing closed behind him. As I rinsed our cups in the sink, I chuckled over the bewildered look on his face when he found himself flat on his back in the snowdrift. Like my brother Joe had always done, James McCall had underestimated me.

Yawning, I tiptoed from the kitchen, past the closed library door, and on up to my room. It would feel good to get out of my damp clothing. And a little extra sleep sounded pretty good too.

During the next week it snowed three more times. The men spent much of their time repairing harnesses and getting the six-passenger sleigh ready for winter use. I did notice, however, the little attentions Drucilla showered on Ian, everything from sewing a replacement button on one of his work shirts to serving the biggest baked apple to him at dinner.

At breakfast one morning, Ian announced that he needed to make a trip into town. He asked if anyone needed provisions.

I brightened. "Would you mind mailing a pack of letters to my family? They're all written and ready to go."

Drucilla smiled and glanced shyly at Ian, then at me. "We'd be glad to."

Stunned surprise swept around the table. James stared at his blushing brother. When Drucilla noted our reactions, she stated demurely, "Earlier, when Ian mentioned he was going, I figured I might as well go too. You can handle things here, can't you, Chloe?"

"I-uh, sure, no problem," I stammered.

"Good! Then it's settled." She bounced her blond curls about enthusiastically. Casting a coy glance at Ian, she announced, "I can be ready in a half-hour." He nodded. She pushed her chair from the table. "If you'll excuse me.

She didn't wait for our answers but sprang from the table and flitted from the room.

James shook his head in wonderment. "Shorty, will you help Ian hitch up the team to the sleigh?"

Shorty wiped his mouth with his napkin. "Sure, boss, right away."

I excused myself and ran upstairs while James and the rest of the ranch hands discussed the work schedule for the day. I hurried to the desk and opened the bottom drawer to scoop up the stack of letters to Hattie, Ma, and Joe that I'd written since we'd returned to the ranch. Maybe there would be some letters waiting for me at the depot. Maybe Pa …

I stopped myself. "No!" I announced to the empty room. "I won't allow myself to get discouraged again. I won't allow myself to feel guilty for a sin God has forgiven. It's up to you now, Pa."

Removing the leather change purse from the night stand beside my bed, I counted out the postage money. My gaze fell on the Montgomery Ward catalog lying on the floor beside my bed. It would only take a minute for me to fill out the order sheet and send it along with the letters. I hurried over to the desk and sat down.

I'd just figured the total on the third order when Drucilla knocked on the door. She peeked around the door. "We're ready to leave, Chloe. Are your letters ready?"

"Here they are. And here's the postage money. If it runs more, I'll pay you when you get back." I handed her the letters and cash. "Thanks so much for doing this. I really appreciate it."

She beamed with happiness. "Glad I can do it for you." Leaning forward, she touched my sleeve and whispered, "Wish me luck with Ian."

Chapter 14

Forever Friends

Snuggled in the crook of my arm, Jamie turned to the first page of the book The Night Before Christmas. I pointed as I read the words aloud, stopping at key words to allow the child to fill in the blanks. " 'Twas the night before - "

"Christmas,"

"... and all through the - "

"... house ..."

"But it's not night, Miss Chloe," Jamie reminded. "It's morning."

After I'd discovered a copy of the familiar Christmas classic on James's library shelves, I talked with James about teaching his son to read. He'd been delighted.

With Ian and Drucilla having left immediately after breakfast for Hays and the men working in the barn, the big house was pleasantly quiet for a few minutes. Zerelda would be arriving soon, and the rare and delicious solitude would disappear in a whirlwind of stripping bedding from mattresses and scrubbing clothes on the washboard in the kitchen sink.

"Not a creature was stirring, not even a - "

"Mouse!" Jamie giggled. "Do mouses stir?"

"Mice, Jamie," I reminded. "When you have more than one mouse, you have mice."

Jamie looked up at me, his eyes wide with sincerity. "Daddy says that when you have more than one mouse, you have trouble."

"Err! He's right!" I shuddered. "I hate mice."

"Do we have mice in our house?"

I nodded. "I imagine so."

Jamie's brow furrowed in thought. "Maybe we need a cat. Do you think Daddy would get us a cat? I'd like a cat like Muffin."

I laughed and hugged him. "I guess it wouldn't hurt to ask, huh? Shall I read on?"

He nodded and with his finger traced the pen-and-ink drawings of the mice wearing nightcaps and sleeping in miniature four-poster beds. When the kitchen door slammed, Jamie leapt from my lap and ran toward the kitchen. "Daddy, Daddy," he called, "Miss Chloe says we need a … Oh, it's you, Mrs. Paget. I thought you were my dad."

Zerelda laughed. "Sorry, half pint. Where's Miss Chloe?"

I placed the book on the end table and arose from the sofa. I hate washdays. Oh, well, gotta get to work, whether I like it or not.

I didn't have to help Zerelda with the wash, but I couldn't sit by and watch her lug those waterlogged sheets to the lines alone. And the job wasn't so tedious when we did it together. James had strung a pulley line from the back porch to the elm tree, which meant we never had to leave the dry surface of the porch.

The library door swung open and banged against the plant stand behind it. "Chloe, Chloe, hurry. Jenny Evans needs you desperately. She went into labor just before sunup. Jenny's husband Herbert went to town for Doc Farley. He's down with the grippe, and Doc Madox and his wife took the train to Abilene to see her relatives yesterday afternoon. They won't be back until after the weekend." Zerelda paused for breath. "Herbert rode to our place for help just as I was leaving to come here. I told him about you and sent him home to Jenny. I can take care of Jamie for you."

I rushed past Zerelda into the hallway. There was no telling how long the woman would be in labor. "I'll need to take a batch of chamomile as well as dandelion. Not everyone can abide the taste of chamomile tea. Is this Jenny's first child?"

"No." Zerelda dogged my heels. "She has two boys, five and three years old."

I rounded the stairwell and dashed over to the door that led to the attic. "Ooh, that means her labor could go faster."

Upon reaching the top of the stairs, Zerelda turned and thundered back down. "I'll have one of the men harness the team to the sleigh. The wagon or the buggy would never get through. There are drifts between here and my place that could swallow a buffalo."

At the mention of the sleigh, my hand flew to my mouth. "Oh, no, Ian and Drucilla took the sleigh to Hays this morning. I'll have to ride horseback."

"Not alone. You can't go alone. You don't know the way. I'll find one of the men to go with you."

The sound of Zerelda's running feet grew distant as I flung open the attic door. "Chamomile. Dandelion. Comfrey." I measured the crushed dried leaves into the envelopes I'd fashioned out of brown wrapping paper. Then I rifled through the carefully wrapped and marked packets for one more medication Auntie Gert always swore by - Pa's tonic for women in labor.

In Kansas I'd had difficulty finding the ingredients for the perfect blend of chamomile, comfrey, licorice root, and dried juniper berries. But the medication was well worth my trouble. Besides relaxing the patient's nerves, the hot tea eased the pain of the contractions.

Clutching the envelopes in my hands, I ran down to my room and took off my gray woolen skirt and white cotton blouse. I pulled the bottom drawer of the dresser open and held up one pair of Ma's cream-colored long johns. I shook my head and laughed. "You always did get the last word, Ma."

I chose to wear my heaviest woolen dress. Beneath its full skirt I added two of my winter-weight petticoats and an extra pair of woolen stockings. I buckled my boots onto my feet and stood up. Catching a glimpse of myself in the mirror, I giggled. Ma always said I needed to gain a little weight.

Taking my woolen bonnet and cape from the hook in the closet, I also grabbed my red shawl. Just the thought of the brisk prairie winds sent shudders up and down my spine. I hauled down a small valise from the top shelf in the wardrobe and placed the herbal packets inside and snapped the case shut. Have I forgotten anything? What else do I need?

I glanced at the desk. My Bible lay open to John 14:27, where I'd left it a few hours earlier. "Let not your heart be troubled, neither let it be afraid."

I covered my eyes with my free hand. "Thank You, dear Father. I don't want to go anywhere without You."

When I opened my eyes, I remembered that I needed a pair of gloves. Knowing I had nothing heavier than kid gloves, I ran down the stairs to the hall closet. I knew James kept an extra pair of sheepskin gloves on the shelf above his second work jacket.

I didn't hear Bo step up behind me. "Are you sure that cape will keep you warm enough?"

Turning, I shrugged. "It's all I have."

He reached past me and removed James's jacket from the hook. "I know Mr. McCall would insist you use this if he were here."

"But, I - " I looked at the gloves in my hand and reddened. "I guess arguing about wearing the coat is kind of silly since I already intended to borrow a pair of his gloves without asking."

He grinned and helped me into the jacket. Taking the valise from my hand, he directed me toward the kitchen.

"Wait," I said, "I've got to explain to Jamie where I'm going."

"He's in the kitchen with Zerelda. She's told him all about it. They've already begun making a batch of doughnuts."

"Doughnuts?"

We found Jamie wearing one of my aprons and standing on a stool next to the table beside Zerelda. His face wreathed with smiles, Jamie smashed an egg on the side of the mixing bowl. The rich yellow yoke slithered into the bowl along with egg-shell fragments. He and Zerelda were chanting a rhyme.

One cup of sugar, one cup of milk, Two eggs beaten as fine as silk; Salt and nutmeg, lemon will do, Baking powder teaspoons two.

Zerelda broke the rhythm and handed me a partially filled flour sack. "Here, I packed a couple slices of bread with jam and some cookies for you to put in your saddlebag. And don't worry about Jamie; we're going to have great fun making doughnuts. I'll stay as long as he needs me."

Jamie waved goodbye as Bo and I dashed out the back door and down the porch steps to the waiting horses. Bo set the valise down and helped me swing up into the saddle, then retrieved the valise and hopped onto his mount. He led the way out of the yard and onto the roadway. The wind stung my nose and made my eyes water. Wrapping my shawl about my face, I burrowed farther into James's jacket. Bo was right. My cape never would have kept me warm enough.

The horses followed the tracks the sleigh had made earlier that morning until we turned off the main road toward the Evans's spread. Smoke spiraled eastward from the chimney of the tiny part-sod, part wood-framed cottage.

The front door opened before Bo could dismount, and I could hear Jenny's screams. Two wide-eyed children peered out of the glass-paned window beside the door. Without so much as a greeting, Jenny's husband ran to my horse, hauled me from the saddle, and dragged me toward the house.

Once inside the house, I shed the jacket, my bonnet, and shawl and headed toward the screams. I called out my usual list of orders. "I need a large pot of boiling water and a stack of clean sheets and towels. Find me a teakettle, please."

I entered the bedroom and closed the door behind me. Jenny Evans lay curled up on the bed, holding her knees and moaning. The contraction lessened. She fell back against the pillow, exhausted.

I hurried to her side. "I'm Chloe Spencer. Zerelda told me you needed help." Wringing out a washcloth in a basin of tepid water sitting on the washstand, I bathed her forehead and neck. "While you're between contractions, perhaps you can answer a few questions for me. When did your labor begin?"

"I thought you'd never get here," she gasped. "My labor began around four this morning."

"Five hours isn't so long, now, is it?" I dropped the washcloth into the basin and rounded the end of the bed.

"Easy for you to say. You're not the one in labor! Just how many children have you had?"

I smiled. I knew her anger distracted her from her discomfort. "None of my own, but I've delivered, um, let's see." I counted the deliveries in my mind. "Somewhere around twenty-five, including my own little sister."

Amid a barrage of questions about her previous deliveries, I examined my patient. She wasn't making much progress; obviously this baby was in no hurry to be born. I glanced at the homemade cradle beside the bed. "I'm going to brew you a cup of hot tea to help you relax."

She nodded and closed her eyes. I opened the bedroom door to four frantic faces, two adults and two children. Tears streaked the younger boy's face. The older son stood tight-lipped; only his eyes revealed his terror.

I walked to the dish cupboard along the back wall and found a teacup and saucer. "Mr. Evans, your wife is fine, but this birth will take a while. If you will lend Bo your sleigh and team, I would recommend that he take your sons back to the McCall place, where Zerelda can watch over them."

All four watched as I opened my valise and took out the herbal packets with the special mixture inside. Finding a bowl on the shelf, I filled it half-full with cold water from the pump and set it on the table. "Boys, you can help Zerelda and Jamie make doughnuts this morning. Please, Mr. Evans."

The man grabbed his jacket from the hook by the door. "Come on, Bo; help me harness the team."

"What about you, Miss Chloe?" Bo called as Herbert dragged him toward the door.

"I'll be fine. You can come back for me this evening when you return the Evans children." I measured out a handful of dried juniper berries and dropped them into the bowl, then covered the bowl with a saucer. "Boys, put on your heaviest clothing, then go and tell your mama goodbye. Tell her you'll bring home some doughnuts for her and the new baby."

The boys obeyed. Fear drained the color from their faces as they tiptoed to the side of their mother's bed. She opened her eyes and took their hands in hers. I explained the plan to her, and she smiled up at me gratefully. When her brow wrinkled and she again began to draw her knees up in pain, I led the children from the room.

The sleigh pulled up in front of the house. Bo jangled the sleigh bells and called to the boys, who bounded out of the house. I stood by the door and waved. "Come and get me tonight after chores. If all goes well, Jenny will be cuddling a new baby in her arms by then."

Mr. Evans followed me inside the house. I added the herbs and berry liquid to the kettle and placed it on the hot burner to boil. Herbert started when a moan erupted from the next room.

"Mr. Evans, please time the teakettle. When the liquid has boiled for five minutes, divide it into four equal doses. Then bring one portion in a teacup for Jenny to drink."

I reentered the bedroom. Sweat beaded Jenny's forehead. Picking up the basin, I opened the door once more. "I need a basin of fresh, cool water, please, plus a new face cloth and towel."

Herbert returned almost immediately with the basin of water and the linens. After rinsing her face and neck with the fresh water, I massaged the back of Jenny's neck and shoulders, all the while talking about myself and my family back in Pennsylvania. Pa claimed the best way to calm an anxious patient was to talk him to sleep.

After the contraction passed and her husband had returned with the hot brew, I sent him back to the stove to boil more water in the teakettle. Though Jenny grimaced at the taste, I insisted she drink all of the concoction.

When she finished, she handed me the teacup and fell back against the pillow. Brushing my hand across her brow, I said, "In a few minutes, the tea will help you relax between contractions. Ill be in the next room when you need me."

I stepped out of the room and closed the door behind me. "She's mighty anxious over this baby for a woman who's had two normal births."

Mr. Evans paced between the stove and the front door, glancing out the window beside the door at every pass. "Jenny swears there's something different about this pregnancy. She's not felt good about it since about the fifth month."

"As far as I can tell, everything seems normal. There's no doubt it's a big baby, though." I eyed the man as he passed in front of me. No wonder Jenny was anxious and frightened. "You know, if you have chores to do, Mr. Evans, you might as well do 'em. It's going to be a while."

"Are you sure? I do have a mare that's threatening to foal this morning as well. Now that you're here for Jenny, I really should check on her."

The man turned and stared as I threw back my head and laughed. "Mr. Evans, go check on your mare. I'll let you know if I need any help."

He threw me an uncertain smile, grabbed his jacket, and bolted from the house. Sighing with relief, I made myself a cup of chamomile tea and sat down to relax and enjoy a moment of peace. It had been several months since I'd delivered a baby, and I'd forgotten how rattled new fathers could become. I thought of James. Had he been there for Mary when Jamie was born? I couldn't imagine him in a situation where he'd become upset or uncertain of himself.

When the contractions became more frequent, I stayed with Jenny, massaging her shoulders and talking to her. Partway through the afternoon, I insisted she drink another dose of the brew. This time she did so more willingly. As darkness overcame the gray, sunless afternoon, a girl-child was born. I had turned to wash the infant when Jenny doubled over with pain.

"Chloe! What's happening? I think there's another baby coming!"

Placing the child in the cradle by the window, I hurried to Jenny's aid. Twins! Jenny was having twins. My pulse raced as I guided Jenny's second daughter into the world. I'd never before seen, let alone delivered, twins. I knew I was babbling nonsense as I placed the second child at the opposite end of the heavy oak cradle. But then, so was Jenny.

"Twins! Can you imagine twins?" Jenny repeated over and over again as I changed her bedding and helped her into a clean nightgown. Placing one baby in each of her arms, I told her I was going to get her husband. Her cheeks were pink in spite of her exhaustion. "Don't tell him that it's twins."

I winked and grinned. "Don't worry. He won't know until he steps through the bedroom doorway."

Mr. Evans met me at the barn door. The man could tell by the grin on my face that his wife and baby were fine. Before I could say a word, he bounded past me and over to the house.

I heard the new father's Texas-style whoop before I reached the house. Once inside, I tiptoed over to the bedroom door and closed it gently. Jenny and Herbert needed time to enjoy this special moment alone.

I fixed each of us a plate of scrambled eggs and buttered toast, then sat down to enjoy mine by the stove. Beyond the bedroom door I could hear the new parents talking softly to one another and to the new babies. I leaned my head back against the chair and closed my eyes. Suddenly I heard the jangling of sleigh bells. It must be Bo returning with the Evans boys.

I opened the door. Big, lazy snowflakes drifted earthward, tickling my nose and eyelashes. The children tumbled from the sleigh and raced past me into their parents' bedroom. I called as the driver alighted from the sleigh, "Come on in, Bo, and get a cup of hot tea."

Hurrying back inside, I poured the tea into a clean cup. I heard the driver step inside the house. "Here," I said, turning as I spoke. "You must be ..."

Instead of Bo, James stood in the doorway, brushing the snow from his hat and jacket. "I'm sorry, Chloe. I know you were expecting Bo, but I thought it best if I came for you instead."

"Oh, that's fine. Here, warm yourself with a cup of tea while I gather my things together. You might want to pay your respects to the Evans's lovely new daughters before we leave."

"Daughters? More than one?"

I held up two fingers. "Daughters."

After the Evans showed off the latest additions to their family, I asked the men to leave the room so I could examine my patients once more before leaving. I promised Jenny I would drop in on her and the babies in a day or two to see how they were doing.

As I prepared to leave, Jenny grabbed my hand. "Thank you so much, Chloe, for all your help. I don't know what it is, but you have a healing touch. I hope you Ye going to settle in Hays."

"For now I am." I patted her hand and smiled. "Thank you for the privilege of helping to bring two beautiful little girls into the world."

James was waiting for me when I emerged from the bedroom. He helped me into the oversized jacket. "You're wearing this more than I am."

"And that's not all." I blushed and held up his pair of gloves. "I borrowed these too. Bo thought you wouldn't mind."

"Bo thought? Hmm." The space between his eyebrows narrowed. "Of course I don't mind. Using the coat and gloves was the intelligent thing to do."

"By the way, Herb, I'll have one of my men drop off your sleigh and team first thing tomorrow morning." James took my arm and hurried me out of the house. He helped me into the sleigh, then climbed aboard next to me. Two lanterns swung from hooks on each side of the sleigh, the harness bells jangled, and we were off.

"Here." He lifted a heavy woolen blanket. "Put your feet next to mine on the hot bricks. You'll stay a lot warmer."

Timidly, I inched my feet closer. He wrapped the carriage blanket around our feet and legs. "Tuck it under you."

Only the jangling harness bells broke the silence for the first few minutes, making me think of Christmas and

Pennsylvania. I thought back a year. I never dreamed then that I'd be spending the next Christmas in Kansas. And where will I be next year? I sighed and glanced down at the sleigh's black leather-upholstered seat. For the first time I realized we were riding in the

McCall's sleigh instead of the Evans's sleigh.

"So Ian and Drucilla got home safely from town?"

"Just before sunset. Look, Chloe, I'm sorry for disappointing you."

I frowned. "Excuse me, but I don't think I'm following you."

"I should have let Bo come for you as you expected. I'm sorry ..."

Shrugging my shoulders, I replied. "It really makes little difference to me who came to get me, as long as someone did."

He turned and scrutinized my face for a moment. "Surely you realize that Bo is smitten with you. For that matter, so is Darcy."

I looked James straight in the eye. "As much as I cherish both gentlemen as my friends, that's as far as it goes, I assure you."

Averting his eyes, he continued, "It's all right, you know. For that matter, I'd feel comfortable with either one courting you."

"How very nice of you. However, as I told you once before, I am perfectly happy without a beau, Mr. McCall." My toe tapped out my irritation on the hot brick.

"Let's make a deal. I won't try to match you up with any young women in the community, if you will pay me the same courtesy."

James's eyebrows shot up in surprise. "Hey, I feel responsible for you. Besides, I promised your mother I'd take good care of you."

I snorted. "Hmmph! Like my father tried to do by planning to marry me off to the first available male who rode up to our front door? No, thank you!"

"Look, I'm sorry, all right?" He snapped the reins, urging the horses forward. Under his breath, he mumbled, "You wouldn't be a half-bad wife if you could control that waspish temper of yours."

Without thought of the consequences, my Irish burst forth. "And you'd make some woman a moderately good husband if you weren't so overbearing!"

"O-o-over - " His mouth snapped shut. James cracked the buggy whip over the heads of the horses, and we lurched forward.

I listened to the swoosh of the runners sliding over the snow. The wind had obliterated the tracks made earlier by the horses and sleigh. Finally, I couldn't stand the silence any longer. Like it or not, I needed to apologize to my employer. I turned my head and looked up at him. At exactly the same moment, he glanced down at me.

Simultaneously, we said, "I'm sorry"

"No, I'm sorry," I insisted.

"No, I'm the one who should be sorry." His intense gaze refused to back down.

I glared and sputtered, "Overbearing!"

"Waspish!" Even as he hissed the word, his mouth broadened into a grin. The foolishness of our argument struck us both.

He chuckled and then threw his head back and laughed. I joined him.

"You know, Chloe Mae Spencer, you are good for me. I must confess that, at times, I can be overbearing."

I chuckled again. "I'm glad you realize that."

"Well, aren't you going to admit to being short-tempered?"

I faked a look of surprise. "Why should I? I wouldn't want to lie."

His jaw dropped. When I giggled at his reaction, he just shook his head. "You leave me speechless." "Impossible," I muttered.

"Seriously." He turned his attention to the road ahead as he spoke. "You're a good friend. You listen when I talk with you about Mary, about the ranch, about my son. I've come to trust your judgment." He paused. "I hope I haven't jeopardized that friendship tonight - or the other day, for that matter."

I considered his words before replying. I realized that I had come to appreciate him also. I thought about the tender care he'd given Mary during her illness and the gentleness he showed his confused son. "James, you haven't done anything to jeopardize our friendship yet, unless you try to match me up with someone again."

"I promise never to try again." He grinned and paused. "And the other morning?"

"When?" The other morning1? What in the world is he talking about? "I don't understand."

"At the barn - and the subsequent snowball fight? I hope you didn't take it wrong."

"What do you mean?"

He shrugged with frustration. "It just happened. I wasn't trying to, um, well, oh, you know."

I lifted one eyebrow. "Mislead me? No, you didn't mislead me. I believe we both made ourselves perfectly clear the day I agreed to stay on with Jamie."

"Good."

The first indication that we were nearing home was the light shining from the library window. He turned the horses into the yard and stepped to the ground. I allowed him to help me down. When my boots touched the snow, he released my waist and stepped back, extending his right hand toward me.

"Friends?"

I accepted his handshake. "Friends." My breath caught as he held my hand and studied my face for an extra couple seconds. The door to the bunkhouse swung open, and Shorty and Sam walked toward the team. "We'll take care of the horses, boss," Sam called.

James helped me into the house and excused himself immediately. He disappeared into the library and closed the door. As I passed the closed door, I knocked gently and whispered, "James? Thank you for driving over to the Evans's for me. Good night."

The voice from behind the closed door replied, "Good night, Chloe."